"Alex, I have something to tell you about your daughter.

"I should have told you before, but I was…" Gina's voice broke. She rummaged in the pocket of her jeans, took out her billfold and extracted a photograph from one of the side pockets. Wordlessly, she handed it to Alex.

He studied the smiling girl in the picture, his eyes widening. "It's Steffi," he said at last, then hesitated. "Isn't it? She looks older."

"It's not Steffi. It's my sister, Claudia, when she was Steffi's age. You can see a difference in her mouth. Steffi has your mouth."

"I don't understand. How can they look so alike?"

"Because they're related. Claudia is Steffi's aunt."

"Her aunt? What are you saying, Gina?"

"I'm Steffi's biological mother.…"

ABOUT THE AUTHOR

A Family Likeness, Margot Dalton's sixteenth Superromance novel, is set in the Okanagan Valley, British Columbia, Canada, where the author has lived for the past seven years and been inspired by the spectacular beauty and natural wildness of her surroundings.

This bestselling author has also written seven books in Harlequin's popular CRYSTAL CREEK series, two mainstream titles for MIRA Books, and has contributed to two anthologies.

Books by Margot Dalton

HARLEQUIN SUPERROMANCE

558—ANOTHER WOMAN
576—ANGELS IN THE LIGHT
622—KIM & THE COWBOY
638—THE SECRET YEARS
664—MAN OF MY DREAMS
693—THE HIDING PLACE

MIRA BOOKS

TANGLED LIVES (February 1996)
FIRST IMPRESSION (March 1997)

Margot Dalton

A FAMILY
LIKENESS

Harlequin Books

TORONTO • NEW YORK • LONDON
AMSTERDAM • PARIS • SYDNEY • HAMBURG
STOCKHOLM • ATHENS • TOKYO • MILAN
MADRID • WARSAW • BUDAPEST • AUCKLAND

ISBN 0-373-70714-2

A FAMILY LIKENESS

A FAMILY
LIKENESS

CHAPTER ONE

"NOW, LET'S SEE...it's seven inches down to this little bunch of flowers, and four and a half inches up from the bottom..."

Gina made a pencil mark at one end of the strip of wallpaper stretched out on the floor, then crawled briskly over the hardwood, pencil clamped between her teeth, to make a corresponding mark farther down on the roll.

"Did I say four and a half inches?" she muttered, pausing to frown at the paper. "Or did I say four?"

"Who are you talking to?"

Gina glanced up at the doorway, then gestured toward the wall behind her. "Hi, Mary. Isn't this pretty?"

Her housekeeper strolled into the room, wiping her hands on her apron, and looked at the strips of new wallpaper that partly framed an upholstered window seat.

"You were right," she said in surprise. "I thought it was too yellow, but it looks really nice on the wall."

"I knew it would. This paper is exactly what I wanted."

"Listen to her," Mary said indulgently. "The girl who always knows what she wants. You're too young to be talking to yourself."

Gina crawled back around to measure the strip again. "Four and a half inches," she said. "I thought so."

Mary dabbed with her dishcloth at a tiny soiled patch near the edge of the window seat. "I've got to find the time to clean all these before the summer rush," she murmured.

"Now *you're* doing it." Gina held the ruler in place to make a pencil line, then started cutting.

"Doing what?"

"Talking to yourself."

"I'm sixty years old," Mary said placidly, smiling and looking out the window as a pair of white butterflies danced an aerial ballet near the lilacs. "I can talk to myself anytime I want."

"Well, I'll be thirty-six next week."

Gina rolled the strip of wallpaper and plunged it into a narrow plastic trough. She stood erect, holding the dripping sheet of paper over the trough, and glanced at the other woman.

"You know, Mary," she said, "there are times when I can hardly believe it."

"What?" Mary sat down on the window seat, fingering the yellow chintz upholstery with a dreamy faraway look.

"That I'm almost thirty-six years old. Where have all the years gone? It seems like yesterday that I bought this place."

"There've been a lot of yesterdays," Mary said in her gentle voice. "And you're right, they're really flying by."

"Well, I guess that means we're having fun, right?" Gina said dryly. "Even though it doesn't always feel like it."

"You love this place," Mary said.

Gina carried the wet length of paper across the room and climbed the ladder. She frowned in concentration as she fitted the strip into place, matching the pattern carefully. "You're right," she said. "This was the only thing I ever wanted to do with my life. But that doesn't mean I don't find it pretty frustrating sometimes."

She took a sponge from the tray on the stepladder and began to smooth the paper. Mary asked, "The only thing?"

"Beg pardon?" Gina was still wiping briskly at the damp paper.

"Gina, you've got a big wrinkle there on the edge, right under that yellow basket."

Gina smoothed the wallpaper while Mary watched her with a thoughtful eye. "I just wondered," the housekeeper went on, leaning back against the broad oak window frame, "whether that's really true. I mean, that running this business is the only thing you ever wanted."

"Of course it's true. What else have I ever wanted to do?"

"That's what I'm asking."

Gina's face shadowed and she turned away quickly. "If you mean a husband and babies, I've never wanted them. You and Roger are my family."

Mary smiled. "Some family," she said.

"It makes me happy." Gina climbed down from the ladder to smooth the bottom of the wallpaper, then trimmed it above the wide baseboard. "Families come in all shapes and sizes, you know."

"I know." Mary got to her feet and headed for the door. "But you and me and Roger, we're a mighty strange family by anyone's standards."

Still kneeling at the baseboard, Gina looked over her shoulder. "Speaking of Roger, don't forget to tell him about that cracked toilet seat in the blue room, all right?"

Mary's cheeks turned pink with distress. "You'll have to tell him yourself," she said. "I'm still not speaking to him."

Gina sighed and got to her feet. "*Now* what are you two fighting about?" It seemed the housekeeper and the handyman/caretaker were always at odds over something.

"The man keeps insisting on sneaking food to Annabel, even though I've specifically asked him not to."

"But Roger loves Annabel. You know he does."

"She's *my* dog," Mary said firmly. "And the vet says she's too fat. She needs a low-calorie diet. How can she lose weight if that man insists on giving table scraps to her behind my back?"

"Roger's just too softhearted. He can't stand to hear the way Annabel whimpers in the pantry during every meal. It really is a heartbreaking sound, you know."

"She's *my* dog," Mary repeated with uncharacteristic stubbornness. "I guess I know what's best for her."

"I'm sure you do." Gina gave up the argument. "I'll talk to Roger, all right?"

Mary nodded, looking somewhat mollified, and paused in the doorway. "Oh, by the way, I just remembered what I came up here to tell you. A man called a few minutes ago."

"What man?"

"Name's Alex Colton. Said he wanted to talk to you about a room."

"Did you get his number?"

Mary shook her head. "He's in town. I gave him directions and he said he'd drive out this afternoon to make arrangements with you in person."

Gina looked at the messy scraps of wallpaper and the damp floor. "Well, I hope he doesn't get here until I've had time to finish this," she said. "I was really hoping for just one day when I could work without any interruptions."

"There's no such day in this business." Mary smiled, her sunny nature apparently restored. "After fourteen years, you should know that, dear. It looks real nice," she added, gesturing at the wall. "You're doing a lovely job."

Then she was gone, vanishing down the gleaming oak staircase that descended to the lower foyer past a wall of stained glass.

Gina stood in the doorway and watched, thinking about her housekeeper. Mary Schick was worth her weight in gold. She'd been here almost since Gina had first opened the old mansion as a bed-and-breakfast. It was hard to imagine the place without her. A small spare woman with graying hair worn in a careless perm, the housekeeper was the kind of quiet efficient person upon whom people seemed automatically to depend. In fact, she'd spent her entire life looking after others. She'd settled in right after high school to run her family's restaurant and look after her parents. She'd never married, had never even left Azure Bay. When her mother died and her father soon afterward, she'd sold the restaurant, happy to be free of the responsibility, and come to work as a cook and housekeeper for Gina Mitchell.

A few months later, Mary had sold her parents' little house in the village, as well, and moved into the bed-and-breakfast as a permanent resident. She and Gina had been together ever since.

Fourteen years, Gina thought as she walked back into the guest room shaking her head in disbelief. She knelt to measure the next strip of wallpaper, then squinted up at the wall to determine the pattern match.

But Mary's visit had set Gina's thoughts on another track, and keeping her mind on the job at hand became increasingly difficult.

"Almost thirty-six years old," she said, sitting back on her heels. "Lord, I can't believe it. Where has the time gone?"

She got up, the pencil in her hand forgotten, and wandered over to look out the window. Beyond the leaded-glass panels, a willow tree swayed and rustled in the warm breeze, partially obscuring her view of the lake. Gina stared into the trailing green branches, thinking about the swift passage of time.

Framed by the window, she could have been a boy. She wore loose denim shorts, a white cotton shirt with the sleeves rolled up and frayed sneakers. Her body was slim and sun-browned from hours of working outside in the yard and garden, and her curly dark hair was cropped short. She had hazel eyes, high cheekbones dusted with freckles, and a sober level gaze that belied the boyishness of her face and body.

Fourteen years, she thought again, opening the casement window and leaning out to look across the lake. Almost half her life had been poured into this place.

But Gina had no regrets. Edgewood Manor *was* her life; it was her passion, her dream come true. Few people ever had the chance to live out a fantasy the way she had, right from the beginning.

She remembered the first time she'd seen the old mansion, and the powerful visceral surge of yearning she'd felt when she looked at its stately facade, its spacious grounds. From that moment, at the edge of twenty-one, she'd wanted the place for herself, and she would have done anything to get enough money to make the down payment.

In fact, what she *had* done to raise the money had been almost unthinkable...

Gina's face tightened. Those were memories she never allowed herself to dwell on. They were buried deep in the past, and she intended to leave them hidden there forever. It was enough to know that Edgewood Manor was hers. As long as she could keep her business operating at a modest profit and make the mortgage payments on time, nobody could ever take the house away from her.

Nobody, she thought fiercely, gripping the window frame.

She swung her gaze to the orchard. It was early June, and the blossoms on the fruit trees had vanished, replaced by a drift of fresh green leaves. Soon the fruit would ripen, and they'd pick baskets of apples and pears and luscious apricots, and Mary would make jam and preserves. Then the frost would come and the leaves would fall. Snow would drift across the mountains, hiding the lake in shrouds of mist.

And another year would pass, and another...

Gina caught sight of a solitary figure down in the side yard, under one of the apple trees.

"Roger!" she called, leaning out the window. "What are you doing?"

The caretaker looked up and waved a length of wood he appeared to be whittling.

"Don't go away," Gina said. "I'm coming down."

She glanced at the unfinished wall, the partial roll of wallpaper on the floor and the untidy clutter of scissors, rulers and paper scraps. With a rueful shake of her head, she left the room and ran lightly down the stairs.

An elderly couple were in the plant-filled sunroom when she passed, reclining in wicker chairs among the ferns and reading peacefully. Gina paused to smile at them.

"Hello," she said. "Are you enjoying our Okanagan sunshine?"

"It's heaven," the woman said, lowering her book. "We came all the way from Pennsylvania to stay at this place, you know. Friends of ours were here two years ago, and they never stopped talking about how wonderful it was."

"Really?" Gina said, pleased. "From Pennsylvania?"

The man nodded. "The Piedmonts," he said. "Allan and Sheila."

"Oh, I remember them," Gina said. "They were here in the fall, I think. In fact, I seem to recall that Mr. Piedmont spent most of his time outside taking pictures of the autumn foliage."

"Allan's a real camera nut," the woman said. "Sheila gets so annoyed with him."

Gina lingered for a moment, exchanging pleasantries with the guests, then excused herself and went out through the French doors.

She crossed the flagstone courtyard, where a young honeymoon couple shared one of the wrought-iron benches near a rose-covered trellis, talking in low tones.

They looked up at Gina with shy smiles as she passed, then returned immediately to their conversation, heads close together and fingers intertwined. Gina ignored the tiny pang of envy she felt. The young couple had a closeness, an almost palpable aura of love that shut the rest of the world out.

She moved to the gate set in the honeysuckle hedge, then trotted across the clipped grass to the orchard.

"Hi, Roger," she said, approaching the tall man in a plaid shirt and denim overalls who sat under the apple tree whittling. "What's that?"

"One of the spindles on the back stairway is warped. I'm carving a new one."

Gina looked in awe at the length of oak, which had been partially turned on the lathe in Roger's workshop at the back of the house and was now being hand-finished to match the other spindles.

"It's amazing," she said, bending to run her fingers along the wooden shaft. "When you're done, I probably won't know which spindle you replaced unless you point it out to me."

"Well, I certainly hope not," Roger said placidly. He returned to his carving while Gina leaned against the tree and considered how to tell him that his habit of sneaking food to Annabel was a source of great distress to Mary.

It was funny about this pair. Roger and Mary were about the same age, and Roger, like the housekeeper, had wandered into Gina's life just when she'd needed him most.

She'd still been fairly new in the business then, struggling to make a success of her bed-and-breakfast

operation and cope with the mortgage payments.
Mary had helped a lot in those early years, with her
housekeeping skills and her genius in the kitchen. But
Gina was still crushed by the constant repairs that
needed to be done, and the prohibitive expense of
getting tradespeople out from the city.

Then, one mellow autumn day, Roger had dropped
into her world like a gift from the gods, and things had
begun to run smoothly.

Roger hadn't arrived looking for work. He'd actually been a paying guest, an executive from a Vancou-
ver-based lumber company trying to deal with burnout
and job stress by taking a holiday in British Columbia's lovely Okanagan Valley.

Despite his desk job, Roger was a man who could
turn his hand to almost anything. He'd entertained
himself during his vacation by helping Gina with leaky
pipes, ill-fitting windows and warped doors.

When it was time for his holiday to end, he decided
he didn't want to leave. So he simply mailed in his
resignation, moved his accounts to the bank in Azure
Bay, bought a snug little house and property just down
the road from the hotel and stayed on as Gina's handyman and caretaker.

"I don't know how I ever ran this place without
you," she told him now, watching as he carved neat
grooves into the bottom portion of the spindle. "What
on earth would I ever do if you left?"

"You'd manage," Roger said comfortably. "You're
not a girl who needs help from anybody, Gina. You're
a real survivor."

She thought about that, enjoying the way the long
curls of wood fell away from the oak shaft under his
hands. "Everybody thinks I'm so tough and inde-

pendent," she said at last. "But lots of times I don't feel that way at all."

He smiled up at her. Roger was nearly bald, with a tall angular body and eyes that were blue and tranquil under silvered brows.

Gina sometimes wondered how he'd adapted so readily to this life-style, which must have been, after all, a radical departure from his old existence.

Roger never talked about his past. Apparently he had no family or emotional entanglements, and seemed to be financially independent. At least, he managed without apparent discomfort on the small salary that was all Gina could afford, ate most of his meals with Gina and Mary in the hotel kitchen and passed his free time happily in his little farmhouse. For hobbies, he had his woodworking and a lovely old cello he played with surprising skill in a local chamber-music group.

"Mary's upset with you again," Gina said at last. "I promised I'd talk to you."

Roger sighed. "What did I do this time?"

"It seems you've been sabotaging Annabel's diet."

Roger looked up, feigning innocence. "Is Annabel on a diet?"

"Roger, you know she's too fat."

"She certainly is. She's probably the most obese poodle in the province."

"So why do you insist on feeding her table scraps?"

Roger grinned and began to carve another neat groove. "That animal was howling so loud yesterday the couple in the patio room were complaining about the noise. I just gave her an old soup bone to chew on, that's all."

"With a bit of meat on it?" Gina asked wryly.

"Maybe a little," he admitted.

She chuckled, then sobered. "You're a sweetie, Roger, and you know how much I love you. But you've got to stop upsetting Mary that way. Someday this will escalate to the point where I'll lose one of you, and then I'll probably have to close the business."

"Nobody's indispensable," Roger said mildly. "Always remember that, Gina. You could get along perfectly well without either one of us. We're just a habit, you know. A well-worn groove."

Gina glanced at him sharply, caught by something in his tone. "You keep saying things like that."

"Do I?"

"Lately you're always talking about how capable I am, and how perfectly well I could manage on my own. Are you setting me up, Roger? Is there something you want to tell me?"

He shook his head and went back to his careful whittling. "I don't like hearing you say you'd have to close the place down if one of us left, that's all. It doesn't sound like you, Gina. You're a fighter, not a quitter."

"I know. But I've grown used to having companions in the battle, that's all. I'd really hate to be all alone again."

"So why don't you find some nice young man to work at your side?"

Gina kicked his leg gently with the toe of her sneaker.

"Stop that," she said. "Immediately."

Roger moved his leg slightly. "I mean it," he said, holding the shaft of wood to his eye like a rifle and squinting down its length. "You're not that bad-looking, and still reasonably young. Aren't there any decent prospects out there who don't mind a skinny, freckled, hot-tempered girl with a will of iron?''

Gina relented and sank onto the grass, sitting cross-legged next to him and frowning at a ragged tear in the hem of her shorts. ''All the men I meet fall roughly into two categories,'' she said.

''Okay.'' He put the wood down and rubbed his knife on a small whetstone, then tested the blade with his thumb. ''I'll bite. What are they?''

Gina plucked a stem of grass and chewed on it thoughtfully. ''Well, there's the kind of man who feels really threatened by a woman living alone and running her own successful business. Those men seem to need to put me down in all kinds of subtle ways just to prove they're still dominant.''

''Mmm. That's attractive,'' Roger said. ''What's the other kind?''

''The ones who think what I'm doing is great, because they could move in with me and have a nice free ride on my efforts.''

''Equally attractive. So which category's worse?''

''I don't know,'' Gina said gloomily, throwing the grass away. ''I hate them both.''

''Not an attitude that's going to get your dance card filled, my dear.''

She grinned and got to her feet. ''Oh, there are a whole lot of openings in my social calendar, all right. And it's probably a good thing, because I never have enough time to get my work done as it is.''

''Speaking of work, what are you doing in the gold room this afternoon?''

''Putting up new wallpaper. You should come and see it, Roger. It looks terrific, especially around the window seat.''

"Isn't that the paper Mary thought was going to be too yellow?"

"Yes, but now she admits she was wrong."

"She does?" Roger's eyebrows went up in surprise. "Now, *there's* a first. For such a timid little thing, Mary can be pretty hardheaded in her opinions, you know."

"You be nice," Gina told him severely.

She left him under the tree with his whittling, strolled across the grass and let herself through the gate into the courtyard, recalling, too late, that she still hadn't told Roger about the cracked toilet seat in the blue room.

No rush, she decided. Roger was busy with other things at the moment, and the blue room wasn't booked for at least a week.

She paused inside the hedge and looked up at the house. Even after all these years, the sight of its massive vine-covered bulk against the distant violet of the mountains and the cloudless blue sky was enough to make her heart beat faster.

"It's really beautiful, isn't it?" a feminine voice said at her elbow, echoing her thoughts. "Like a scene out of *Sleeping Beauty* or something."

Gina turned and smiled at the honeymoon couple who, dressed in bathing suits now and carrying towels, were on their way down the path to the beach. They were an attractive pair, both medical students from Minnesota who'd just completed their residencies before their June wedding. This Canadian honeymoon had been a gift from the groom's parents.

"The house is more than a hundred years old, fairly ancient by local standards," Gina told them. "Actually it's quite a romantic story."

"Tell us," the girl commanded, leaning against her young husband and gazing up at him. "We're in the mood for romance these days."

Gina smiled, thinking about their cozy love nest up in the rose pink dormer room with its little stone fireplace.

"The house was built by Josiah Edgewood," she began. "Josiah was a Scottish nobleman and adventurer who came out to Canada when he was a young man and discovered gold up north in the Caribou region. Josiah made a fortune at his mine and fell in love with the area. He picked the Okanagan Valley for its spectacular scenery and mild winters, and started trying to convince his new wife to come and join him here."

"But she wouldn't?" the young bride asked, still looking up at her husband as if unable to believe that any woman would be reluctant to follow her man to the ends of the earth. He dropped a kiss on her nose.

"She was afraid. Poor little Lady Edgewood," Gina said. "She was barely out of her teens and quite frail, and she thought this whole country was overrun with wolves and grizzly bears. She refused even to consider living in the wilderness unless Josiah could provide her with some decent accommodation."

"So he built this big house?" the groom asked.

Gina smiled. "Wait till you hear the story. Josiah *moved* the house. Most of this is the original Edgewood Manor from the family estate near Kilmarnock in Scotland. Josiah had the whole structure dismantled and every piece marked. It was shipped across the ocean in crates, a proceeding that took several years to accomplish. The house was reassembled like a huge jigsaw puzzle right here on the shores of Okanagan Lake. All to please his darling Elizabeth.''

Both young people gazed at her, enchanted. Gina understood their rapt expressions, because she, too, always felt a little thrill whenever she thought about Josiah's great venture.

If she could ever meet a man like that, a real man with a generous spirit and a strength to match her own, maybe then she wouldn't be so reluctant to share her life...

"So what happened?" the girl asked. "Did Elizabeth come and live here with him? I hope she didn't die on the ship coming over and leave him all heartbroken or anything.''

"She certainly didn't," Gina said cheerfully. "She arrived to find her manor house completely reproduced on the shores of a Canadian lake, right down to the chandeliers and the stained glass on the stair landings. She was so happy she gave Josiah a big hug and a kiss and settled right in to have babies.''

"How many?"

"Eight. Six girls and two boys. She became the queen of local society and a generous patron of the arts and charities, too. She lived in the house until she died more than seventy years later. That was about 1960, I believe.''

"What happened to the house after that?"

"It went through some pretty hard times," Gina said. "None of Josiah Edgewood's offspring wanted to live here, so they tried various money-making projects, like opening the manor up for day tourists and dividing it into apartments. Both the value and appearance declined rapidly, and about fifteen years ago they decided to put it on the market.''

"And?" the young man asked, toying absently with a strand of his wife's long blond hair.

"And I bought it," Gina said. "I'd just finished a degree course in hotel management. I was on my summer vacation, like you are. I came out to Azure Bay with a friend to spend a day swimming and lazing on the beach, saw this tumbledown old place and fell in love at first sight. I knew it would be perfect for a bed-and-breakfast, which was something I wanted to run."

"But you must have been so *young!*" the bride said in awe. "Younger than we are, even. How could you ever buy a big place like this?"

"Well, for one thing, I had a small inheritance from my grandmother." Gina's voice was offhand, but her stomach tightened at the memory of that awful time. "And the bank was really impressed with my plans for restoring the building and developing a business."

"Bankers aren't all that easy to impress." The young doctor looked at her with frank admiration. "Nowadays it seems they only lend money to people who already have lots."

Gina gazed across the rippling turquoise waters of the lake. "I know. It all happened so long ago the details are pretty hard to remember. But I managed it somehow," she said with forced casualness. "So, you two are off for a swim?"

"If the water's warm enough. Yesterday it still felt like *ice.*"

Gina laughed at the girl's expression. "Okanagan Lake is more than eighty miles long from one end to the other, you know, and it's mostly fed by snow melting up in the mountains. The water doesn't really warm up for another month or so. But with the hot weather we've been having, it should be getting tolerable."

"Jenny's just scared of the lake monster," her husband said, ruffling his wife's hair fondly. "What's his name again?"

"Ogopogo," Gina told him. "Lots of the local people say they've seen him. He's supposed to be about sixty feet long, quite playful, with several humps and a head much like a horse."

"Have you ever seen him?" Jenny asked.

Gina smiled. "Maybe," she said. "But I'm not telling. Hurry up and go for your swim, or you won't be back in time for tea."

"I *love* teatime," the husband said with enthusiasm.

"Forget the tea and cakes," his wife teased. "The sherry's what he really likes."

The young man grinned, then ran off along the path to the beach, laughing as his wife came scrambling after him.

Gina watched them until they disappeared behind a rocky promontory. At last she turned and headed back up to the house, climbing the stairs to the gold room with its piles of wallpaper scraps.

SOON SHE WAS ABSORBED in her task again, lulled by the mechanics of the job, the careful measuring and fitting and the almost magical transformation as the fresh new paper covered the faded walls.

Gina hummed softly, thinking about curtains. The old lace panels looked limp and discolored against the new paper. Maybe she'd make a set of white priscillas for the window seat. Or some muslin panels on fling rods, trimmed with macramé lace...

She frowned, considering, and took a step closer to examine the window frame. In most of her decorating projects, she tried to stick to an authentic Victorian look, which was in keeping with the rest of the house. But window coverings, those were a real challenge.

She preferred a light fresh look in draperies, something that let in the marvelous scenery and the fragrant breezes from the garden and the lake. She hated the Victorian habit of swathing windows in yards and yards of heavy brocade and damask, often further cluttered with fringes and valances, all designed to keep the sun at bay. She paused to look out the window, pleased by the sights and sounds of her little world. Far below on the beach, she could see the honeymoon couple lying on the beach, stretched out on their dark blue Edgewood towels, their hands touching.

The elderly couple had left the sunroom and were strolling in the garden, admiring the geraniums. No other guests were in evidence, although five of Gina's nine rooms were currently occupied. People tended to scatter after breakfast, off exploring the countryside or visiting one of the resort towns along the lake.

But they were usually careful to get back in time for afternoon tea, served with cakes and sherry in the wood-paneled library. This charming custom had been established with great success during Gina's early years at Edgewood Manor, and was one of the features that brought people back year after year.

Through the open window, she could hear a gentle medley of sounds. Bees hummed drowsily among the flowers in the garden, Mary's pudgy poodle whimpered somewhere nearby—obviously still suffering from hunger pangs—and sea gulls cried around the dock.

It was heaven, Gina thought, absently fingering one of the lace panels. The place was simply heaven.

"Hello?" a voice said behind her, startling her. "Are you Gina Mitchell?"

She dropped the curtain, whirled around—and found herself staring in confusion at one of the most attractive men she'd ever seen.

CHAPTER TWO

GINA STUDIED the newcomer. He appeared to be about forty, no more than average height, but powerfully built. He wore casual pleated slacks and a white polo shirt, and had curly dark hair, heavily frosted with gray at the temples. His face, with its finely chiseled features and clear intelligent blue eyes, was severe in repose, despite the fullness of his lower lip. She thought his mouth hinted at a sensual nature, well controlled but very intense.

"I'm sorry if I startled you." His tone was courteous. "My name's Alex Colton. I phoned earlier to say I'd be coming out this afternoon."

"Oh, that's right. My housekeeper mentioned your call. But I've been so busy today I forgot all about it."

Colton looked around at the wet scraps of paper littering the hardwood, then at the flowered walls, now almost completely covered. He turned back to Gina with a smile. "It looks great. You're quite the decorator."

The smile surprised her. It transformed his face, driving away the severity and making him seem happy, almost boyish. But as suddenly as it had appeared, the smile faded and the severity returned.

Or was it sadness? Gina wondered. If a woman lived with this man, she'd probably spend a lot of her time trying to make him smile.

Gina wiped her hands briskly on her shorts and moved past him to the door. "My housekeeper mentioned that you were interested in renting a room?" she asked over her shoulder.

"I wanted to discuss terms," he said. "If you have a few minutes to spare."

"I always have time to spare for business."

Gina led the way down the stairs, conscious of Alex Colton just behind her. For such a powerfully built man, he had a tread as light as a cat.

"That window is magnificent," he said, gazing upward. "Do you happen to know who did the stained glass?"

Gina paused in the foyer by the newel post, fingering an intricate carving of grape leaves in the polished oak. For the second time that afternoon, she told the story of Josiah Edgewood and his reluctant bride.

Colton stood above her on the stairs and listened in apparent fascination, emotions playing visibly across his face. The man was such a good audience that Gina had to force herself to stop talking. She felt as if she could go on for hours, telling him stories about the house and its history, enjoying the way his eyes lit up and that elusive smile touched his mouth.

"Well, it seems my wife was right, as usual," he said at last. "I think this place is going to be perfect for us."

His wife.

Gina was surprised and a little annoyed with herself for her swift surge of disappointment. After all, she was hardly the sort of woman who looked on every man as a romantic prospect.

She led the way across the foyer and into her office. Moving behind the broad oak desk, she gestured to one of the leather chairs nearby and reached into a drawer for the reservation book. Her guest settled in a chair and examined the placid scene beyond the window.

"When were you and your wife thinking of coming to stay with us, Mr. Colton?"

He glanced at her, looking startled and unhappy, and turned back to his study of the yard. "What's wrong with that dog?" he asked.

Gina followed his gaze, watching as Mary's fat white poodle lumbered past the window and settled near a clump of pink alyssum, whining piteously.

"She's hungry," Gina said. "Her name's Annabel and I'm afraid she's on a diet."

"She certainly should be," Colton said with another of those brief shining smiles. "But she doesn't seem to have a lot of willpower, does she?"

"Not a lot," Gina agreed. "Annabel doesn't believe in suffering silently."

She stole a glance at her visitor, who was still watching the dog. He looked so intrigued that once again she had to suppress the urge to keep talking, to tell him all about Mary and Roger and their running conflict over the care and feeding of Annabel.

"We're getting a lot of bookings for the summer," Gina said, studying her reservations again. "But we have a few weekend rooms left in June, and a fair number of openings in the fall, though Christmas is already—"

"I want the whole summer," he said abruptly.

Gina looked at him in astonishment. "The whole summer?"

"That is, if the place looks as great under close inspection as it does on first impression."

She fingered her pen nervously. "I'm not sure if you're aware, Mr. Colton, that our prices are... somewhat higher than normal accommodation rates in the area."

"About a hundred and fifty dollars a day," he agreed calmly. "My wife had a brochure about the place, and I hope it isn't too far out-of-date. Are those prices still accurate?"

Gina nodded. "There's quite a lot of variation from room to room," she said. "Some of the smaller rooms are less than a hundred a day, but the attic suite, for instance, is two-fifty."

"Why?" he asked.

"Because of its size and the amenities. There's a wood-burning fireplace, a king-size sleigh bed on a platform fitted with steps, a large antique bathroom with a two-person whirlpool tub and a covered balcony overlooking the lake."

"Sounds like a honeymoon suite," he said.

"Often it is."

"And is the attic suite occupied at the moment?" he asked.

"There's a young couple from Minnesota staying there for the weekend. They'll be gone on Tuesday."

"Well, it sounds beautiful, but probably not exactly what I'm looking for. What about that room you were working in?"

"That's the gold room," Gina said. "It's about midrange. It has leaded-glass casement windows, a gas fireplace and a small balcony. It's a hundred and seventy."

"And if I took it for two months? Would I have to pay—" he paused a moment to think "—ten thousand dollars?"

"Of course not. I could offer a substantially decreased rate for a long-term stay. And all our guests are treated to a wonderful three-course breakfast and an afternoon tea in the library."

Colton leaned back in his chair. "Would the gold room be free for the entire summer?"

"I think I could make arrangements to have it available," Gina said, keeping her face carefully expressionless. She could never recall having a room booked for sixty consecutive days to the same person. A stay at Edgewood Manor was usually an expensive luxury for her guests. It was a chance to escape from the real world, to be pampered by the staff for a few days and swathed in the sumptuous elegance of a bygone era.

Sometimes travelers from faraway places such as Australia or Japan stayed for a week or more if they had a particular interest in the Okanagan region. But a booking of two months was simply unheard-of. It would require some juggling on her part and moving of guests to other rooms. But she had nothing on file to indicate that anybody had specifically requested the gold room, so it should be all right...

While she was examining the reservation book, Colton startled her again.

"Before you get too involved in that," he said, "I probably should mention that I'll be needing another room, as well."

"*Two* rooms? For the entire summer?" Gina looked up at him sharply.

He was sitting in relaxed fashion in the leather chair and had returned his gaze to the window. The afternoon sunlight etched his profile softly with gold.

Gina felt a rising annoyance.

This had to be some kind of scam. Maybe he was a journalist, planning to do a sensationalist article on inflated accommodation prices in resort areas, without the slightest concept of how much it cost to operate a huge old place like this.

"Look," she began stiffly, "if you're trying to make some kind of point, I'm not sure I understand what it is."

He turned in surprise. "What do you mean?"

Gina's anger faded to uncertainty once more. His gaze was so clear and honest, his face quietly appealing. "We don't normally have such extended bookings," she said at last. "A stay at Edgewood Manor is a weekend luxury for most people, Mr. Colton. It's not the kind of place where people tend to book a room for two whole months. And," she added, looking down at her reservation book to avoid his thoughtful gaze, "certainly not *two* rooms."

Colton sat forward in his chair. His face suddenly looked tired and drawn. "I see. But it's allowed? I mean, you'll still rent me the rooms if I want them?"

"Why do you need two rooms?" Gina asked bluntly.

"My daughter will be spending the summer here, as well. She's fourteen."

Gina still felt nervous and uncertain. She couldn't seem to read the man, couldn't determine if he was utterly sincere or merely feeding her a line for some obscure reason of his own.

She decided to play along and see what happened. Maybe he really was on the level. And renting two rooms for the whole summer was certainly profitable for her.... "All right." She consulted the book again. "But there'll be a problem, I'm afraid, if you want your daughter in a room adjoining yours. On the second floor we only have the blue and gold rooms and the Edgewood master suite, which is quite expensive and also heavily booked."

"Well, what about the blue room?"

Gina shook her head. "A number of couples have strong emotional attachments to the blue room. It's already reserved for quite a few weekends this summer. If your daughter stayed there, she'd have to move out at regular intervals to a different room while the blue room was being used."

Colton shook his head. "Oh, she wouldn't care for that, I'm afraid. Like most teenagers, Steffi travels with a lot of stuff. It takes a small army to move it."

Gina examined the reservation book again. "Let's see. Fourteen years old..." she murmured thoughtfully. "Maybe she'd like the patio room. It's on the main floor, with a French door opening onto the terrace. It's readily accessible to the beach path, and it's also one of the smaller, less expensive rooms. You can see the door to it over there, in fact."

She gestured out the window toward the side wing of the mansion. There was a door at ground level across the leafy yard, with leaded-glass panels set into rails of antique brass that winked brightly in the sunlight.

Colton's eyes sparkled with interest. "May I see the room?"

"Of course." Gina got up and led the way out of her office, conscious again of him following close behind. "It's quicker to go out through the back," she said, opening a door into a wide hallway floored in oak and smelling deliciously of fresh bread.

"What a heavenly aroma," he said, sniffing in pleasure.

"Mary's baking this afternoon. She's the cook and housekeeper. That's the kitchen," Gina added as they passed a big airy room full of glass-fronted cabinets. "Guests are welcome to drop in and visit while Mary's working. And she's always very generous about sharing her recipes."

"I look forward to meeting her."

Gina nodded. "I'll introduce you on the way back. Hello, Roger," she said as the caretaker passed them, carrying his freshly carved spindle and a can of wood stain.

Roger smiled at Gina and Alex Colton, his face creasing with warmth. "I have to match the wood stains," he told them, brandishing the spindle. "It usually takes about seven attempts before I get it just right."

"That's Roger Appleby," Gina told her visitor as the handyman vanished into the foyer. "He looks after things for me around the hotel. He also plays wonderful music on a hundred-year-old cello."

"I'm liking this place more and more," Alex Colton said, smiling down at her.

The two of them went out the back and down the broad steps to the yard. Annabel caught sight of them and trotted awkwardly across the lawn, gazing up at them with wretched appeal.

"She looks even fatter up close," the man said, bending to pet her.

Gina watched, liking the way he caressed the dog. His hands looked strong and competent, but very gentle. She realized she was staring and turned away quickly to cross the yard, heading for the shaded flag-stone terrace.

"Is all the landscaping authentic Victorian, too?" he asked.

"Most of it. Lady Edgewood had a lot of shrubs brought over from Scotland, and they do quite well in this climate. There's even some heather growing on the slope up there. Of course, I've added other perenni-als, and Mary has a big garden that provides most of our vegetables during the summer. And we make all our own jams and preserves."

"Enchanting," Alex Colton said sincerely, looking around at the shimmering lake, the blue-shadowed mountains on both sides of the valley and the roofs of the little town of Azure Bay in the distance. "Really beautiful. I think this summer is going to be good for us."

Gina watched him, struck by the sadness in his face. He looked utterly worn-out, she thought with a rush of sympathy, despite his obvious physical strength.

"I was sure," she muttered, rummaging in the pocket of her shorts, "I had a master key somewhere. Now what did I . . ."

Gina felt a growing embarrassment as he watched her place the contents of her pockets, item by item, on a stone retaining wall. There were two polished stones that she'd found on the beach that morning after her swim, as well as a piece of flint that could possibly be a chipped arrowhead, and a length of bent wire she planned to use on the shed door until Roger could find a lock.

But the key didn't emerge. She went on lining things up on the wall, ignoring his amused glance.

A lottery ticket she hadn't found the time to check on yet, two feathers, a recipe for peach chutney jotted on a table napkin, a couple of pieces of toffee wrapped in gold foil, a tiny plastic replica of Batman, a pocketknife with a wooden handle, a miniature compass in a gold case—

"A compass!" he exclaimed, picking up the little object. "Does it work?"

"Of course," Gina said briskly. "Ah, here's the key," she said in relief, sweeping the other things back into her pockets.

"Why do you carry a compass?"

"You never know when you might get lost in the woods around here. A compass is a really handy thing to have."

His eyes sparkled. "You're just like a ten-year-old boy. Pockets full of interesting stuff. I like that, Miss Mitchell."

He handed Gina the compass and she returned it to her pocket, trying hard to look like the mature and professional manager of a successful business. But it had been so unnerving to have him examining that row of objects.

She resolved to clean out all the junk from her pockets as soon as Alex Colton left and to try harder in future to refrain from picking up every interesting thing that caught her eye.

"Is the patio room occupied at the moment?" Colton asked. "I'd hate to barge in on somebody."

Gina shook her head. "There was a couple here for two days, but they left yesterday morning. I'm afraid they complained to Roger that Annabel was making a lot of noise," she added.

"Steffi is going to love Annabel," Colton said with a fleeting grin. "Although," he added, "there's a very real danger she might be tempted to sneak some food to the poor thing."

"Oh, goodness, I hope not." Gina unlocked the door. "Roger does that all the time. Mary gets very upset with him."

"I think," he repeated, following her into the room, "I'm really going to like this place."

He was immediately charmed by the patio room, which had a curtained window seat, a walk-in closet and a small en suite bathroom.

"Perfect," he declared. "I'll take this room, as well as the gold room, all right?"

"You haven't even asked about the price," Gina said, leading the way back into the yard.

"I'm sure you'll be fair."

Gina paused by the retaining wall and looked up at him. "How can you be sure of that?"

He hoisted himself onto the stone ledge and smiled at her. "Because you carry feathers and a compass in your pocket."

She hesitated, feeling awkward.

"Sit here with me, Miss Mitchell," he said, patting the sun-warmed stone beside him. "I do have a few more questions about the hotel."

"Gina," she said automatically, settling on the ledge a couple of feet away from him. "We're all on a first-name basis here."

"Gina," he repeated. "And I'm Alex."

He extended his hand. She shook it, pleased by the strength of his grip.

"It's nice to meet you, Alex," she said formally. "I hope you'll enjoy your stay at Edgewood Manor."

"Yes," he said, leaning back, his hands braced against the stone. "So do I. We could certainly use a holiday."

He closed his eyes in the sunlight. Gina stole a glance at him, once again struck by his look of strain and weariness.

"When will you be arriving?" she asked.

"On the first of July, right at the beginning of the long weekend. I'll book both rooms for all of July and August, but Steffi might choose to visit a school friend for the first week or two of July, so she'll arrive later than I do."

"I see." Gina wondered why he didn't say "we." Maybe his wife would also be staying home until their daughter was ready to travel to Azure Bay. But it seemed odd that he would come by himself, ahead of his family.

"What's the daily routine here?" he asked, bending to pet Annabel again as she huddled by their feet, nibbling one of her paws disconsolately.

"Well, there aren't any rules. We serve breakfast at eight o'clock, and Mary leaves fruit and baked goods in the dining room all day for guests who like to nibble. Tea is set out in the library from about four o'clock on. Guests are welcome to build a fire in the drawing room or the library on chilly nights and go anywhere on the property that's not marked exclusively for staff."

"How large a staff do you have?"

"Mostly just Mary and Roger and me. But in July and August, our busiest months, I also hire a couple of college girls from town to help out."

"What about the evening meal?" Alex asked.

"The staff eats here, but we don't serve anything to the guests. They usually choose to walk or drive into town for dinner. It's less than half a mile, and there are several restaurants catering to tourists, including a really good seafood place. They also have a Chinese restaurant and a pizza place that both deliver, if you prefer to stay and eat at the hotel."

"Sounds great." He glanced up at the vine-covered facade of the old mansion's other wing. "Can we see the room where you were working from here?"

Gina pointed. "The gold room's that second-floor balcony up there under the dormer."

Alex squinted into the sunlight. "Ah, yes. Would there be an electrical outlet on the balcony?"

"No, but there's an outlet just inside the door. I particularly remember," she added, "because I had to take the plate off today to paper around it."

"Good. I'll probably work out there most days if the weather's nice."

"What kind of work?" Gina asked.

"Computer," he said briefly.

She nodded, not pressing for further details. He seemed reluctant to divulge more.

But then to her surprise he said, "I teach economics at a private college near Vancouver. I plan to do some writing this summer."

"Will your wife and daughter be able to amuse themselves all day?" she asked. "I'm afraid there's not a lot going on in the town of Azure Bay—though Kelowna is less than half an hour away, and it's a good-size resort city."

"Steffi's an outdoor girl," Alex said. "She loves hiking and swimming, and she's a pretty fair amateur photographer. She's not the type to hang around malls or video arcades.''

''I see.'' Gina paused, thinking about the reality of a two-month stay at Edgewood Manor for anyone unaccustomed to this kind of rural existence. ''How about your wife? Is she—''

''My wife is dead,'' he said quietly.

''I'm sorry.'' Gina glanced at him. He was staring across the lake, his profile cold and unrevealing. ''I thought . . . I was sure you spoke of this holiday as her idea.''

''In a way it was.'' He continued to look at the shimmering expanse of blue-green water. ''My wife died three months ago after a lengthy illness. When I was going through her papers, I found the brochure about Edgewood Manor.''

''I see.''

''My wife was the one who planned our vacations,'' he went on. ''I was always too busy to bother with details like that. Besides, she had a flair for finding the perfect place and organizing quirky offbeat holidays that were perfect for us. So when I found that brochure in her desk, I looked on it as a sort of message from her.'' He gave Gina a tired smile. ''And it seems she was right again.''

''I hope so,'' Gina said with gentle sincerity. ''I hope you and your daughter enjoy the summer.''

''It's been hard for Steffi,'' he said. ''Really hard. I'm worried about her.''

Gina was silent, recognizing his difficulty with talking about his family's trauma. He was a man who didn't share his feelings easily.

''She's at an age where a girl needs her mother,'' he went on in a low voice. ''It was bad enough for Steffi to lose her, but to watch how terribly Janice suffered at the end..."

He fell silent.

Gina glanced at him again, wanting to reach over and squeeze his hand, or put her arm around him and give him a sympathetic hug. But she kept her hands folded tightly in her lap.

"What...what was your wife's illness?" she inquired hesitantly. She knew she was prying, but something about the man compelled her to ask.

"She had Huntington's," he said, still staring at the lake.

"Oh," Gina murmured, wrung with sympathy. "Oh, I'm so sorry."

She was silent a moment, trying to remember what she'd heard about the condition. "I always thought..." she began.

He turned to face her. "Yes?"

"About Huntington's. I thought it didn't affect people until quite late in life."

"Usually it doesn't," Alex said. "But it can strike in the early thirties. That's when my wife first started to develop symptoms—about ten or eleven years ago. Her father and an uncle both died of it," he added, "so we knew what to expect. But the children of people with Huntington's still have a fifty percent chance of escaping it."

"And until the symptoms appear..."

"You keep hoping," he said bitterly. "You cling to hope until the last minute. You tell yourself maybe the tremors are just fatigue, and the dizziness is some kind of allergy. You grasp at straws as long as you can."

"But hasn't a test been developed recently? I thought there was some kind of genetic marker that can be isolated and identified."

"That's true," he said, looking at Gina in surprise. "You're very well-informed."

"I watch public television," she said, "and read a lot. I've always had an interest in scientific things."

"Of course you have," he said with a quick smile. "Anybody can tell that by looking at the things you carry in your pockets."

She smiled back. "My mother was a chemistry teacher until she retired a few years ago. She always encouraged me to have an inquiring mind."

"What about your father?"

Gina tensed, reluctant to get into a personal discussion. But he'd told her about his own family tragedy, so it seemed graceless not to respond to his questions.

"My father was in sales," she said. "He traveled a lot. When I was about eleven, he left on a trip to Ontario and wound up staying there. My mother raised us all alone."

"Us?"

"I have a sister who's ten years younger than I am. She and my mother live in New Brunswick. I came out here almost twenty years ago to go to college, fell in love with the province and never left."

"Why did you decide to go to school so far from home?"

"I have an aunt who lives in Vancouver near the university," Gina said. "It was cheaper to stay with her than in a dormitory somewhere. And UBC offered a really good course on hotel management, which was always my career choice."

"I see."

Alex leaned back again, lifting his face gratefully to the warm rays of sunlight.

"In answer to your question about testing," he said after a brief silence, "it was something my wife never wanted to do, even after the test became more readily available. She said she refused to live with a death penalty over her head. As it happened, the disease progressed a lot more rapidly than is usual once the symptoms appeared, so maybe she was wise."

Maybe, Gina thought. But it wouldn't have been her own choice. She always preferred to know what she was dealing with, to confront the reality head-on no matter how awful it might be. She wondered about Alex's daughter, though. Had she been tested? Surely—

Alex suddenly got to his feet, then waited courteously while she did likewise. "We'd better get this deal concluded," he said. "I have to be back in Vancouver before nightfall."

She walked with him back into the hotel, relieved that their painful conversation was ended.

But as they strolled through the hallway with Annabel at their heels and paused in the kitchen to greet Mary, Gina was alarmed to realize she was already counting the days until the first of July....

CHAPTER THREE

ROGER STROLLED into the kitchen and patted Gina's shoulder as she worked at a little side table near the window.

Outside, the late-evening sun was setting behind the mountains, casting long purple shadows across the yard. The lake glistened with fiery streaks of orange, and the twilight air was warm and murmurous with crickets and the music of bullfrogs by the water's edge.

"What's this one?" he asked.

Gina squinted at the scrap of wire and golden feathers in her vise. "A yellow nymph," she said. "Like the ones I made last year, but with some minor improvements."

"Those yellow nymphs were great flies. Remember the big trout I caught, Gina?"

"How could I forget? You've mentioned it practically every day for the last year."

"You're just jealous," he said placidly. "We should try to get up to Bear Creek again. We've hardly been fishing at all this spring, and June's almost over."

Gina sighed, winding her thread carefully. "It's always so busy around here."

"Well," Roger said, pouring himself a cup of coffee from the pot on the counter, "if we wait till we're not busy, we'll never go."

"That's certainly true." Gina frowned at the partly shaped fishing fly on her vise, then rummaged in a tackle box full of colored feathers, scraps of fur and spools of thread. "I think I'm going to add some black antennae," she said. "Something that wobbles a bit."

"Do nymphs have antennae?" Roger asked.

He crossed the room to the big oak table, the antique lights overhead reflecting on his bald pate with its scant fringe of silver.

"Who cares?" Gina said cheerfully. "Never question an artist. I'm the one who tied the fly that caught your prizewinning trout, remember?"

Roger sat at the table, stirring cream into his coffee. "I remember, all right. Speaking of being busy," he said thoughtfully, "when do Mr. Colton and his daughter arrive?"

"Next week. At least, that's when the rooms are booked, but he's going to be arriving on his own. He faxed a confirmation last week. I gather she's going to be coming a week or two later."

"It seems strange," Roger said. "I mean, booking the patio room just to have it available, even though the girl won't be here for maybe two weeks. At a cost of more than a hundred dollars a day, too. Isn't that a real waste of money?"

"It appears," Gina said, "that money isn't a problem for Mr. Alex Colton."

"I didn't think college professors made that kind of income."

"Neither did I. But, you know, he seemed so casual about the cost. He was perfectly willing to accept my terms. In fact, I could probably have charged him twice as much and he would have agreed without an argument."

Roger sipped his coffee and looked out the window at the glowing sunset colors reflected in the waters of the lake. "Well, it's sure an advantage to have those rooms booked full-time. No turnover. Less work for you."

"Maybe." Gina snipped at the colored thread. "And maybe not."

Roger glanced at her in surprise. "What do you mean?"

Gina selected a bit of black wire, wrinkling her brow thoughtfully. "What if they're awful guests?" she asked. "What if we find after a while that we can't stand them, like that Kimmer family last summer, but we're stuck with them for two whole months?"

Roger grinned. "Remember how Mrs. Kimmer demanded a computer printout of the fat and cholesterol content in every breakfast?"

"And Mr. Kimmer kicked Annabel, and he and Mary almost came to blows over it?"

"And—" Roger grimaced "—the way they kept letting those awful kids of theirs slide down the banisters all the way from the attic, and take their towels outside to play in the mud."

"Oh, they were a charming group, all right," Gina said dryly. "That's my point." She put the wire down and turned to look at her caretaker. "What if these two are horrible like the Kimmers and turn out to be really disruptive? We've never had somebody here for two whole months, Roger."

"I'm not worried," he said calmly. "I met Alex Colton and had a talk with him that day he booked the rooms. He struck me as a decent sort of fellow. I liked him."

Gina was silent, idly flexing her pliers.

"His daughter sounded nice, too," Roger went on. "In fact, Colton told me she's a real outdoors type. I was wondering," he added almost shyly, "if maybe she'd want to go fishing with us sometime. Wouldn't it be fun to have a kid along, Gina? Somebody young and enthusiastic?"

Gina considered this, startled by the idea. "I'm not sure," she said at last. "I don't know much about teenage girls."

"Didn't you grow up with a little sister?"

"Sure," Gina said. "But Claudia's ten years younger than I am, Roger. She was eight when I left home, and I've hardly seen her at all since. It's too expensive to travel between here and the Maritimes."

"How long ago was it that time she came out here? Five or six years ago?"

Gina considered. "It would have been eight years, I guess. That trip was my gift to Claudia the year she graduated from high school, when she was eighteen. My goodness—" Gina sighed "—I can't get over the way the years fly past."

"Does she still have that trouble with her leg?"

"Not much. She hardly limps at all anymore." Gina turned to stare out the window. "But it's taken years of hard work and therapy."

"What happened exactly?" Roger asked. "I don't think you ever told me the whole story, just that she'd been in some kind of an accident."

"It was after I'd been out West a couple of years, when Claudia was ten. I was in Vancouver when I heard." Gina shuddered. "My mother decided to take Claudia with her for a summer holiday in New England. She'd been driving all day and was exhausted, but I guess she didn't realize *how* exhausted. She dozed off on the freeway in Maine and drove under a semitrailer parked by an off-ramp.''

Roger took another sip of his coffee and listened in sympathy.

''It was so awful,'' Gina went on. ''Mom's injuries were mostly superficial, but Claudia's right leg was almost severed just above the knee. They rushed her to the hospital and used all kinds of microsurgery techniques to reattach the nerves and tendons, then did bone grafts to restructure the leg.''

''Wonderful, isn't it?'' Roger said. ''What they can do with medical science these days.''

''Oh, it's wonderful, all right,'' Gina said gloomily. ''Really wonderful.''

''Gina?'' he asked, puzzled.

She met Roger's gaze, thinking about the nightmare her family had been forced to endure. ''My mother's kind of an absentminded professor, Roger. Not practical at all. She didn't think to buy medical insurance for herself or Claudia before traveling out of the country.''

His eyes widened. ''My God,'' he breathed. ''So how much did a procedure like that cost?''

Gina brushed a hand across her forehead. ''Some of the surgeons donated their time, and we had Claudia transferred back to the Maritimes as soon as she could travel. But the bill for her treatment was already over forty thousand dollars by the time she was moved.''

''Could your mother afford that?''

''My mother could hardly afford to put meals on the table,'' Gina said bleakly. ''She was about to lose her little house, her teaching job, and any possibility of earning enough in the future to pay for the years of extended therapy that Claudia was going to need.''

"So what did you do?"

"We managed." Gina stared at the lake. The sun had completely retreated behind the mountains now, and the black still depths of the lake seemed to echo the void in her heart, the aching sorrow and yearning that never went away. "We managed somehow. We all made some . . . pretty big sacrifices."

Roger studied her thoughtfully for a moment. "Your sister is a real stunner, as I recall," he said at last.

"She certainly is." Gina gathered herself together. "Claudia looks a lot like our mother. I wasn't lucky enough to get the red hair or the peaches-and-cream complexion."

"Well, you're a beauty in your own way, Gina," he said gallantly. "Red hair or not."

She smiled at him. "And you're a sweetie. But I'm realistic about myself, Roger. I know what my strengths and weaknesses are."

"I'm not sure you do. I don't know if you've ever been fully aware of your strengths."

Gina shook her head. She and Roger had been friends for almost twelve years, but except for some casual teasing, they usually tended to avoid this kind of personal discussion.

"Speaking of strengths and weaknesses," she said, removing the completed fly from her vise and picking up another bit of wire, "do you ever regret moving here, Roger? Do you miss having a desk and an expense account and a brass nameplate on your door?"

"Not a bit. I live alone, and I'm sixty-two years old. Why would I want to sit behind a desk all day? I want to enjoy my days, because if I can't, what's the sense in living?"

"But do you really enjoy it here?" she asked, suddenly anxious to hear his answer. "I mean, looking after the hotel for me and keeping things running smoothly, is that enough of a challenge for you?"

"At my age, I don't want challenges anymore, Gina. What I want is comfort. And I find my life here very comfortable."

"Good," she said in relief. "Sometimes I'm afraid you're getting restless."

"You're supposed to quit saying things like that," he reminded her, then pushed his chair back and got up to open a cupboard door. "What happened to the banana loaf Mary baked this morning?"

"The guests gobbled every last crumb with afternoon tea."

"Too bad," he muttered, still peering moodily into the cupboard. "Where is the woman, anyhow?"

"She's at choir practice. You'll get as fat as Annabel if you keep eating Mary's baking," Gina warned him, though from the look of his long angular body she doubted there was much fear of that.

She paused suddenly and narrowed her eyes. There was something different about Roger tonight.

"Why are you here now?" she asked. "You don't usually come over after supper."

"I needed to pick up something."

"What?"

"Just some tools," he said evasively.

"Why?" Gina asked.

"I'm working on something."

"But you don't even have a workbench at your house, do you? I thought you did all your woodwork here at the hotel."

"What is this?" Roger asked mildly. "An inquisition? Am I not free to drop by the hotel after hours if I want to?"

"Of course you are," Gina said. "But you look...different tonight, that's all."

"In what way?"

"I don't know." She studied him. "Maybe you've changed your hairstyle."

He chuckled. "And *you*, young lady, are becoming far too impertinent."

Gina smiled and returned to her task, while Roger poured himself a second cup of coffee. For a while there was a companionable silence in the kitchen.

But after a few minutes the peace was broken by the closing of a door, a noisy storm of barking and a gentle tread in the hallway. Mary entered the room, laden with books. Annabel tumbled at her heels and yelped hysterically.

"For God's sake," Roger said. "Feed that animal, won't you? She's being even more annoying than usual."

Mary lowered her books onto the table and gave him a level stare. Then she sniffed dismissively and turned away. Gina smiled to herself.

"How was your choir practice, Mary?" she asked.

"It was exciting." Mary crossed the kitchen and took a can of dog food from the cupboard. She opened it and measured the contents into a bowl with calm deliberation, while Annabel writhed on the hardwood floor in an agony of anticipation.

"Choir practice was exciting?" Roger asked.

Mary washed her hands at the sink and continued to address Gina as if he hadn't spoken. "Mr. Bedlow gave the soprano solo to Marianna Turner."

Gina's eyes widened. "No kidding. Even though everybody knows?"

"What does everybody know?" Roger asked, watching with a bemused expression as Mary put Annabel's bowl on the floor and the animal began to wolf it down as if she hadn't eaten in weeks.

"About Mr. Bedlow and Marianna Turner," Gina explained.

"What about them?"

"Oh, Roger," Gina said. "How could you have possibly missed such a juicy tidbit of gossip?"

His look of surprise was almost comical. "Dried-up old Cecil Bedlow? And that plump young schoolteacher? There's *gossip* about those two?"

Mary forgot she was no longer on speaking terms with the caretaker. "There certainly is," she told him, tying on her apron, then began opening doors and cabinets, assembling the ingredients to prepare batter for the next morning's fruit crepes.

"Was Marianna embarrassed?" Gina asked.

"I think so. *Whatever's* happening, it's more on his side than hers, in my opinion. I think poor Marianna just doesn't know what to do about him."

"You're always so generous, Mary," Roger said. "Other women would probably be catty about a situation like that."

Mary ignored the compliment. "So we didn't get much of anything else done," she concluded, "except for the opening bars of the 'Hallelujah Chorus.' We're singing it at the Canada Day picnic next weekend."

"Well, of course," Roger said solemnly. "That's a rousing picnic song. Handel should blend right in with the fried chicken and the kids' sack races."

Mary gave him a stern glance. "Well, that's good. Because your chamber-music group is booked to do four sets of Elizabethan madrigals on the entertainment stage by the hamburger tent."

"Elizabethan madrigals!" he exclaimed, recoiling in alarm. "You're joking."

"It's right there on the program, next to the Tiny Tots Highland Dancing."

Roger subsided behind his coffee mug again. "This town is a mad, mad place," he said sadly. "Utterly insane."

"Oh, come on," Gina said. She left the worktable to get herself a mug of coffee, pausing on the way to drop a kiss on the top of Roger's shiny bald head. "You love living here. And you have lots of fun at the picnic every year, no matter how much you complain and make fun."

"My goodness." Mary paused with a sifter of flour in her hand. "I almost forgot," she said, staring at Gina. "The choir practice wasn't the only exciting thing this afternoon."

Gina carried her mug back to her table and began construction of another yellow nymph. "So what else happened, Mary?"

"I got some library books."

"How does the woman ever survive her days?" Roger asked with a grin. "Fraught as they are with such drama and excitement." He rolled his eyes eloquently in Gina's direction, making her giggle. Unruffled by his teasing, Mary began to mix the batter for her crepes in a big blue enamel bowl.

"I went to the library," she repeated, "and picked out a lot of books for myself. I also got some new books on gardening and furniture restoration for you, Gina, in case you ever have time to read."

"Thanks," Gina told her. "That was thoughtful of you, Mary."

"How about me?" Roger asked. "Did you get any books for me?"

"Two political biographies and a new mystery," Mary replied calmly. "Although I probably needn't have bothered, since you seem to be so *busy* these days."

The words were innocent enough, but Gina was surprised by the unusual edge in Mary's voice and the way Roger seemed to duck his head in embarrassment.

Suddenly the room was full of tense undercurrents. Confused, Gina looked from one to the other, about to ask what was going on, when Mary resumed her story.

"And while I was browsing through the newspapers, I discovered the most amazing thing."

"An appropriate location to make amazing discoveries," Roger murmured, his equilibrium apparently restored. "Among the well-stocked shelves of the Azure Bay Library."

Mary ignored him and addressed Gina. "Remember the day you brought that man into the kitchen and introduced him to me? The one who's staying all summer with his daughter?"

Gina nodded. "Alex Colton. He's arriving in a few days."

"And remember how I told you after he left..." Mary paused to add more milk to her batter. "I told you I was absolutely positive I'd seen him somewhere, and you said I was probably wrong because he'd never been in the valley before?"

Gina nodded, baffled. "I remember. Why?"

"Well, I was right," Mary said, crossing the kitchen to rummage through the pile of books and magazines.

Gina got up again and crossed to the big central table, cradling her coffee mug in her hands and sitting down next to Roger.

Mary opened a recent copy of a newspaper and laid it out on the table in front of them. "See?" She stood back with an air of triumph.

Gina gazed in astonishment. Alex Colton's picture appeared at the top of a newspaper column on the financial pages. She studied the image, struck once again by the man's appealing masculine look, and the contradictory mixture of sensuality and asceticism in his face.

"I'll be damned!" Roger exclaimed. "Alex Colton is a columnist? I thought he was a college professor."

"Not just any columnist. He's Alexander Waring." The usually reserved Mary clearly enjoyed the sensation she was causing. "He writes this column about investment and personal finance," she told Gina. "It's syndicated, and Roger and I read it all the time. His column's in a lot of the big papers, but it never used to have his picture at the top. He also has four or five books in the library."

Roger leaned closer to examine the paper. "Well, I'll be damned," he repeated. "Alexander Waring. I have two of his books at home, you know. He has terrific money sense." Roger shook his head in amazement. "And to think I talked with the man about woodwork and cello music, and didn't even know who he was."

"Well, I don't know as much about the world of high finance as you two obviously do." Gina took the paper from Roger and studied the picture. "Is he really good?"

"He's one of the best," Roger said. "His books give down-to-earth advice on investing and money management, things an ordinary person can actually use. And sometimes," he added with a smile, "they're really funny. The man must have a great sense of humor."

"Can I borrow one of them?" Gina asked. "It's probably... it's time for me to start learning something about money management," she said lamely when the other two looked at her in surprise.

Roger's eyes were bright with teasing. "That's all you want to learn?"

"Of course," Gina said. "You know, I just remembered—he did say that he planned to do some writing this summer. He asked me about electrical outlets on the gold-room balcony for his computer."

"I suppose he has to keep writing even during the holidays," Mary said. "He could hardly take two whole months off, after all. A lot of people swear by that column of his."

"Really? You think he'll still be doing the column?" Gina asked with sudden excitement. "Maybe he'll mention the hotel. Anything that brings us to the attention of the public is good for business."

"As long as he writes about how good the food is," Mary observed placidly.

"And doesn't devote whole columns to disruptive pets." Roger glanced at Annabel, who'd emptied her dish and was now clattering it noisily around on the floor in a vain attempt to discover stray morsels clinging to the sides or bottom.

Mary glared at him. "*Most* people," she said coldly, "have better things to do with their time than sit around insulting poor defenseless animals."

"Ah, yes. My cue to depart."

Roger got to his feet, smiled at the two women and strolled from the room. They could hear the sound of a truck starting outside, followed by the slow rumble of his departure along the lakeshore road.

"He isn't going home," Gina said, leaning forward to peer out the window. "He must be going into town."

She seated herself at the worktable again, setting the newspaper down carefully next to her tackle box. Mary continued to work at the central table, mixing batter in the bowl with fierce strokes.

"Mary?" Gina said.

"What?"

Mary bent down to take Annabel's feeding dish away. The poodle sank onto her fat haunches and watched with a comical look of dismay.

"Did you notice something different about Roger tonight?"

"Of course I did," Mary said curtly.

"What is it?"

"He's all dressed up. He's wearing his second-best pants, those gray pleated corduroys, and the new sweater I gave him for Christmas."

Gina's eyes widened. "You're right," she said, putting down her pliers. "I remember when he got that sweater, but I don't think I've ever seen him wearing it before."

Mary murmured something to the poodle, then returned to her task.

"Why would he be all dressed up?" Gina said, puzzled. "This is just an ordinary Saturday night, isn't it? I mean, their chamber group isn't playing anywhere. He always tells me when they have a concert in case I want to go along."

"Oh, it's certainly not a *concert,*" Mary said.

Gina pushed her chair back, completely intrigued by now. "Mary, I want you to tell me what's going on."

"Nothing very important. Roger has a lady friend, that's all."

"You're kidding." Gina gaped at the cook, astounded, while Mary continued to whip the batter. "How could Roger possibly have a girlfriend without me knowing?"

Mary remained silent and tipped the contents of the blue bowl into a pitcher, then stored it away in one of the two oversize fridges along the wall.

"Look," Gina persisted, "are you serious? I mean, about Roger having a lady friend?"

Mary poured herself a mug of coffee and sat wearily at the table. "Oh, yes," she said. "I'm quite serious."

"I can't imagine," Gina said, "who the woman could be. I don't think there's anybody in town who'd be even faintly eligible. Although—" she frowned thoughtfully "—when one considers Cecil Bedlow and Marianna Turner, I guess anything's possible."

"It's not somebody from town," Mary said, bending to stroke Annabel. "It's a stranger. A woman who's staying at Fred's motel out near the winery."

"How did Roger meet her?"

"Apparently she came to one of their chamber concerts and struck up a conversation with him. Roger's taken her out several times since then for drives and coffee."

"Why," Gina said plaintively, "does nobody ever tell me anything?"

Mary shrugged. "I thought it was no big deal at first. Apparently this woman is one of the shareholders in the winery, and she wanted to come out and look at her investment firsthand. At least, that's what Fred says."

"Well, Fred should know. He runs the motel, after all."

"Fred's not all that bright," Mary said sadly. "Even if he is my second cousin."

"So how long has this woman been staying at the motel?"

"About two weeks."

"Have you met her, Mary?"

"Annabel, stop that whining!" the housekeeper warned with unusual sharpness. "Stop it this instant!"

The poodle slunk away into the hallway, casting a bitter glance over her shoulder as she did so.

"Mary?" Gina prodded.

"Yes," the housekeeper said, rubbing the back of her neck with a weary sigh. "I've met her, all right. She was in the drugstore yesterday, and Maybelle introduced us. I knew the woman was interested in Roger, so I took a real good look at her."

"What's her name?"

"Lacey Franks."

"And how old is she?" Gina asked.

"Probably about fifty, but she looks ten years younger than she is. Dyed hair," Mary said. "Bright clothes and lots of makeup, but she's careful with it so you can't tell."

Gina wound another fishing fly onto her vise, gripping the pliers in silence.

"She's very stylish." Mary looked down ruefully at her cotton dress and brown cardigan. "And she dresses to show off her figure, too. Yesterday when Maybelle introduced us, she was wearing a little yellow tennis dress with a sweater tied over her shoulders like the women in the television ads."

Gina shook her head in amazement. "And our Roger is interested in her? He's actually taken her out on a *date?*"

"More than once," Mary said darkly. "Maybelle told me she saw them sitting in a booth at the Clamshell eating lobster, holding hands and laughing together like teenagers."

"Well, for goodness' sake," Gina said, pleased by this image. "Isn't that nice."

Mary folded a plastic covering over one of the mixing bowls.

"Where does this Lacey Franks live?" Gina asked. "Does the local gossip network know anything about her?"

"Only that she's supposed to be rich and her home address is somewhere in West Vancouver."

"That's a pretty posh area, isn't it?"

"I wouldn't know," Mary said. "I really wouldn't know."

The cook got up, removed her apron and hung it in the pantry. With a softly worded good-night, she made her way out of the kitchen, leaving Gina sitting alone at the window, gazing thoughtfully out at the darkness.

ALEX COLTON, TOO, was gazing into the darkness through the window in his study. The sun had vanished below the horizon in a fiery ball of orange, and the light across the waters of English Bay had faded quickly.

At last he got up and prowled restlessly around the little room, picking up papers and setting them down again, scanning the shelves for a book to take up to his room later. But nothing looked interesting.

"Lord, how I need a holiday," he muttered, returning to the window. "Or at least a change of scene."

He thought about the vine-covered mansion in the Okanagan, and the newly papered room where he would soon be staying. The place was enormously appealing, especially with that air of bygone elegance that so perfectly suited the peaceful drowsy warmth of its rural setting.

It was odd, Alex mused, that Janice had never mentioned the hotel to him. She'd obviously learned about it years ago and set aside that brochure in anticipation of a time when they could travel there on a family vacation.

But for the past two years, Jan hadn't been well enough to travel anywhere. And in the final months of her life, she often hadn't even been able to remember her husband's name or their daughter's face, let alone the address of a resort hotel.

Alex gazed blindly out the window at the dark silvered water, trying to fight off the image of Janice's twisted face, her body ravaged by an illness so brutal that in the end, it destroyed every vestige of dignity and composure. With a little shock of alarm, he realized he could no longer remember her as she'd looked before the illness. He picked up a photograph from his desk and studied the smiling image in the gold frame.

Jan had been slim and blond, with a delicate, almost angelic beauty that belied her determined nature. When they were first married all those years ago, he'd been surprised and a little taken aback to learn just how formidable—and stubborn—a woman she really was.

But even Jan's strength had been no match for the crippling illness that was hidden in her body, biding its time, waiting to claim her.

He shook his head moodily, still watching as the last of the twilight glow faded beyond the horizon and the first stars began to glimmer over the waters of the bay. He found his mind returning to the old hotel on the lake and the young woman who apparently owned it. She'd been in his thoughts a lot these days, more than he liked to admit.

Slowly Alex sank into an armchair by the window and allowed himself to reconstruct the image of Gina Mitchell's face. Everything about the woman was appealing. He liked the open frankness of her expression, the level brows and calm hazel eyes, her dusting of freckles and that cropped curly mass of dark hair. He even admired the boyish athletic look of her body.

He smiled, recalling the way she'd emptied her pockets and solemnly lined up those delightful little objects along the top of the stone wall. At that moment he'd been completely enchanted by her. He would have liked to reach out and touch the skin of her bare arm, ruffle her hair, maybe—

Alex shook his head abruptly, the smile fading.

Not a very attractive line of thought, he told himself, for a man whose wife had been dead for little more than three months.

But Jan had been lost to him for a long, long time. When her symptoms had become too obvious to ignore and she'd finally allowed herself to be examined, the diagnosis itself had been a sentence of death. Both of them knew it. But before death had finally claimed her, the illness had been lingering, so excruciatingly painful both physically and mentally that it had drained every bit of strength from all three of them.

For the last three years, Alex and his wife had no physical relationship apart from the care he gave her and the comfort he could sometimes provide by holding her in his arms. Toward the end, even his touch was too painful for her to endure.

Alex didn't like to dwell on his own suffering, because he knew that his daughter had endured far more pain. As a girl just entering adolescence, growing into the knowledge of her own womanhood, Steffi had watched her mother fade from strength and beauty to utter dependence. She'd witnessed the deterioration of that lovely body and powerful mind, and gradually come to understand that nobody in her life, not even her father, could protect them from this horror.

He and Steffi had once been so close. Alex was desperately concerned about his daughter's moody silence and increasing withdrawal. No matter what he did, she seemed to retreat farther from him every day into a place he couldn't follow.

He put the worried thoughts from his mind and returned to his computer, forcing himself to spend a couple of hours in concentrated work on the final column before his trip to Azure Bay.

At last, when he was too tired to see the computer screen clearly, he got up and pulled the draperies across the darkened window, then went into the kitchen to make coffee and help himself from the bowl of cold pasta salad left in the fridge by his housekeeper. Finally he cleaned up the table and climbed the stairs, stopping outside a closed door in the upper hallway.

"Steffi?" he called softly. "Are you awake?"

No answer. After a moment he pushed the door open and went inside, pausing by his daughter's bed to look down at her. She was in her long plaid nightshirt and sleeping soundly. Her lips were parted, hands curled under her chin like a small child, and she was bathed in the soft pink glow of a night-light shaped in the form of a rosebud, which had been in her room since she was a baby.

Alex smiled at the delicate cluster of glass petals. Every year or so, Steffi declared that she was old enough to sleep without a light. But after a couple of days the rosebud would reappear, and nobody would comment until her next attempt to leave it behind.

Nowadays he cherished any little habits of childhood that still clung to her. They helped to reassure him that he hadn't completely lost her. At fourteen his daughter almost had the face and body of a woman. Only when she was sleeping like this could he see traces of the enchanting little girl she'd been.

There were people who'd considered them irresponsible for having a baby when they were aware of

Janice's illness. But those people, of course, didn't know the truth about Steffi's birth.

He felt a painful lump in his throat as he remembered how he'd adored that red-haired baby they'd brought home from the hospital all those years ago. What a miracle she'd been to him and his wife. Their lives had been transformed. The growing tensions between him and Janice had almost disappeared, replaced by happy sun-flooded years of laughter and absorption in the growing child they both so dearly loved.

A few years of heaven, Alex thought grimly, followed by years of utter hell. Life had a harsh way of balancing things out.

He could bear it for himself. But he hated his daughter's having to endure those cruel checks and balances, Steffi, who had never done anything to deserve the kind of suffering inflicted on her family. During all her growing-up years, Steffi had been a pure delight, a ray of sunshine. How he missed that happy generous loving little girl.

Now she was as tall as her mother had been, with a curving figure and a sulky hostile expression that chilled him. Her lips, which were exactly like his own, were usually pressed together in a taut line, and her smiles were rare. He hardly knew what to say to this beautiful stranger, how to fight his way past her anger and pain to the child still living in there.

He reached down gently to brush a strand of hair back from her sleeping face, then adjusted the blankets. As he did so, he saw that Steffi had gone to sleep clutching her old stuffed bunny.

This favorite toy had once been soft pink plush, with a yellow velvet waistcoat and a jaunty expression. But years of love had worn the plush almost bare in places, and the long ears were limp and droopy from constant handling.

As far as he knew, she hadn't slept with the bunny for eight or nine years. The sight of it now, cradled in her arms, was almost unbearably painful to him.

How lonely and distressed she must be feeling!

If only she would talk to him, even yell at him. Maybe then, Alex and his daughter could start to breach this grim wall of silences and be a family again. But Steffi was so cold and remote. After school and on weekends, she hiked by herself along the trails near their home, fished for hours down in the cove, tramped alone through the woods or sat up in her room with a book.

He should probably be glad she was spending the first two weeks of the summer with Angela Sanders and her parents on a long-planned trip to Disneyland.

As far as Alex knew, his daughter had almost as little to do with her school friends these days as she did with him. Steffi had once been such a bubbly gregarious child, but now she was usually solitary. Maybe a couple of weeks with her friend would be a good thing, though he yearned to have her with him at Edgewood Manor.

But she'd be home from California in a couple of weeks, and then they'd have the rest of the summer together.

Again he thought of the old hotel on the shore of Okanagan Lake. Alex hoped that the tranquillity of that lovely old house and the beauty of its setting would work a miracle, that somewhere within the sun-dappled walls of Edgewood Manor, he would find the touch of magic that would bring his daughter back to him.

CHAPTER FOUR

"WHY DO YOU KEEP looking down the road?"

"What road?" Gina burrowed among the strawberries. "You know, some of these are really huge."
She held up a fat strawberry for Roger's inspection.

He nodded, leaning on his hoe in the sunshine
among the neat little hills of potatoes. "How many
roads are there leading to this place?"

"One," Gina mumbled. "Last time I looked."

"Which was about four seconds ago."

Gina sat back on her heels and gave her caretaker a
stern glance. "Roger, you've got to quit teasing me
about that man, or..."

"Or what?"

"Or I'll wrap a shovel around your neck," Gina
said cheerfully.

Roger rolled his eyes and plied the hoe on a patch of
weeds near the fence. "Half the time she worries and
frets about me leaving, and the other half she's
threatening to attack me. Women are so hard to understand."

Gina crawled along the row, digging more plump
strawberries out from under their sheltering dark green
leaves. "Mary tells me you've been learning a whole
lot about women these days," she said casually.

Roger grunted and removed his baseball cap to
scratch his head. "And how would Mary know? When

she's not working in that kitchen, she spends all her time at choir practice or buried in the library.''

"Mary knows a lot of things." Gina stood up and carried her plastic bucket to the next row of strawberries. "Roger..."

"Yes?"

"Why didn't you tell me about your new friend? You know I'd be interested. I'd love to meet her."

"What friend?" he asked, scraping busily with his hoe.

"You know." Gina knelt and started on the next row. "Lacey Franks. The city lady who's been staying over at Fred's motel. Apparently the two of you are getting really... well acquainted."

Roger straightened his lanky body and leaned on the hoe, resting his chin on the handle and staring gloomily across the lake. "This town is the damnedest place for gossip."

"Of course it is. All small towns are the same way. So?" She looked up at him expectantly.

"So what?"

"*Tell* me about her," Gina said, exasperated.

"Nothing to tell. Are any of those wax beans ready yet?"

Gina gave up, knowing it was hopeless to press him further. She reached over to examine a long yellow pod on one of the bean plants nearby.

"Yes, I think they are. A few of them, anyway."

"Could we pick enough for our supper?"

Gina checked the plants again. "I think so. You'd better tell Mary before she plans something else."

"You tell her. She hardly speaks to me anymore."

"Oh, for goodness' sake," Gina said. "I get so tired of all the squabbling you two do."

But her annoyance was immediately overcome by pleasure at the idea of fresh-cooked buttery beans for their evening meal in the kitchen. She was still riffling through the laden bean plants when a shadow fell across the garden.

Roger looked up with a cordial smile.

"Hello there," he said, leaning on his hoe again to address someone behind Gina. "We've been expecting you."

Gina's heart began to pound. She got up, holding her plastic pail, and brushed dirt from the knees of her jeans.

Alex Colton smiled and extended his hand. "Hello, Gina. Nice to see you again."

He looked happier today, Gina thought, examining him closely as she shook his hand. His face was still tired and worn, but he seemed much more relaxed than on his first visit. Today he wore jeans, a yellow cotton shirt and a jaunty straw fedora, and was the image of a man embarking on a long holiday in the country.

"So, Alex, are you ready to settle in and be pampered for a whole summer?" she asked.

"More than ready. I feel like I've finally arrived in heaven." Alex gestured at the lush garden, the stone mansion within its screen of vines and flowers, the shimmering lake and sleepy town in the distance. "I've been waiting for this day."

"So have we," Roger said with a teasing glance at Gina, who bent hastily to collect her bucket of strawberries.

"I'll get you registered and show you to your room," she said. "Unless Mary's already helped you?"

Alex shook his head. "I just drove up and saw you two out in the garden, so I came right over. What's in the pail?"

Gina fell into step beside him, heading across the lawn toward the back door. She held out the pail so he could see. "Mary's planning to make strawberry waffles for breakfast tomorrow."

"I *am* in heaven. Real whipped cream with them, I suppose?"

"Absolutely. And it's fresh, too. We get all our dairy products from a farm up the road."

Alex smiled down at her, one of those transforming smiles that tended to leave her at a loss for words.

"I have to drop this off in the kitchen," Gina said at last, pausing by the back steps. "Roger will help you with your luggage, but first I need to check you in at the front desk. If you don't mind waiting a couple of minutes while I wash my hands..."

"May I come to the kitchen with you? I'd like to say hello to Mary."

"Of course. Come in."

He climbed the steps lightly and held the screen door for her, then removed his hat and followed her into the cool wood-paneled interior of the house, with its pleasant scent of spices and fresh bread, flowers and furniture polish.

Gina was conscious of his quick intake of breath and the admiration in his eyes as he looked around.

"Well, is everything as nice as you remembered?" she asked, pushing open the door to the kitchen.

"Even nicer, if that's possible. You don't know how much I've been needing this holiday. Hello, Mary," he said, smiling at the cook, who was lifting a tray of raisin-filled scones from the oven.

Mary straightened and smiled almost shyly, self-consciously rubbing a hand across the smear of flour on her cheek. "Hello, Mr. Colton. It's nice to see you again."

"Please. Call me Alex."

Mary ducked her head and said, "All right...Alex." She gestured at her baking. "And you've arrived just in time to have scones with your tea this afternoon."

"He still has to unload his luggage and get registered," Gina said, putting her bucket of strawberries on the table.

Mary looked at the berries with approval and carried them to the big enameled sink for washing. "Are the wax beans ready, Gina?" she asked over her shoulder.

"Some of them are. Enough for tonight, anyway. Roger said I should tell you."

"Couldn't tell me himself, I suppose." Mary began to run water over the strawberries.

Alex and Gina exchanged a glance and moved toward the door.

"Still at odds, are they?" Alex murmured when they reached the hall, bending so close that his hair brushed her cheek.

"I'm afraid so," Gina whispered. "And not just over Annabel's diet, either. There are all kinds of new complications."

His eyes danced. "Like what?"

Gina was tempted to confide the details about Roger's glamorous new girlfriend. But just at that moment Roger came through the front door and into the reception area, carrying a couple of well-traveled leather suitcases, a garment bag and a small case.

"Thanks, Roger," Alex said. "I could have looked after those."

"No problem. I might as well take them right up to the gold room."

"All right." Alex reached for his wallet, but Gina touched his arm and shook her head.

"No tipping," she told him quietly. "We don't believe in it around here. As soon as you've registered, you become a welcome guest in our home, not a paying customer."

He relaxed and nodded. "Thank you, Roger. Be careful with the smaller case, all right? I've got a laptop computer in there. Most of my life is on that hard drive."

Roger paused at the foot of the staircase. "I read your column all the time. It's really good."

Alex gave Gina a look of comical dismay. "I guess I've been discovered."

"Mary found your picture in one of the newspapers at the library. Do you mind?"

"Not really. The pseudonym used to give me some privacy, but now that they've started attaching a picture to the column, I get recognized a lot."

"Would you prefer that we keep your identity to ourselves while you're here?"

"Yes, if it's possible," Alex said gratefully. "This is my holiday, after all, and I'd just as soon not have other guests asking me for stock tips during breakfast."

Roger paused halfway up the steps and peered over the carved banister with a cheerful grin. "How about the staff? Would you mind slipping us a few investment tips?"

"Roger!" Gina said.

Alex winked up at him. The caretaker chuckled and vanished into the depths of the upper landing.

"Sorry," Gina murmured. "I'm afraid I have absolutely no control over the household help around here."

"They're terrific." Alex watched as she sat at the big mahogany desk in a corner of the front hall and took out a heavy brassbound ledger.

He leaned over to sign his name, then added his daughter's name on the line below.

"Steffi," Gina read aloud. "Short for Stefanie?"

"That's right. Janice always loved the name. She thought it had an aristocratic sound."

Gina smiled. "When will Steffi be arriving?"

"Well, she's in Disneyland with a friend and her family right now. They plan to get back to Vancouver on the tenth. If all goes according to schedule, she'll be flying into Kelowna on the twelfth."

Gina took his credit card and ran it through an imprinter concealed in a bottom drawer.

"You know," she said thoughtfully, "there might be a few other young people booked to stay with their parents around that time, but I'm not sure."

"It doesn't matter," Colton said, a shadow crossing his face like a cloud drifting across the sun. "These days, Steffi doesn't seem keen to talk to other kids any more than she talks to me."

The bitterness in his voice was as unexpected as it was chilling. Gina glanced up at him in concern. But he was turned away from her, examining the oil painting that hung above the console table with its huge vase of fresh flowers.

She finished his registration card in silence, wondering about the problem Alex Colton was apparently having with his daughter.

"STEFFI, AREN'T YOU coming with us?"

Huddled in an armchair, Stefanie Colton exchanged a quick glance with her friend Angela, then looked back at the woman standing in the doorway of the girls' cluttered hotel room. "I'm sorry, Mrs. Sanders," she muttered. "I have a...kind of a stomachache."

Angela's mother came into the room, her pleasant face creased in concern. "Oh, dear. Shall I stay at the hotel with you?"

She turned to her husband, who appeared in the doorway with Angela's little brother.

"Jim, why don't you take Angela and James over to Disneyland today, all right? I'll stay here with Steffi."

"*Mom!*" the little boy wailed. "You promised we'd *all* go to the Magic Castle today. You *promised!*" James ran into the room and clutched his mother's arm. Angela slumped near the window, rolling her eyes and sighing heavily, while Jim Sanders watched in helpless silence.

Steffi felt like dying.

For the thousandth time, she wondered what had possessed her to come on this stupid holiday in the first place. It was mostly her father's idea. He'd been nagging for weeks about how much fun the trip was going to be.

Fun, she thought bitterly, looking at the little boy's contorted face and the obvious misery she was causing for the rest of Angela's family.

"Please, Mrs. Sanders," she said at last. "You don't have to stay here. You can go with them. I'll be fine by myself."

Angela's mother looked at her uncertainly. "But I wouldn't feel right leaving you all alone. What if your stomach gets worse, dear? It could be appendicitis or something."

"It's nothing like that. I get this all the time," Steffi lied. "It's just . . . cramps," she whispered, giving the woman a pleading glance.

Mrs. Sanders's face cleared. "Oh, I see." She stood erect and ruffled her son's hair. "James, go back to the other room and wait for me." She turned to her husband. "Jim, would you take him? I'll be there in a minute."

Steffi sighed and braced herself. When the two girls were alone with Angela's mother, the older woman smiled sympathetically at Steffi. "Do you have everything you need, dear?" she asked gently. "Sanitary supplies, I mean."

"Yes," Steffi replied in an agony of embarrassment. "I have all that stuff. Mostly I just want to lie down and be quiet."

Mrs. Sanders hesitated. "Are you *sure* you'll be all right? Because Angela could—"

"No, it's fine," Steffi said hastily. "Angela and I talked about it already. She really wants to go with you today to see the Magic Castle."

In fact, Angela had struck up a friendship two days earlier with a young man who sold balloons near one of the rides. Wild horses wouldn't have kept Angela from Disneyland this morning. Besides, Steffi was so tired of her friend that she honestly thought she'd scream if she had to spend a whole day alone with her at the hotel.

Mrs. Sanders continued to hesitate, but Steffi could tell that the woman was wavering. She pressed her advantage by leaning forward in the chair and gripping her hands over her abdomen, moaning softly.

"Oh, they must be so painful," Mrs. Sanders murmured, stroking Steffi's hair back from her forehead. "You poor darling."

Get your hands off me, Steffi thought. *Just don't touch me. You're not my mother.*

She was really afraid that if they didn't leave soon, she'd start saying some of these awful things out loud. Mercifully Mrs. Sanders made her decision at that moment and started toward the door.

"We'll leave some information at the hotel desk," she said. "If you have any problems, you just have to dial zero on the phone and somebody will be here right away. And I'll call at noon to check on you." She hesitated in the doorway. "Are you *sure* you'll be all right, dear?" she asked.

I'm positive. Just go away, all of you, before I start screaming.

But Steffi merely nodded gratefully, whimpered again for effect and climbed into the messy bed, pulling the blankets up over her and squeezing her eyes shut.

"Hey, Steff," Angela whispered, pausing by the bed after her mother had disappeared out the door.

Steffi opened one eye to look at the other girl, who wore a tight pink T-shirt and baggy jeans belted low on her hips. "What?"

"Are you faking?"

Steffi contemplated her roommate's heavy makeup, wondering what had ever made her think Angela was such a good friend. During the time they'd spent together these past few days, she'd learned all kinds of unpleasant things about the girl.

Angela was sly and selfish, really cruel to her little brother when their parents weren't looking. And she seemed able to lie without any pangs of conscience at all. Steffi found this kind of deceit deeply troubling.

Still, she shook her head and gave Angela a piteous glance. "My cramps are really awful," she whispered.

"Bummer," Angela said, looking bored. "Jason told me he might have a friend along with him today."

Steffi shuddered in distaste and gripped the blankets. Jason was the young man who sold balloons—and Angela's new crush. He had two earrings in his left ear and a mostly shaved head with a long topknot pulled into a ponytail.

"Too bad I won't be there," she said, wondering if she'd managed to inject regret into her voice. "Maybe tomorrow."

"Okay." Angela cracked her gum and moved off toward the door, where her parents and little brother now stood waiting.

"Be sure you take your key if you go down to the lobby, dear," Mrs. Sanders called anxiously to Steffi. "We've left some money here on the dresser in case you get hungry and want to call room service. And remember, you mustn't ever answer the door for *anybody* unless you check first and know who it is."

Steffi nodded under her mound of blankets, wondering how dumb they thought she was.

At last the door closed and she was alone. She lay for a long time beneath the sheltering covers, hardly daring to move, savoring the bliss of having the Sanderses all gone. At last, when it felt safe, she scrambled from the bed and crossed to the window, peeking out through the heavy curtains.

Now that she was alone, she could abandon all pretense of sickness. She pulled off her plaid nightshirt and dressed rapidly in denim cutoffs and a baggy shirt, then sat down at the dressing table and looked at herself in the mirror.

She picked up a hairbrush and began to ease the snarls and tangles out of her long red hair. While she worked, she studied her image in the mirror.

"I hate being here," she said to her pale unhappy face. "God, I want to go home."

But there was nobody at home, either. Her father was already at that dumb place where he'd decided they had to spend summer vacation.

Steffi scowled at her reflection.

She didn't want to go to some boring bed-and-breakfast place for two whole months. She didn't like the sound of it, and she especially hated the way her father's face lit up when he talked about the lady who owned the place.

Steffi wanted to spend the summer at home, where her mother felt so close. She wanted to be quiet and still, surrounded by her mother's things. Sometimes it seemed that if she stayed quiet enough in the house, she could even hear her mother's voice.

Her father called it "moping around" and said it had to stop. But he didn't understand. Nobody did. They didn't know what she was suffering, or why.

Steffi got up and wandered back to the window. She curled up in the chair, hugging her bare knees, and pulled the curtain back so she could watch the people and cars streaming past.

It would be possible to go down there and get lost in those crowds. She could vanish into their midst so completely her father would never find her. And if somebody hurt her or killed her, what would it matter? At least the pain would be over. The terrible things that lurked in her future would never happen to her.

Steffi knew all about the monstrous disease that had killed her mother, even though her father had tried to keep the details from her.

They'd never really talked about the sickness. Her father was always so anxious to protect her, but he didn't know how often she listened at doors while he talked with the doctors, or the way she'd learned to look up medical facts in the encyclopedia at the school library.

She understood exactly what Huntington's disease was, how it hid inside the body for years and then crept out from its hiding place to disfigure your body and destroy your mind. Worst of all, she knew that she'd inherited the disease from her mother. Her hands shook a lot of the time and she often had dizzy spells, and those were the first symptoms.

When you carried a death sentence inside your body, did it really matter when or how you died?

For a long time Steffi sat there and watched the colorful throngs moving below. At last she let the curtain fall, burying her face on her knees. She began to cry, deep gulping sobs that made her body tremble in harsh spasms.

ALEX COLTON UNPACKED his bags, hanging shirts and slacks in the closet, filling the drawers with writing equipment and personal supplies. While he worked, he looked around the room with pleasure.

The gold-flowered wallpaper was fresh and bright. A pair of new curtains had been added, too, since his last visit. They were frothy white muslin, arranged in a charming crossover pattern that framed the tranquil scene beyond the windows.

Alex wandered over, a shaving kit in his hand, and sat for a moment on the chintz-covered window seat. Below him he could see the side yard and the stone retaining wall where Gina had lined up all those little objects from her pockets.

He chuckled, remembering, then watched as other guests, in couples and groups, drifted out of the mansion and headed for the little town farther along the shore to eat their evening meal. When at last it seemed they were all gone, a blissful stillness and peace descended. He glanced toward the the patio room where Steffi would be staying, noting how the dying sun glittered on the leaded glass.

Feeling wistful, he crossed to one of the armchairs, upholstered in faded tapestry, and sat. He reached for the phone on the antique drum table beside him, then flipped through his wallet for the California phone number and his calling card.

"Room 3411, please," he said when the receptionist answered.

After a brief silence, a young girl's voice came on the line, sounding bored.

"Hello, Angela," Alex said. "Is Steffi there?"

"Yeah," Angela said. "Hey, it's for you," he heard the girl say, her voice fading. "Your dad."

"Hi, Dad," Steffi said a moment later.

"Hi, honey. How was your day?"

"All right, I guess."

Alex listened closely, trying to glean some information from her tone. But she sounded as distant as ever.

"Did you go to Disneyland?"

"Not today. Everybody else did, but I stayed here. I had a stomachache."

"You did?" Alex felt a stirring of alarm. "Did you see a doctor?"

"It was just cramps, Dad. No big deal."

"Oh. I see."

Alex had been the one to instruct his young daughter in the mysteries of puberty and womanhood, because Janice hadn't been capable of the task by the time Steffi reached that critical age. As a result there were few secrets or constraints between Steffi and her father.

At least, there hadn't been until recently.

"So you stayed alone at the hotel all day?"

"It was fine. I watched TV and read my book."

"I really don't like the idea of you spending your day alone, Steffi. Look, if you're still not feeling well, would you like to fly back early? I could arrange a flight for you tomorrow and drive out to meet you in Vancouver."

"And then we can go home?"

Alex drew a deep breath, trying to be patient. "No, sweetie, we can't go home. You know that. All the carpets are being replaced and the house is in a mess. We're staying here at Edgewood Manor for the summer, remember? After you get to Vancouver, you're coming straight out here."

"Are you there already? At that place?"

"Yes, I'm here in the gold room unpacking all my stuff. And just out the window I can see the patio room where you'll be staying, and the path to the beach and a lot of flowers. Oh, look," he added with deliberate cunning. "There's Annabel, the fat poodle. She spends most of her time lying on the grass down by your room. Maybe she's waiting for you, sweetheart."

But Steffi wasn't buying any of his tricks. "I have to hang up now," she muttered. "We're going to a movie or something."

"So you don't want to come home early?"

"Not if I have to go straight to the bed-and-breakfast place. I might as well stay here." She made it sound like a death sentence.

"Okay, honey." Again Alex struggled to curb his impatience. "Whatever you want. I'll call you in a couple of days, okay? And you've got the number here at the hotel in case you need me, right?"

"Whatever."

"Are you sure you've got the number, Steffi?"

The girl sighed. "Yeah, I'm sure. G'bye, Dad."

She hung up. Alex stared at the phone for a minute, shaking his head ruefully. Finally he got to his feet, finished unpacking and admired his tidy room for a few moments, then wandered downstairs.

Fragrant aromas drifted up from the kitchen, reminding him that he was desperately hungry. But the cooking smells were coming from the meal that Mary prepared for the staff. Guests, he recalled, were expected to look after their own evening meals.

Alex hesitated in the lobby, enjoying the dark paneled walls and gracious furnishings. He felt as if he'd

somehow traveled back a hundred years, to a gracious bygone era.

The plant-filled sun room and veranda opened off
the lobby, while the kitchen, offices and rooms be-
longing to Gina and Mary were somewhere in back.
Through another door he could see the cozy interior
of the library, filled with old books, hunting prints and
bronze sculptures. One of the shelves held a pile of
board games and well-thumbed magazines for guests
who wanted to spend a lazy evening in front of the
hearth.

The atmosphere of the old mansion was infinitely
soothing. Maybe, he thought wistfully, even Steffi
would relax and start being herself again when she'd
had the chance to spend a few days here.

"Are you pleased with your room?"

Alex looked around to find Gina in the hallway, her
arms full of snowy bed linens. Behind her stood a
couple of young women both similarly laden. Obviously the college girls who provided summer help.

"My room's beautiful." Alex smiled at all three of
them. "Those sheets smell so good," he added.

"I like to keep them fresh," Gina said. "Every
couple of months we take all the linens, even the ones
in the storage closets, wash them and dry them on a
line out in the sun."

He moved closer and sniffed appreciatively. "I
haven't smelled linens like that since I was a boy."

"It gets even better." Gina nodded at her two young
helpers, who disappeared up the back stairway in a
swirl of giggles. "After they're folded and ironed, we
pack them away in the airing cupboard with packets

of rosemary and lavender we make up from Mary's herb garden.''

Alex looked at the woman with covert interest. When she was talking about her hotel, Gina Mitchell lost any trace of awkwardness or reserve. Her eyes sparkled, and her boyish form was animated with energy.

''You love this place, don't you, Gina?''

She nodded, meeting his eyes directly. ''I really do. I guess I'm one of those lucky people who've been allowed to do exactly what they wanted with their lives.''

''Best of all, you're generous enough to share it with others.''

''That's not generosity, I'm afraid. That's how I make my living.'' She laughed lightly. ''Still, nothing makes me happier than having people come here and fall in love with Edgewood Manor.''

Alex smiled, delighted by her vivid tanned face and the drift of freckles across her nose. She reminded him of someone, but he couldn't seem to track down the elusive mental connection.

''What?'' she asked, catching his expression.

''Nothing. I just wondered if I've seen you somewhere before.''

''Not likely. I've been hidden out here for most of my adult life.''

''And your family's in the Maritimes, didn't you tell me?''

''That's right. Except for an elderly maiden aunt who doesn't look like me at all.''

''Okay,'' he said, giving up. ''It must be one of those déjà vu things.''

Gina smiled and began to mount the stairs. "Have you had your dinner?" she asked over the railing.

He shook his head. "I've been busy unpacking. But those smells from the kitchen are making me feel weak at the knees. What did you people eat?"

"Oh, I'm sorry," she said in distress. "We had stew and biscuits and a salad along with the wax beans. But I'm not sure if there's enough left for—"

"No, no," he interjected hastily. "I'm not asking for special treatment, Gina. The other guests never take an evening meal in the kitchen with the staff, do they?"

She shook her head. "It wouldn't be fair to Mary really, when she has to work all day."

"Of course not. I'll walk into town like everybody else." He started to move away, then asked, "What time's breakfast?"

"Eight o'clock. Nine on Sundays. And it's always marvelous. Wait till you taste Mary's strawberry waffles tomorrow."

"Ah, yes. With the real whipped cream. Waiting will be difficult." He watched as she mounted a few more steps.

"Oh, by the way..." She paused on the upper landing.

"Yes?"

"I hate to tell you this, but we're going to be on skeleton staff tomorrow once breakfast's been served. I'm concerned, because it's your very first day. There'll hardly be anybody here to look after you if you need anything."

"Where's everybody going?"

"To the Canada Day picnic in Azure Bay. We all have jobs with the entertainment committee," Gina said. "Roger's playing his cello, Mary's singing in the choir, and I'll be at the housewares booth giving decorating tips."

"So who's minding the store?"

"Stacey and Kim will be here most of the day." Gina gestured upstairs, where the two young women could still be heard chattering as they put away the bed linens. "And Mary will be back by midafternoon to serve tea for the guests."

"So," he said, "if I happened to stop by the housewares booth tomorrow, would you give me a few tips? I'm having all the carpets replaced in my house and making some other changes, as well."

"I'd be happy to," Gina told him solemnly.

"And if I caught you at an opportune moment, do you think I might be able to entice you away from your post for a glass of lemonade or a soda?"

"Well, maybe. It can get pretty hot and tiring sitting in that booth all day." She smiled at him over the railing, then finished mounting the stairs.

Alex watched her until she disappeared. On his way out, he paused in the marble-flagstoned lobby, enjoying the play of colorful light and shadow through the tall stained-glass windows. Then he pushed the door open and wandered out into the twilight, heading for town along a path lit by the dying sun. As he walked, he mused about Gina, her slender tanned body, her intriguing mixture of competent businesswoman and shy waif.

Something stirred within him, a feeling so unfamiliar and powerful that he was afraid to analyze it. All he knew was that he was looking forward to the coming day with keen anticipation. In fact, he felt positively lighthearted.

He plunged his hands into his pockets, kicked at a pebble in the road and began to whistle.

CHAPTER FIVE

THE TOWN SQUARE was swarming with people by the time Roger arrived at the makeshift entertainment stage and began unpacking his cello. The Canada Day parade had just dispersed at the end of Main Street near the dock. Family groups wandered back to the park to set out their blankets, unload picnic boxes and stake a claim on their patch of grass for the day.

A baseball tournament was already under way on the three ball diamonds adjoining the park. Midway rides clanked and soared in the distance, and vendors dressed as animal figures moved through the crowd, selling balloons and small Canadian flags.

Roger bought a flag from a despondent-looking moose. He paid his dollar, meeting the moose's blue-eyed gaze in the depths of the furry costume.

"Must be pretty hot in that getup," he said with sympathy.

The moose dipped his antlers. "Hey, man, it's awful." The voice was hollow and youthful behind the rubbery snout. "And the day's barely started."

Roger patted the moose's furry shoulder. "Buck up, kid. Just a thousand more flags to sell and you can quit for the day."

The moose groaned and shambled away. Roger was fitting the bright red-on-white maple leaf into his hat-band when Gina came by, carrying stacks of wallpaper books, drapery samples and brochures describing Edgewood Manor.

She set her load at the edge of the stage and sat down with a happy sigh.

"Well, well," he murmured, replacing his hat. "Aren't you pretty. You look like a daisy."

She wore a white sundress splashed with big yellow polka dots, and a pair of dangling yellow earrings that contrasted pleasantly with her tanned skin and freckles. Roger, who hardly ever saw his employer in anything but jeans or baggy shorts, smiled his approval.

Gina smoothed her flared cotton skirt and looked up ruefully. "I'll bet you didn't know I was a girl, did you?"

"Well, I've heard rumors to that effect, but I never really believed them. So, when do you start working in the booth?"

She glanced at her watch. "Ten more minutes. Do you think I have enough brochures?"

Roger chuckled. "You're not the least bit interested in helping these ladies with their decorating problems, are you? This is just an excuse to do a whole lot of free advertising."

She lifted her chin with mock hauteur. "I have a business to run, you know."

"I know you do." Roger patted her shoulder. "And I keep forgetting what a good businesswoman you are. Have you seen Mary?" he asked, plucking idly at the strings of his cello as he peered into the crowd.

"The choir's having a secret practice over in the Anglican Church tent. Nobody's allowed inside."

Roger chuckled. "Cecil Bedlow is so pompous. You'd think they were performing at Carnegie Hall."

Gina laughed. "Mary says they'll be doing their first set in a few minutes. Will you be able to go over and listen, or will you be playing?"

"I'm not sure. Mickey Taunton had to go all the way back home on his brother's motorcycle to get his flute, so we might be slow getting started."

"How could he forget his *flute?*"

"He's also pitching in the baseball tournament," Roger said mildly. "He's got a lot on his mind."

But Gina wasn't listening. She leaned forward, gazing at the throngs of people. "Have you seen anybody else we know this morning?"

Roger smiled at her glistening boyish curls and her slim brown shoulders in the pretty sundress. "Anybody *else?*" he teased. "Like who?"

She shrugged awkwardly. "You know. Neighbors, guests from the hotel..."

"He's around somewhere," Roger said. "In fact, I saw him just a few minutes ago talking to a grizzly bear."

Her cheeks turned pink. "Oh, is there a grizzly bear, too? I thought there was just a moose and a beaver this year."

"Yes, there's a grizzly bear, my child. And there's also a well-known financial expert wandering the grounds, who's probably going to forget all about stocks and bonds when he sees you in that dress."

Gina's color deepened beneath the freckles. "Look, Roger," she began earnestly, "you've got it all wrong. I don't really—"

"Go away." Roger took a soft cloth from the bottom of the case and began polishing his cello. "Go over there and get to work."

She clambered down from the stage and gathered her supplies. "Do you want to meet us for lunch?" she asked.

"Where?"

"At the hamburger tent by the fountain. Mary and I are having lunch there at one o'clock. You can stop by if you're not busy."

"Is Cecil actually going to let the choir have a lunch break?"

Gina grinned. "All except for Marianna Turner. I understand he's making her stay behind to practice her scales."

Roger made a face. "All of you are such awful gossips. Go away and quit bothering me."

Gina laughed and made her way toward the display booths. Roger watched until her curly head was out of sight. Then he glanced wistfully toward the Anglican Church tent where Mary was practicing with the choir.

The housekeeper hardly spoke to him anymore. Roger was surprised by how much he missed her views on life. Once you got past her shyness and reserve, Mary had a really good mind. Over the years they'd had absorbing discussions about politics, music, people and everything else under the sun.

Mary Schick, once roused, was also a worthy opponent in a verbal battle. Roger liked the way her mind worked. If the truth were known, he sometimes took the other side in an argument just to get her going, even when he secretly agreed with her.

But lately she'd been remote and hard to reach. He couldn't understand what was bothering her. It couldn't just be the conflict over Annabel, because they'd had lots of disagreements in the past over the care and feeding of that poodle.

Something else was on her mind, and he couldn't for the life of him figure out what it was.

He shook his head, still looking longingly at the striped tent, hoping to catch a glimpse of Mary's small erect figure. But there was no sign of her.

He wondered what she was wearing today. Probably one of her shapeless cotton dresses, the same as always. He frowned. Her drab clothes were another source of irritation. Dammit, the woman had a nice shape. She'd kept her waistline and her legs were really good. So why did she—

"Well, hello there," a feminine voice said, interrupting his thoughts. "You're a *terrible* man, you know."

Roger blinked in surprise. "I am?"

Lacey Franks stood near the stage, regarding him archly.

"You didn't call me last night, you naughty boy. I waited and waited."

"Was I supposed to call you?" Roger asked, confused.

Lacey's hair was upswept, bright gold in the sunlight. She wore high-heeled sandals and a red dress that fitted snugly to her attractive curves. Only the lines in her face hinted at her real age, but they, too, were downplayed with skillfully applied makeup.

Again Roger thought of Mary's careless graying hair and shapeless clothes. For some reason he felt even more annoyed.

"We didn't have a formal *arrangement.*" Lacey pouted. "But I just assumed you might call and make some plans for the day."

Roger sighed. It was harder than he'd thought, this whole business of dating. Apparently there were all kinds of mysterious things expected of a man.

"I told you when we had coffee the other day, Lacey," he said patiently. "I'm going to be busy for most of the day. We're playing at least four sets. I said I'd probably see you around."

She continued to pout, but reached up to fiddle with his tie, straightening the knot. "I was hoping we could make some definite plans for the evening. There's going to be a fireworks show down on the beach, you know. I just *adore* fireworks."

While she was talking, the choir members spilled out of the tent and moved past in a tight group, heading for the band shell in the center of the park.

Mary was with them. Roger waved, then felt embarrassed when the housekeeper saw Lacey Franks in her tight red dress still fondling his tie. He pulled away from Lacey and reached up nervously to straighten his hat brim.

"Hi, Mary," he called, trying to sound casual. "All set to warble like a meadowlark, are you?"

She said nothing, just looked away and moved on, clutching her armful of sheet music.

"She's a timid little thing, isn't she?" Lacey said, watching the choir members mount the steps of the band shell. "And such unfortunate clothing sense." She gave a small shudder. "That navy blue dress on a day like this..."

Other musicians began to arrive at the entertainment stage, where they exchanged banter and unpacked their instruments. "Lacey, I have to tune my cello," Roger said curtly. "I'll see you in a little while, all right?"

"Why, honey, I'm not going anywhere." Lacey stroked his arm. "I'm sitting down right here so I can listen to you."

A crowd was beginning to gather in front of the stage for the musical performance, and Roger watched as Lacey made her way through the rows of folding chairs and found a seat.

She looked beautiful, he had to admit. There was an air of glamour about Lacey Franks, a glossy sophistication that set her apart from most of the locals, as well as the other tourists. Heads turned to look at her as she crossed her legs and put on a pair of designer sunglasses, then stashed her handbag under the chair and waggled her red-tipped fingers at him.

He couldn't imagine why this exotic creature was interested in him, but she made no secret of the fact. Indeed, from their first meeting right after her arrival in Azure Bay, Lacey had made it obvious that any advance from him would be more than welcome. Roger was both flattered and baffled.

Across the way, in the band shell, the choir swung into the opening verse of "The Old Rugged Cross."

Roger picked up his bow and began to saw lightly at the strings of his cello, listening to the violin behind him while Lacey watched raptly from her chair.

IN THE BAND SHELL, Mary tried to concentrate on the page of music in her hands. But her gaze kept wandering to the entertainment stage where Roger was seated behind his cello, the flag in his hatband dipping rakishly as he bowed the strings.

Mary joined in automatically on the alto portion of the hymn, her gaze shifting to Lacey Franks, whom she could see in profile sitting in front of the stage, a brilliant figure with her red dress and shining gold hair.

Who was this woman? Where had she come from and why had she focused her attention so determinedly on Roger, who lived a quiet and unassuming life on his little farm?

But, of course, Mary knew the answer.

Lacey Franks was simply another unattached woman in her fifties, more attractive than most, with lots of resources and a good deal of sophistication. Nevertheless, she was alone, and part of an age group where the women seemed to far outnumber the men. Almost any single male would look good to a woman like that, as long as he was reasonably presentable.

Roger, with his quiet charm, his dry wit and courtly, old-fashioned gallantry, was probably irresistible.

Mary gripped the page of music. Her voice blended with the others in the choir as she tried to put the unhappy thoughts from her mind and enjoy the day. But she couldn't stop brooding over Roger and the city woman, wondering how far their relationship had progressed.

Mary pictured them holding hands, even kissing, and felt a flood of emotion so intense it made her shiver. She couldn't bear to think of Roger touching the woman. She didn't even like to imagine their conversations or contemplate the idea of Roger's sharing his whimsical humor and wry observations about life with somebody else.

Again she allowed herself to glance in his direction, brooding over his rapt look as the chamber group swung into the chorus of "Greensleeves." Roger had such beautiful hands, Mary thought. She'd always liked his hands, with their long callused fingers and utter competency.

Miserably she wondered how women like Lacey Franks managed to be so open about their feelings and desires. How did you let a man know you thought he was wonderful? How did you pick somebody and then find the courage to announce your choice to the world, leaving no doubt about your feelings?

Her voice broke suddenly. The woman next to her gave her a glance of concern.

"Sorry," Mary whispered during a break in the music, trying to smile. "I must be getting a cold or something."

As the voices soared all around her again, Mary forced herself to take part, blinking at the hot tears that stung her eyelids.

As soon as Gina opened the decorating booth in the exhibit tent, she was flooded with people wanting to discuss color schemes, draperies and period furniture. This was the fifth year she'd operated her booth during the Canada Day celebrations. Townspeople now expected her to be at the fair, and they lined up to visit the booth.

The day was long and grueling, but Gina enjoyed the questions and the opportunity to hand out a stack of brochures on Edgewood Manor. Every year there were several guests at the hotel who told her they'd first learned of the bed-and-breakfast at the Azure Bay fair, so she considered her annual day in the decorating booth to be time well spent.

She talked briefly with a young couple who were studying the wallpaper book, then returned her attention to a local housewife who was contemplating an addition to her seventy-year-old house.

"We'd like to keep it authentic," the woman said. "But we don't know where to find all those old moldings and things."

Gina opened a catalog and displayed a number of products available for period restoration. The woman leafed through the pages, fascinated. She wrote down some addresses, murmured her thanks and wandered off with a couple of brochures.

Taking advantage of the brief lull, Gina bent down and rummaged in her bag for the roll of peppermints she'd dropped in it earlier.

"I don't like anything about my house anymore," a deep voice said nearby. "What should I do, Miss Mitchell?"

Startled, she looked up to see Alex Colton standing right in front of her, gazing down with a teasing grin. He was more attractive than ever this morning, rested and refreshed, clearly enjoying the outdoor fun and holiday atmosphere.

Gina grinned back. "If you don't like *anything* about the house, you've got real problems. Are you planning to redecorate?" She offered him a mint, then took one herself.

"I'm not sure," he said, popping the candy into his mouth. "Maybe I should just sell the place and move."

Gina watched as he leafed through one of the decorating books, once again asking herself why she found this man so appealing.

Probably the combination of intelligence and virility, she decided. He was a real study in contrasts, this summer guest of hers. He seemed to combine authority with courtesy, power with gentleness.

And overall, there was that air of sadness that tugged at her heart and threatened to breach all her careful defenses.

"What kind of house is it?" she asked, making every effort to sound normal.

"A house that's too full of unhappy memories." He closed the book abruptly and seated himself on the counter. "Actually, I don't really want to think about my house today. I'm on holiday."

"Still," Gina ventured, "it might not be a bad idea to consider a redecorating project, you know. A complete change might be really uplifting."

He nodded thoughtfully. "I'm having the carpets replaced, but I hadn't considered anything else. If I did a few sketches of the place, would you give me some advice?"

"I'd be happy to. I love decorating. Especially," Gina added with a smile, "when I get to spend somebody else's money."

He smiled in return, then his eyes clouded with doubt. "I think you're probably right about the change of scene being healthy. The problem is, I'm not sure how Steffi would feel about it. She's so protective of her mother's memory. She might be upset if I started changing all the color schemes."

Not for the first time Gina wondered just how formidable this fourteen-year-old was going to be when she arrived at the hotel next week. Alex gave every indication of being a strong confident man, but he seemed so cautious and troubled whenever he spoke about his daughter.

A young couple approached the booth just then, and Gina handed them a couple of brochures, answering their question about the use of drapery rods in bay windows. Alex waited nearby, listening with apparent interest.

"You really know your stuff, don't you?" he said when the couple had wandered off.

"I've spent a lot of time learning about decorating. Especially period restorations." Gina straightened the books on the counter and lined up a few more brochures, conscious of him watching her.

"That's a pretty dress," he said.

"Thank you. Roger said I look like a daisy." Gina glanced down at her outfit. "I'm not entirely sure it was a compliment."

"Oh, I think it probably was." Gina felt herself grow warm under his scrutiny. Then he said, "Do you ever get a break here, or will you be on duty all day?"

"Pretty much. I stay in the booth till five, with a half hour off for lunch. I'm meeting Mary," she added almost apologetically.

"Uh-huh. And what happens at five? Are you going straight back to the hotel?"

She shook her head. "Not right away. I'll probably stay and watch the fireworks. It's really quite an impressive display."

"So if I dropped back around five, would I have any chance of taking you for dinner and watching the fireworks with you?"

Gina's heart began to pound, but she kept her face carefully expressionless. This was just a casual invitation, she told herself. The man didn't know anybody in town, and he was being friendly, nothing more.

But she felt a treacherous surge of fear and excitement when she thought about the long mellow twilight, the gathering darkness and the fireworks exploding over the lake in soft fiery blooms...

She knew she should refuse the invitation. Alex Colton had the potential to be far too dangerous to her careful well-managed life. In addition to his undeniable attractiveness, he was newly bereaved. Most troubling of all was the knowledge that his unhappy daughter was waiting in the wings.

The best thing would be to say no and avoid all the problems that might ensue. *Just keep saying no, and nothing can ever hurt you,* she told herself.

But she couldn't seem to form the refusal.

"All right," she said at last, distressed by her weakness. "I'll see you at... at five o'clock."

"Great. I'll look forward to it." He gave her one of those warm unsettling smiles, then moved aside to let a group of women peruse the wallpaper books. The last Gina saw of him was his powerful body and curly graying hair as he made his way through the crowd.

ALEX SPENT A HAPPY DAY browsing though the delights of the outdoor fair. He spent a good deal of time at the livestock exhibits, admiring the fat glossy pigs with their polished hooves and prize cows with ribbons woven into their tails. He ate corn on the cob and homemade peach cobbler, then listened for a couple of hours to Roger's chamber group and Mary's choir. Both were remarkably skillful. It was obvious the little town took its music seriously.

Later in the afternoon while he waited for Gina to finish her duties, Alex wandered down to the lakeshore, away from the crowds. He sat on a rock, gazing across the water. Sunlight glimmered on the tranquil expanse like a carpet of diamonds, and a great blue heron sailed majestically over the water.

Alex tipped his head back slightly to let the sun fall directly on his face. Again he found himself wishing Steffi were here with him.

It was a healing place on the shores of this mountain lake. The climate was pleasant, the air pure, the people honest and warmhearted. The gentle ambience was like a balm to his spirit, and he felt sure it was exactly what Steffi needed.

He remembered her flat unhappy voice on the telephone and the news that she wasn't feeling well. Damn. Maybe he should call and insist that she leave. The Sanders family could put her on an early flight tomorrow, then go on with their holiday. But Alex was afraid to suggest the plan, knowing how scornful and bitter Steffi had been in past months about anything he proposed.

Since he couldn't seem to do anything right, Alex thought ruefully, it was probably safest to do nothing at all.

He looked at his watch and felt a surge of excitement. It was almost five, time to go and meet Gina at the booth. He stood up, smoothing his hair with a pocket comb, then laughed at himself.

Forty-three years old, and he had a date. For the first time in recent memory, he was about to take a lady out on something other than a business meeting.

He thought about Gina's vivid face, her pockets full of peculiar odds and ends, the endearing boyishness that contrasted so sharply with her obvious competence as a businesswoman. And because he was only human, his thoughts also dwelled on the way she'd looked in that sundress this morning, with her bare shoulders and small pert breasts.

It had been so long since he'd held a woman in his arms for any kind of sexual purpose. In fact, he could hardly remember the last time...

Alex swallowed hard and hurried toward the display tent. Gina was closing up the booth, packing her samples and brochures in a couple of cardboard boxes. Despite the busy day and the heat inside the tent, she still looked cool, sweet and full of energy.

"Fresh as a daisy," he said to her bent head.

She glanced up, flustered.

"You," Alex said. "You're beautiful."

Her cheeks turned pink. "Actually, I'm exhausted and I'm sure I must look it. But it's nice of you not to point that out."

"Can I help with anything?"

Gina shook her head. "I'm just leaving these boxes under the counter. Roger will come by and collect them on his way home."

"Are you sure?"

"Positive." Gina stretched and sighed, then moved out from behind the counter. "I'm so glad to be finished."

Alex offered his arm, liking the feeling of having her at his side as they walked through the crowds together. The two of them were such a good fit. Their shoulders almost touched, and their strides matched easily. Her hand was warm on his arm. Alex patted it and glanced at her.

"What?" she asked.

"I like this," he told her simply. "I could get really used to walking with you."

Her cheeks warmed again beneath the drift of freckles, making him smile.

"Do you always blush like that?"

"It's a curse," she said, pausing to look at a display of cereal grains, wrapped into huge sheaves and tied with ribbons. "I've always blushed easily. Just ignore it. Those blushes mean absolutely nothing."

"I see." He nodded solemnly as they moved along the tables containing a display of garden produce. "So how can I tell if you're embarrassed?"

"Well, if I were to crawl into a hole, curl up and die, that would be a pretty fair clue."

He chuckled. "Did you get a chance to see any of the other exhibits, or were you stuck in that booth all day?"

"Mostly. But after all the years I've spent in this town, none of it's really new to me. What did you like best?"

He paused to consider. "The pigs were great," he said at last. "And Roger's chamber group was, too."

Gina gave a delighted peal of laughter, making him smile again. "Wait till I tell Roger he came second to the pigs."

Alex laughed with her. He could feel the dark bands gradually loosening from around his heart, the clouds rolling away. He threw an arm around Gina in a friendly sort of fashion, loving the feel of her slim body against his, but forced himself to release her almost immediately.

"Where would you like to eat?" he asked. "Do you want to walk into town and have a steak?"

"Goodness, no!" She looked at him, shocked. "Not while we can have nutritious things like chili dogs or greasy hamburgers. This is a country fair, after all."

"It certainly is. Okay, let's go look at a few more exhibits, then find a booth and see how much damage we can do to ourselves."

They looked around for an hour or so, nibbling at ice-cream cones to soothe their hunger pangs and even riding on a couple of the tamer midway rides.

At last, when they were both too famished to endure the wait any longer, they bought a plateful of hamburgers, buttery cobs of corn and fried onion rings, added plastic cups of lemonade and took their picnic to a table near the water.

"This is so *good*," Gina said happily, wiping her mouth with a paper napkin. "Why is it that all the really delicious things are bad for you?"

Alex was watching her face and hair, etched with gold by the dying sun. All at once, he couldn't seem to find his voice.

"Come on," she said. "Do your part. I'm not eating all those onion rings by myself."

"We'll have to jog all the way back to the hotel to work this off."

"That sounds like a good idea. I like jogging."

"You have so much energy." Alex helped himself to a couple of the crusty onion rings. "Are you always like this?"

"Pretty much. I love what I'm doing, that's all. I'm living exactly the way I want to."

"No regrets?" he asked.

Gina glanced up at him. "Like what?"

"Don't you ever look back and think of specific moments in your life when you wish you'd done something differently?"

He was surprised by her reaction. Though she was staring across the lake with her face in profile, he could see the way her jaw tightened and her face clouded suddenly. But when she turned back to him, her expression was bland.

"Not really," she said. "Everybody's life is full of hard choices, but I'm mostly satisfied with the ones I've made. How about you?"

Her clear hazel eyes rested on him thoughtfully. Alex toyed with the edge of a paper wrapping, knowing she wanted an honest answer. Gina Mitchell was a straightforward person, and she no doubt expected the people in her life to be just as straightforward.

Her honesty was one of the most attractive things about her, but also one of the most disconcerting. Because if Alex was honest with this woman, he'd have to let her see how very attracted to her he was. She'd soon realize he was beginning to yearn for a lot more than just companionship.

"I guess," he said at last, "I'd make the same choices, but I wish I'd made a lot of them earlier."

"How's that?" She sipped lemonade, watching him closely.

"Probably it was Jan's illness that made me feel this way. When you lose somebody close to you, it gives you a real sense of how fragile and fleeting our lives are. I wish I'd had the courage to start writing my books and the column a lot earlier, because it gave us more freedom and independence. I wish Steffi had been born earlier, so Janice would have been able to see her grow up. That sort of thing.''

Briefly the old pain came back, settling around him with a dark rustle of brooding wings.

Gina reached out and squeezed his hand. ''I'm sorry,'' she murmured. ''Those last years must have been so hard for all of you.''

He held her hand gratefully. She had a small firm hand, with slender fingers and a callused palm, and he loved the way it felt in his.

''Alex...''

''Yes?''

''Weren't you afraid to... I mean, having a baby, with your wife's illness...''

His heart contracted. ''Steffi is adopted,'' he said.

''Oh, I see,'' Gina murmured.

An awkward silence fell, while both of them looked out across the water.

''Look,'' Gina said at last. ''They're getting ready for the fireworks.''

''We're going to have a ringside seat.''

''Do you want to stay here?'' Gina glanced around uncertainly. ''We could find a spot on the grass somewhere...''

Alex moved around the table and sat on the bench next to her, relaxing and stretching his legs.

He took off his jacket and draped it over her bare shoulders. ''Is that warm enough?'' he asked. ''When the sun gets low, it'll be pretty cool here by the water.''

''I'm fine,'' she replied. ''How about you? Are you comfortable?''

"I'm so comfortable," he told her huskily, "that I think I could happily stay right here, just like this, for the rest of my life."

In the fading light, Alex could again see the delicate flush of color on her cheeks before she turned away from him. It was all he could do not to gather her into his arms.

CHAPTER SIX

BREAKFAST AT EDGEWOOD Manor was a lavish leisurely affair, served in the gracious old dining room where Josiah and Elizabeth Edgewood had sometimes entertained forty guests at sit-down dinners.

Gina disposed of Edgewood's huge oak table soon after she'd bought the manor. She replaced it with seven smaller tables, each set with dark blue place mats, fine china and gleaming silverware. Flowers from the garden adorned the tables, and the shrubbery beyond the windows made the room into a cool green cave, dappled richly with sunlight.

A week had passed since the Canada Day fair in Azure Bay. Several of the guests had become quite friendly, and as they sat down to a breakfast of fruit compote and spinach quiche, fresh preserves and warm oatcakes served in baskets lined with blue gingham, conversation flowed easily. The paneled walls fairly echoed with lively voices.

Gina was carrying a silver coffeepot down the hallway when she heard Alex's hearty burst of laughter. She came into the dining room and smiled at him.

He sat with a couple from Atlanta, both archaeologists who were combining their summer vacation with a chance to study the petroglyphs along the lakeshore. One of the places at their table was empty, a mute reminder that Steffi Colton would be arriving in just a couple of days.

Gina moved around the room with the coffeepot, exchanging banter with the guests. The old hotel was filled to capacity these days, practically bursting at the seams. Kim and Stacey, the two college girls, were working full-time.

Several of the rooms even had children sleeping on roll-away cots, although normally there weren't a lot of children at Edgewood Manor. The staff always found the busy summer months both exhilarating and exhausting, but even more so now.

"What's all this noise?" Gina asked with mock severity, pausing at Alex's table. "I'm afraid laughing isn't allowed. The three of you will have to leave."

Alex turned to grin at her, and it was all she could do not to drop her hand on his shoulder or reach out to stroke his hair.

Gina had never known such an overwhelming physical attraction to another person. Every day it seemed harder to keep herself away from the man.

He looked up at her with a searching gaze. "Did you sleep well, Gina?"

"Very well, thank you."

"Gina and I worked until almost midnight last evening," Alex told the other two. "We were out in the lake helping Roger fix the old raft so the kids could use it for swimming."

The woman smiled at Gina. "You're very lucky to have such a helpful guest," she said in her rich Georgia drawl.

Gina thought about the moonlight rippling on the water, their laughter and teasing, Alex's muscular wet arms encircling her as they bobbed along the side of the raft. She shivered briefly, then returned to her task.

"Coffee?" she asked the two archaeologists.

"Is it the same blend you served yesterday?" the woman asked. "I just loved that touch of hazelnut."

Gina nodded. "It's our house blend. Roger grinds the beans every morning."

"Then I'll be glad to have a cup. How about you, Gerald?"

Her husband nodded with enthusiasm. "You bet, Sue Anne. I never turn down anything they offer me at this place. It's all so delicious."

"It's guests like you," Gina said, filling his cup, "that make my job so much fun. Coffee for you, too, Alex?"

He looked up at her again, his eyes sparkling. "I agree with Gerald. I won't turn down anything you offer."

She felt the annoying telltale blush creeping up her cheeks. "I almost forgot," she told him. "There's a fax for you in the office."

"From Vancouver?"

Gina nodded. "The third fax in two days. Your boss must be getting anxious."

"Okay. I'll come by and pick it up after breakfast."

"What kind of work do you do?" Gerald asked.

Alex and Gina exchanged glances. "I teach economics at a private college in the Lower Mainland," he said.

"And they're bothering you during your summer holiday?" Sue Anne asked. "Now, I think that's real mean."

Gina filled Alex's cup calmly. If he chose to keep his identity a secret, then certainly she wouldn't reveal it. Still, she fully expected some alert guest to find him out before the summer ended.

"What are you doing today, Gina?" he asked, touching her arm.

"I thought I'd take the canoe up the lake a bit and see if I can find any ripe blueberries back in the woods."

"Isn't it too early for them?" Sue Anne asked.

"Maybe," Gina said. "But it's been pretty hot this year. I think there might be a few ready to pick. Wait till you taste Mary's blueberry cobbler with sweet cream."

Gerald closed his eyes in ecstasy, making his wife chuckle.

"Can I come along?" Alex asked.

"I thought you had to work today. What about all those faxes?"

"I worked until after midnight last night. I'm ready to take the day off. Come on, Gina," he pleaded. "Let me come with you. I'll even do all the paddling. I'll be your gondolier, and you can ride in the canoe like a grand lady. You can carry a parasol and trail your hand in the water."

She laughed. "That's a tempting offer. Will you pick all the berries, too?"

"Buckets of them," Alex said promptly.

"All right," she agreed. "I have to go over some accounts with Mary, so I'll probably be leaving at about—" she glanced at her watch "—ten o'clock. Okay?"

"Great. I'll put on my hiking boots and find a big stick to scare the bears away."

Ten minutes later Alex pushed his chair back and got to his feet, along with most of the other guests. People were dispersing, getting ready for a day of outdoor fun on the beach and the hiking trails.

"Don't forget that fax," Gina called, crossing the room to pour coffee for the few who still lingered at their tables.

"Come with me to the office." Alex returned and took the empty coffeepot from her. "We'll drop this off in the kitchen and I'll pick up my fax. Then you get your business done and we can head for the water."

"Has anybody ever told you how pushy you are?"

"Damn right." He put an arm around her and gave her a squeeze. "I want to get you safely into that canoe before somebody else comes along and snatches you away from me."

"I don't see anybody trying very hard," Gina said dryly.

She pulled away from him and headed for the kitchen, hurrying out of sight before he could see how much she was affected by his touch.

GINA LAY BACK in the canoe, gazing at the cloudless sky. True to his word, Alex had even provided her with a pile of cushions from the patio chairs, fitted against the rear seat and arranged in the bottom of the canoe so she could recline in comfort while he paddled.

Plastic pails were stacked neatly in the bottom of the canoe, one of them containing a packet of sandwiches and cookies provided by Mary, along with a flask of coffee. Gina had a pleasant holiday feeling, like a child on a picnic.

She closed her eyes to enjoy the warmth of the sun on her face, and listened to the gentle dip and splash of his paddle. This was heaven, pure heaven.

"You work too hard, you know," Alex said from the other end of the canoe. "I hardly ever see you relaxing like this."

Gina opened her eyes and squinted at him. She liked everything about him, from the darts of silver in his hair and the gentle humor of his eyes to his powerful shoulders and arms as he dipped and swung the paddle.

"You should be wearing a life jacket," she said drowsily. "I'd hate to lose you."

"You would?" he asked, his eyes crinkling. "Why?"

"Because you're the best-paying guest I've ever had. This is going to be a record-breaking summer."

He laughed. "Just as long as you appreciate my finer qualities. How come *you* aren't wearing a life jacket?"

"I was a provincial champion in freestyle swimming when I was fifteen. I could swim all the way across this lake." Gina waved her hand at the vast expanse of shimmering blue water.

"Have you ever done it?"

"Twice. And you can get that glint of competition out of your eye, Alex Colton. I'm not about to race you across the lake."

"Why not?" he asked innocently. "Come on, let's try it. I'll bet you'd win. After all, you're a lot younger than I am."

"How much younger?"

"Well, let's see." He rested the paddle on the gunwales. "Mary tells me you had a birthday a few weeks ago and turned thirty-six. I'm forty-three. So you've got seven years on me."

Gina smiled and leaned back, closing her eyes again. "You're right. I could probably beat you. But why humiliate a high-paying guest?"

He chuckled, then looked over at the shoreline as they drifted by. "This is really isolated, isn't it? We haven't seen a house for ages."

"Not isolated enough for me."

"Why?" he asked in surprise. "Don't you like having neighbors along the lake?"

"The more I live here," she said dreamily, "the more I wish we could all magically disappear and leave it the way it was in ancient times. I hate seeing those cabins that pump their sewage straight into the lake, and docks renting Jet Skis, and hamburger stands and bait shacks. It's all so... so ugly."

"But necessary," he argued, "for people to enjoy the lake. Including you."

"That's my point. I'm not sure it's necessary for us to take advantage of every single thing on earth just because it's here and accessible. Some things are so beautiful they should be left alone."

"I'll be damned. You're a conservationist," Alex teased. "A real tree-hugger."

"I guess I am," Gina said, unruffled. "I didn't used to be, but living here has made me passionate about the environment. We're going to lose so many precious things if we're not careful."

His eyes were on her, so warm and intent that she shifted nervously on the cushions and looked over her shoulder.

"Almost there," she said. "About another half mile to the blueberry patch."

Alex began to paddle again, his muscles flexing and rippling with the powerful strokes. He wore tattered cutoffs and a loose gray tank top, leaving his legs, shoulders and much of his chest bare. He already had a tan from sunny days spent at the beach, and the warm brown of his skin contrasted pleasantly with the dark mat of hair, shot with silver, on his chest.

Gina watched him through slitted eyes and shivered. Alex looked even better in this scanty attire. When he was dressed, he had a square stocky look. But now, half-naked, he was all muscle and hard masculinity.

"You're in pretty good shape," she observed, trying to sound casual. "For a professor."

"The faculty at the college has a gym and weight room. I work out all the time." He made a broad sweep with the paddle, steering their way deftly around a couple of partially submerged logs. "At first, when Jan got sick, it was mostly a way to relieve stress. But as time went by, I got kind of addicted to the physical challenge."

"Challenges can be addictive, all right."

"Like running a hotel single-handed?"

"I'm not exactly single-handed. I have Mary and Roger."

"Speaking of whom, do you have any idea what's happening with those two?" Alex asked. "The atmosphere in the kitchen seems pretty icy. Is it all just because of Annabel's diet?"

Gina shook her head, feeling a tug of worry. "I'm not sure. They've had arguments about Annabel in the past, but never anything that's lasted this long. I'm getting worried about Mary. She's so quiet and . . .

private, in a way. It's always hard to get her to talk about anything that's troubling her."

"I'd be more worried about Roger." Alex frowned, examining the dense underbrush along the shore.

"Why?" Gina asked in alarm.

"Well, he's got this glamorous city lady for a girlfriend, right? If they get serious, I can't picture the lady staying indefinitely in Azure Bay."

"You think Roger might leave?"

"It could happen."

Gina frowned. "You know, I still haven't met her. It seems everybody knows Roger's girlfriend except me."

"You really should get out more often. Want to come into town with me for a drink tonight?"

Gina shook her head.

Despite the fact that she and Alex seemed to spend much of their days together around the hotel, she'd resisted all his attempts to take her out for anything more formal. Almost subconsciously, she knew there was no point in starting a social relationship that would have to end as soon as his daughter arrived.

Alex left no doubt about how important Steffi was to him and how fervently he wanted her to have a happy holiday. Gina suspected that his days and evenings were going to be fully occupied once the girl was staying in the patio room.

She felt a pang of loss—which she suppressed at once, deeply ashamed of herself.

After all, Stefanie Colton was only fourteen years old, and she'd suffered the devastating loss of her mother just a few months earlier. Gina could hardly begrudge the girl her father's attention.

Still, it was painful to realize that she and Alex had only two more days of privacy to enjoy the sweetness of their developing friendship.

"Stop here," she commanded. "Over in that little cove, there's a strip of gravel where we can beach the canoe."

Alex peered dubiously at the wall of dark green foliage. "Are you sure there's a blueberry patch in there?"

"Positive. I found it years ago when I was out hiking."

"What about bears? Maybe they've found the berry patch, too."

"Oh, come on," Gina scoffed. "Bears hardly ever wander down this far."

He climbed from the canoe and hauled it up onto the gravel, then reached down to help Gina step out. "Roger says there've been a lot of bear sightings this year. All along the shores of the lake, he said. The police are warning people to be careful."

"Bears won't hurt you if you don't startle them. It's important to let them hear you first so they can get away. We'll just be careful to sing and fool around a lot while we're working."

He grinned and moved closer to her. He still had hold of her hand, and now he put his other hand on her shoulder. "Well, I'm not much of a singer, but I really like the idea of fooling around."

She didn't respond to that, just stood there, conscious of the deep silence and complete isolation of this place, conscious of his touch.

"It feels," she said at last, trying to smile, "as if we're the only human beings in the world. Doesn't it?"

He nodded, gazing at her intently. "I love the feeling. Don't you?"

"I...I'm not sure," she murmured as his arms closed around her.

She sighed, nestling in his embrace, burying her face against his chest. After so many days of yearning and wondering, it felt good to yield, simply to relax and let him hold her. And when he drew back slightly, lifted her chin and covered her mouth with his, the sensation was at once strange and utterly familiar. His lips were warm, sweet, firm, and the kiss went on and on. Gina was aware only that she never wanted it to end.

But at last he pulled away to touch her chest above the open neck of her shirt. "Look at you," he whispered. "Your heart's beating like a trapped butterfly in there."

She took a deep breath and released it slowly. "This isn't exactly normal behavior for me, you know. I can hardly believe it's happening."

"Me, too. I can't remember the last time I kissed somebody like this. You feel so good. So...wonderful."

Part of her wanted to end the embrace, to draw away and plunge into the deep woods beyond the shore, leaving him alone on the beach. But the urge to kiss him again was too strong.

She moved back into his arms, pulling his head down and kissing him hungrily, her mouth opening against his.

"Gina," he whispered when they were both able to speak again. "You take my breath away."

He held her, running his hands up and down her body, pulling her closer.

"What a woman you are," he murmured. "Why do you live like this, Gina? Why have you shut yourself away out here like a nun in a convent? A woman like you should be married to some lucky man, raising a houseful of kids."

A cloud drifted across the sun, making her feel chilled and bleak though his arms were still warm around her. She pulled away and bent to take the plastic pails from the bottom of the canoe.

"We'd better get going," she said, avoiding his eyes. "I need to be back before teatime."

"Gina," he said softly.

She ignored him. "Here, you take all these pails, Alex, and I'll carry the lunch. Do you think we'll need our jackets?"

He moved nearer and put his hand on her shoulder. "Gina, what's the matter?"

"Nothing," she said, forcing herself to sound casual. "Nothing at all. I just don't want things to get complicated, that's all."

He took the pails and moved off beside her on the path leading into the underbrush. "Define complicated."

She shook her head. "You're the writer. You know the meanings of words."

He fell in step behind her when the trial narrowed. "Am I still allowed to touch you?" he asked over her shoulder. "I haven't dated anybody for a long time, Gina. I don't know what the rules are in situations like this."

"There aren't any rules. We've got the whole summer ahead of us. I don't want to rush into anything, that's all."

He was silent. But Gina could tell, without even glancing back at him, that Alex was thinking the same thing she was.

They didn't have the whole summer. They only had two more days before his daughter arrived.

She hurried to change the subject. "This trail seems to be a lot better than it was last year. There must be animals using it regularly, because nobody ever comes here."

"What kind of animals?"

"Deer and rabbits mostly."

"And bears?"

Gina chuckled. "Quit worrying so much. I'll protect you if a bear comes along. Look, here's a big patch of berries already."

They made their way into a small sun-dappled glade surrounded by thickets laden with ripe blueberries.

"You start over here." Gina put their lunch down in the shade of a tree, then took a pail from him. "I'll do this side."

"Is there some kind of prize for the first one to fill a whole pail?"

"You're awfully competitive," she said cheerfully. "Why are men always like that?"

"I don't know. Why do women always generalize about men?"

They laughed together, then settled in to pick berries, chatting amiably as the sun filtered through the leaves overhead and a magpie scolded them from a tall pine.

"How did you get started writing your column?" Gina asked.

"At first it was a contribution to our college paper, something to give the students advice about investing

and handling money. Then one of the big city newspapers picked it up and started running it twice a
month. I was thrilled."

"Did they pay you for it?"

"That was the thrilling part," he said. "I couldn't
believe I was actually being paid for something that
was so much fun to write."

"And now it's syndicated all over the continent."

He nodded, plucking energetically at the bushes.
"The column's carried in hundreds of newspapers. I
even have a literary agent. Sometimes—" he smiled up
at the raucous magpie "—I think about everything
that's happened and I can't believe it."

"But you've still kept your teaching job?"

"I don't have a full teaching load anymore, just a
few classes in introductory economics. I like the contact with the students."

"I suppose you have to travel a lot to get material
for your columns," Gina said.

"I used to go to New York and Toronto all the time,
but that was before Janice got sick. The past few
years, I've stayed pretty close to home."

She nodded, aching with sympathy when she
thought about what those years must have been like
for Alex and his daughter.

"What about you?" He strolled across the glade
and started on a patch of berries closer to her. "Have
you traveled much?"

"Just between the Maritimes and British Columbia
when I came out here for college. My job is to provide holidays for other people. I don't often get a vacation myself."

"So where would you go if you could travel anywhere in the world?" he asked.

"And money was no object?"

"Of course. What's the point in daydreaming if you're going to fret about money?"

"Okay. Let me see." Gina's hands stilled. She stood with the half-filled pail dangling in her hand and squinted thoughtfully at the treetops.

Alex went on stripping berries, waiting.

"I'd like to go to Costa Rica," she said at last.

He glanced at her in surprise over the top of the bush. "No kidding. Why Costa Rica?"

"I've read about this tour. It's kind of a safari through the rain forest. You sleep in tents and see all kinds of marvelous things along the way. Birds and plants, exotic animals, waterfalls and secluded rivers..."

"Sounds pretty rugged."

"Apparently the trip itself is really tough, but when you come out of the forest, you spend three days in a luxury resort hotel. I think the contrast would be great."

He looked at her in amazement. "That's quite a wish. You know, Gina, you constantly surprise me."

"Why?"

"I don't know." He frowned thoughtfully. "You're such a study in contrasts. You're a clever business-woman with all kinds of vital interests and goals. But at the same time you're a sort of...fairy-tale princess. You're like Sleeping Beauty, hidden in your enchanted castle, locked away from the real world."

"That's ridiculous," Gina said, stung. "I'm very much in the real world, Alex."

She bent and picked furiously at the lower branches so he wouldn't see her face and realize the accuracy of his casual observation.

Nobody would ever know the dreadful secret that kept Gina Mitchell locked away from the world. And, she thought miserably, no prince was ever going to come along with a healing kiss that would make all the pain disappear. Because hers was one fairy tale that could never have a happy ending. . . .

"Why don't you?" he was asking.

"Why don't I what?"

"Go to Costa Rica."

Gina glanced at him in disbelief. "Alex, the tour costs more than twelve thousand dollars. I could never in my wildest dreams afford a trip like that." She wiped a hand across her forehead. "It's getting awfully hot. How are you doing?"

He moved closer and displayed his pail. "Almost full."

Gina gave him a look of dismay. "You're way ahead of me. I've been daydreaming, instead of picking."

"That's not all you've been doing, sweetheart," he said, laughing.

"What do you mean?"

"You've also been eating those berries, instead of putting them in your pail."

"I have not!"

"Yes, you have. You've got blue lips." He leaned forward and kissed her. "Even sweeter than I remember," he whispered, smiling down at her. "Definitely a blueberry flavor."

"Alex . . ."

He lowered his pail to the ground, then took hers away and drew her into his arms. Gina sighed and gave herself up to the pleasure of his embrace. She shivered with hot waves of desire as his hands began to roam over her body, stroking her hips and waist, caressing her breasts.

"I think," she whispered in his ear, "that I just heard a bear."

"Who cares?" Alex murmured. "Let that bear find his own girl. I'm busy."

She laughed and pushed at him. "Alex, we can't do this."

"Why not?"

"Because... because I'm not ready."

His hands dropped immediately and he turned away to retrieve their pails. "Sorry."

"Don't be sorry. I loved it. Being with you like this is such a wonderful feeling. I just... I want to be really careful. I'm far too old for a summer romance."

"You're right of course. But it's been so damned long since I've felt this way. I don't know how much I can stand."

"I'm sorry," she said with genuine regret.

He laughed. "Now *you're* the one who's apologizing. But my sexual frustration is hardly your problem, Gina. Look, let's stop working and have our lunch, okay? Maybe it'll help me get my mind off kissing you."

Gina hurried across the clearing to fetch their wrapped sandwiches, wondering how much longer she was going to be able to resist him.

Alex wasn't the only one, she thought wryly, whose physical drives hadn't been satisfied for a long time.

Together they were a dangerous combination. Every time he touched her, they faced a potential explosion.

And Gina couldn't imagine what her life would be like afterward, if that explosion was ever allowed to happen.

CHAPTER SEVEN

"SO THE LITTLE GIRL arrives tomorrow?"

Mary passed Gina in the hallway, laden with boxes of jars for her fruit preserves. Annabel trotted briskly at Mary's heels. The poodle's eyes brightened as she neared the kitchen.

"Steffi's not a little girl," Gina said, lifting off the top couple of layers of boxes and following Mary into the kitchen. "She's fourteen years old."

"Oh." Mary put her burden down on the table and wiped her hands with her apron. "Did Roger bring that sack of sugar I asked for?"

"I think so." Gina crossed the hardwood floor. "See? It's here in the pantry."

Mary hauled the big paper sack out into the room. "I'm surprised he found the time. Seems he's... awfully busy these days." Her voice cracked and she blew her nose on a tissue from her apron pocket. Gina glanced over in concern. "Mary? Are you getting a cold?"

"No, I'm fine." The cook dumped a pile of blueberries into a pot, measured water and sugar on top of the berries and carried them to the stove. "Will you be around next Thursday?"

Gina lined fruit jars up in the sterilizer, preparing to run boiling water over the lids and jar tops. "Let's see.

Six days from now..." she muttered, trying to clear her mind so she could concentrate.

But her head kept filling up with images of Alex, his powerful body and sensual mouth, his laughter, wit and gentleness, the amazing sweetness of his mouth on hers...

"Gina?" Mary asked from the stove, giving her a troubled glance. Annabel sat between them in a warm pool of sunshine and hoisted one leg straight up in the air to nibble energetically at her woolly flank. "Will you be here next Thursday?"

Gina brought herself back to the conversation with a guilty start. "Yes. Of course I'll be here."

"That's good," Mary said. "Because we're having a visitor."

"We are?" Gina poured boiling water carefully over the jars, then set the tray to drain on a nearby counter. "Who's coming to visit?"

"Lacey Franks. Roger wants us to meet her."

"No kidding?" Gina paused briefly in her work. "Well, it's about time." She began taking more fruit jars from the boxes. "If they're really getting serious, we should at least know what sort of person she is, don't you think?"

Mary said nothing. She stood at the stove, wielding a big wooden spoon in the bubbling mass of fruit, looking miserable. Gina glanced over at her, puzzled again by her manner. But when Mary wasn't in the mood to talk, there was no point in pressing.

Gina resumed daydreaming about Alex. She and the cook worked together with the ease of long companionship, in a silence broken only by the clatter of Annabel's feeding dish as she hauled it out of the pantry and began to push it hopefully around the floor.

THAT EVENING Gina lay in bed, reading by the light of her bedside lamp. She lived on the main floor of the old mansion in a suite overlooking the garden, comprising a small bedroom, an attached sitting room and bath. Mary's suite was across the hall, next to the kitchen.

Gina had decorated this personal space in her favorite colors, dark green and cream, with touches of rose pink in the wallpaper and cushions. She loved her little hideaway. After a hard day's work around the hotel, she usually retired for the evening with a sigh of pleasure to lose herself in her books, framed prints and needlework projects.

But these days she felt restless.

She slipped from her bed and drew the heavy green draperies aside to look across the expanse of grass to the patio room in the other wing. Tomorrow night Stefanie Colton would be living in that room. Alex was driving to the airport in the morning to pick her up.

Gina planned to be away when the girl arrived, off on another berry-picking expedition with the canoe. Alex didn't need any distractions when his daughter finally joined him at the manor. Gina knew how much he'd been looking forward to this day, and what high hopes he had for Steffi and their summer together.

She let the curtain fall and climbed back into bed, picking up her book and trying to concentrate.

A knock sounded on the door. "Come in," she called automatically.

Mary often stopped by at this time in the evening with a tray of hot chocolate and cookies. She would settle in Gina's armchair, and the two of them would have a comfortable chat about the workings of the hotel. Gina sat up in bed and put her book aside, grateful for the company.

But it wasn't Mary.

Alex Colton stood in the doorway wearing jogging pants and an old college sweatshirt. He carried a sheaf of papers in one hand and his reading glasses in the other.

Gina looked at him, startled, and pulled the covers higher to cover her breasts in the skimpy nightdress.

"I'm sorry," he said, hesitating in the doorway. "I didn't realize you'd already gone to bed."

"Summer's a busy time. I'm pretty worn-out by the end of the day."

"I'm sorry," he repeated. "I'll talk to you about this tomorrow." He started to turn away.

"Wait," Gina said. "It's all right, Alex. Just let me..."

He stayed just behind the half-closed door while she got up, took her robe from the chair and slipped into it. Then she sat on the bed again, arranging the blue terry cloth nervously around her legs.

"Okay," she said. "I'm decent."

The door swung wide and Alex stepped in. Gina looked at him with an awkward smile. "Did you have something to show me?"

He crossed the room and seated himself in the armchair next to her bed. "I have a travel program on my computer. I ran a search and found a lot of information on Costa Rican environmental tours. I thought you might be interested in this stuff."

Gina gave him a teasing smile as she took the papers. "I thought you were supposed to be working on your column today."

He grinned back at her. "I'm like a kid on my summer holiday. Anything to keep from getting down to work. See? I printed out a lot of this information for you to look at."

Gina took the papers in surprise. "You have a color printer up there, too?"

"I have so much technical equipment in that room," he said with a wry grimace, "I could probably run this whole place with a few keystrokes."

"Wouldn't that be nice?" Gina sighed. "We could all go away and have a holiday."

Alex leaned forward to stroke her curly hair, then let his hand rest gently on the nape of her neck. Gina made no effort to move away, enjoying the warmth of his hand on her skin as she read.

"Oh, my goodness," she said at last, putting down the sheaf of pages. "Doesn't it sound *wonderful?* Look at these birds, Alex, and the gorgeous tropical flowers! If I were ever to go on a trip like this, I'd remember every detail for the rest of my life."

"Why don't you plan to go this winter?"

"Because, like I told you before, I could never afford it."

"How about a holiday somewhere else? Maybe out to the Maritimes to visit your mother. You must have some slower times at the hotel in January and February, don't you?"

"Not really. A lot of people come for the skiing, you know. There are hundreds of cross-country trails around here. And the kids from town aren't on staff during the winter, so there's just Mary and Roger to help me look after everything. Besides—"

"Gina." He leaned forward and took the papers from her.

"What?"

"Stop doing this. We both know you can't spend your whole life buried out here. What are you hiding from?"

"I wish you'd quit saying things like that, Alex. I'm simply running a business the best way I know how."

"But everybody needs a holiday from time to time. In fact, I think I'd like to take Steffi on one of those tours in Costa Rica this winter."

"Really?"

"Why not? It sounds terrific," he said, gesturing at the papers. "I'd never heard of these particular tours till you mentioned them. I think Steffi would enjoy it, too."

The soft glow of the lamp cast deep shadows on his cheek and jaw, making him look so ruggedly handsome it almost took her breath away. Gina smiled and reached out to touch his sleeve.

"Alex, you didn't really come to my room this late at night to talk about Costa Rican environmental tours, did you?"

He shook his head, looking a little abashed. "I couldn't sleep. I've been lying awake and worrying about Steffi."

"Why?"

He frowned and stood up to prowl restlessly around the room. "She's been acting so strange lately. Withdrawn and sullen and really moody. Steffi never used to be like that. I'm hoping nothing will go wrong this summer."

"Wrong? In what way?"

"She needs to be handled very carefully," Alex said. "Not teased too much or pushed into doing things or made the center of attention . . . Do you know what I mean?"

"I think so. But don't worry. We're not in the habit here of invading guests' space. We'll be especially careful with Steffi. I'll keep my distance."

He smiled gratefully and returned to the chair.

"Not too much distance," he said quietly. "I want her to get to know you."

"Why?"

He reached out and touched Gina's face, cupped her chin in his hand and looked at her gravely. "Because I'm falling in love with you," he said, his voice husky. "And that's something else Steffi will have to deal with pretty soon."

Gina's cheeks heated furiously. She pulled away from him in rising panic.

"Alex," she whispered. "Please, don't do this."

He moved over and sat next to her on the bed, drawing her into his arms. "I know I shouldn't keep pressing if you're not ready," he murmured. "But I need you so much. This past week after spending a lot of time with you, I'm almost going out of my mind. I lie in bed thinking about you for hours. When I finally fall asleep, I dream about you."

"Alex," she whispered against his chest, "you think I don't know how that feels? But there are so many—"

"Don't," he said urgently, toying with the belt of her robe. "Don't talk about the problems. Not tonight, sweetheart. Let's just . . . be together and forget everything else until tomorrow."

"Do you really think that's wise?"

"I've been wise and grown-up for years," he said, nuzzling her shoulder. "Tonight, just this once, I'd like to be young and foolish. How about you?"

"I forget how it feels to be young and foolish. In fact, I'm not sure I ever knew."

"Why not?"

"Because I've been carrying around such a heavy load of responsibilities for as long as I can remember."

"Oh, Gina..." He untied her belt and opened her robe, pulling it aside and embracing her. "God," he said with a sharp intake of breath. "You feel so good."

She resisted only briefly, then yielded completely, loving the feel of his hands on her body. He kissed her for a long lingering time, until both of them were breathless with passion, then began to tug gently at the nightgown, pulling it over her head while Gina sat up to help. Finally she was in his arms again, her naked body feeling warm and luxurious against his clothes.

Alex lowered her gently and lay beside her on the bed, gazing at her in the glow of the lamp with wondering awe. "Look at you," he murmured. "Pure beauty."

"Hardly," she protested, suddenly feeling shy. "Roger always teases me about being skinny and covered with freckles."

"Obviously he's never seen you like this." Alex ran a hand over her body, cupping her breasts and softly caressing the nipples, stroking her flat abdomen and rounded hip. "What a lovely woman you are."

Gina delighted at his caress, surprised by her own lack of inhibition. His touch and his admiring gaze made her feel beautiful. Her tension evaporated, replaced by a flood of confidence.

"Alex," she whispered, "why don't you take those clothes off..."

He sat up and tugged the shirt over his head, then gazed at her while she stroked the mat of curly hair on his chest.

"Are you sure about what we're doing, Gina? Do you really want this?"

"*Now* he asks," she scoffed softly. "Yes, Alex, I really want this." She tugged at the waistband of his jogging pants.

He stood up and stripped off his pants and undershorts, then slipped into bed next to her and drew her into his arms.

"Wonderful," he breathed as their bodies came together. "I'd forgotten what it's like to be naked with someone."

"How long has it been?" she asked, nestling in his arms and stroking his back.

"God, I can't even remember. A long, long time."

"Oh, Alex. It must have all been so sad and terrible for your family. Especially for you."

"How about you, Gina?" He leaned back to look at her, then pulled her into his arms again. "How long has it been since you did this?"

Gina hesitated, thinking.

"Don't answer that," he said hastily. "I'm sorry, darling. I've got no right to pry into your life that way."

"It's all right. I'm just trying to remember."

He laughed and cuddled her tenderly. "If you have to try that hard, it can't have been too recent."

"It wasn't. But I'm so busy all the time, I don't think about my lack of a love life much."

"I tried not to think about it, either. But it's become impossible since I met you."

Desire spiraled through her. He felt so satisfying in her arms. His body was firm and hard, and the muscles in his arms rippled as he embraced her. His skin was silky and warm, and his clean male scent, without any of the heavy colognes or after-shaves she disliked, was intoxicating.

"You smell so good," she whispered, kissing his shoulder, then licking it. "And you taste good, too. I knew you would."

He shuddered. "Oh, Gina..."

Feeling his mounting excitement, she moved against him with more purpose, caressing him with her hands and tongue.

"Be careful, sweetheart," he muttered raggedly in her ear. "I'm pretty fragile, you know. I can't stand too much of this."

She pushed him onto his back and climbed on top of him, moving her body luxuriously over his. "Then tell me when to stop."

"You'll have to stop pretty soon. Maybe in about a hundred years," he said, making her laugh.

Suddenly he gripped her shoulders and stopped her movements. "Gina, I don't have anything with me."

She looked down at him, puzzled.

"To protect you," he said awkwardly. "I don't tend to carry those supplies around with me."

She smiled and kissed him. "Don't worry. I take birth-control pills. Not because I need the protection," she added dryly. "The doctor prescribes them because they help to regulate my periods."

"So it's all right?"

"It's all right, Alex."

Gina felt a moment of wonder at the strangeness of their situation. Alex Colton was a powerful wealthy man, strong and decisive in every aspect of his life. But here in the warm privacy of her bedroom, Gina was in charge. This man's heart and emotions were completely in her hands.

"I'm going to make you so happy, Alex," she said softly, seductively. "You won't believe how happy I'm going to make you."

He groaned and held her, arching his back as she lowered herself and guided him into her body.

Slowly, tenderly, Gina moved against him, thrilled by the hungry intensity of his response. She brought him to the brink of release, then stopped to prolong their pleasure.

When he could endure no more, Alex grasped her in his arms, rolled her over on the bed and moved above her. Now he was in charge and Gina yielded herself to emotion, letting his thrusting male power carry her out of herself into a breathless world of sensation.

At last, within seconds of each other, they exploded in shattering release. Gina lay sated and limp, holding him close.

After a long time she stirred drowsily in his arms and kissed his neck.

"So, what do you think?" she whispered.

"About what?"

"Was that any good? Are we compatible at all?"

"I'm not sure."

She drew away and looked at him in disbelief. "You're not *sure?*"

Alex smiled and pulled her back into his arms. "I need to do a little more research. In fact, I want to try it again now and see if I can reach some kind of decision."

She laughed. "You're a terrible glutton."

"No, darling." He kissed her and ran a hand gently through her tousled curls. "I'm a starving man, and you've offered me a feast."

"Really, Alex?"

"Really." His voice roughened. "I love you, Gina."

She felt a chill of fear. "Please don't say that."

"Why not? What's wrong with loving you?"

"It's too scary. For one thing, we hardly know each other. For another, we both have complicated lives, with all kinds of responsibilities."

"Does that mean we can't fall in love with each other?"

"It means," Gina said, "that we can't just plunge into something without being really careful."

Alex leaned up on one elbow to study her face in the lamplight. "You're always really careful, aren't you, Gina? You don't give your heart away easily. Part of you holds back and analyzes the situation."

"Always," she agreed.

He stroked the hair off her forehead, then ran a finger down the tip of her nose and around the contours of her lips. "What would it take for a man to capture that elusive part of you?"

"I don't know."

"What if a man could get you alone in the Costa Rican rain forest? Do you think he might have a ghost of a chance there?"

But we wouldn't be alone, Gina thought. *Your daughter would be there. And she certainly won't feel the same way about me as you do.*

"Well, maybe it could work," she said, forcing herself to smile at him. "Especially if the river was infested with snakes and alligators, and you were the only man around to protect me."

Alex chuckled. "I'd love to be the man who gets to protect you from every danger."

He pulled her into his arms and began to kiss her hungrily. Gina responded with rising passion, but his words lingered in her mind, frightening her at some deep unspoken level.

There were so many dangers in the world. And Gina knew that even the love of a man like Alex Colton could never provide enough protection to keep all those terrors at bay.

THE NEXT MORNING Alex drove to the airport in Kelowna, lost in thoughts about Gina. He'd left her room well before daylight and crept back upstairs while the house was still silent, missing her as soon as he was away from her arms, longing to see her again.

But she hadn't made an appearance in the dining room at breakfast, even to bring in the coffeepot. This was unusual enough to be a little worrisome. When he'd gone looking for Gina, Mary said that her employer was already out in the canoe, paddling down the lake to pick blueberries.

Knowing the cautious way Gina approached their relationship, he wasn't surprised she'd chosen to avoid him today. Still, he hungered for her touch, even a glimpse of her face. He gripped the wheel and smiled, thinking about her slim tanned body, her level gaze and endearing smile, and the amazing generosity and tenderness of her lovemaking.

His body was so fulfilled and eased that he felt almost weak with happiness. But his feelings went far beyond the mere pleasure of sexual release. As he'd told Gina, he was in love.

He couldn't believe how quickly this woman had crept into his heart. There were so many things about her he found appealing. He loved her quiet hardworking nature, the way she carried her burden of responsibility with such calm. He loved the whimsical tomboyish self she often showed when she thought herself unobserved. And he was utterly charmed by her conversation, her laughter, the quickness of her mind and the surprising things she dreamed about, such as a vacation in the rain forest.

Alex longed to make her dream come true. He couldn't imagine anything more wonderful than lying at night in a tent with Gina, holding her in his arms while rain drummed against the taut canvas...

Thinking about her body, her warmth and passion, he felt his groin tighten. He shifted uncomfortably on the leather seat and glanced down the highway with a rueful smile. *I'm like a teenager with a first crush,* he thought.

Thinking about teenagers jolted Alex sharply back to the fact that he'd soon be seeing his daughter. Steffi was scheduled to arrive just before noon.

Alex frowned, wondering how Steffi was going to feel about Gina. His daughter was too young to understand the full nature of an adult relationship. Steffi couldn't know, of course, what it had been like for her father to endure the long bitter years of celibacy while his wife's illness progressed, or how quickly a man's desire could flare when he met a woman he found irresistible.

Steffi might feel he was being unfaithful to her mother's memory. She might be hurt and resentful. Alex knew that Gina, in her wisdom, feared a reaction like that. She had, in fact, tactfully given him to understand that she intended to stay well in the background after Steffi's arrival, letting him spend time with his daughter.

Alex loved Gina even more for that, but he didn't want her to withdraw from them. He wanted the three of them to do things together, wanted to create an opportunity for a friendship to build between Steffi and Gina. Most of all he wanted them to love each other and see the good things in each other that he saw.

Apparently he wanted a lot of things, he thought with a humorless smile. Maybe not all of them were going to be possible, but he certainly intended to do his best.

He pulled into the airport parking lot and went into the terminal, settling to wait near the windows where he could see Steffi's plane land. She was one of the last to disembark from the little commuter flight, and he felt a lump in his throat when he saw her unmistakable blaze of red hair.

He watched eagerly as she crossed the tarmac, then entered the terminal. Because she no longer tolerated public displays of affection, Alex held himself in check when she came through the arrivals area to join him. He gave her only a quick hug and a peck on the cheek, taking the duffel bag from her.

"Good trip?" he asked as she followed him toward the door.

She shrugged. "It was okay. They gave us a sandwich and some fruit."

"So you don't want to stop anywhere for lunch? We could run into town and grab a burger."

Steffi shook her head. "I'm not hungry, Dad."

She wore faded jeans with gaping holes in the knees and a baggy plaid shirt that hid most of her slim graceful body. Alex sighed, thinking about the beautiful girl under those sloppy clothes, trying to remember when he'd last seen his daughter wearing something really attractive.

But clothes were another of the many topics that caused tension between them, and he didn't want any tension. At least not today.

"Did you like Disneyland, honey?" he asked, stashing her luggage in the trunk of his car.

"Not really," she replied sullenly.

"Why not?"

"I dunno. It was kinda dumb. And I really hated being with Angela's family."

"Why? Weren't they nice to you?"

Steffi sighed. "They were all right. But Angela's a jerk. And they were all so—" She fell abruptly silent.

He held the passenger door open for her, then went around and climbed behind the wheel. "What were you saying about Angela's family?"

"They were so *normal*," she said at last. "One big happy family, you know? It got pretty sickening after a while."

Alex shifted the car into gear. "I guess it's been a long time since we've been a normal happy family," he said quietly. "I'm sorry, Steff."

"Why?" she asked. "It's not your fault Mom got sick."

"I know. It wasn't anybody's fault, but these past few years have been so hard for you."

He stole a glance at Steffi, but her profile was unrevealing. She stared straight ahead, ignoring the spectacular scenery of lake and mountains as they drove up the highway toward Azure Bay.

"I'm really hoping this vacation will get us back on track," he said after they'd covered a few miles. "It's a beautiful place, Steff. Wait till you see this old house. And there's a lot of things for you to do. You're going to love this summer."

She sighed again, then leaned back in the seat and closed her eyes, leaving Alex to negotiate the highway in troubled silence.

GINA PADDLED her canoe slowly down the lake toward home. She wore khaki cutoffs, a T-shirt and a ragged straw hat to shield her face from the midday sun. In the canoe she had six pails filled with berries, evidence of a morning spent working at top speed in an effort to hold her thoughts at bay.

But now, as she dipped her paddle and sent the canoe smoothly over the surface of the lake, all the images came flooding back. She saw Alex smiling down at her as he lay in her bed, heard his voice, felt the tenderness of his hands.

Her body grew warm and tingly as she recalled their passionate lovemaking. Alex had been so hungry. He'd been in such need, and she'd been able to satisfy him so completely....

"So what are you?" she said to herself. "Some kind of social worker, giving sexual relief to frustrated men?"

She glanced around nervously, but her voice was lost in the vastness of the lake and the surrounding trees.

And what came next? she asked herself. What about tomorrow, now that she'd been foolish enough to let this happen? How could she ever look the man in the eye and pretend nothing was different? He was going to be at the hotel for almost two months, along with his daughter.

So now what?

The warm memories faded, replaced by a flood of worry. She rested the paddle on the gunwales and dropped her face into her hands, letting the canoe drift toward the shore. She was brought back to reality when the hull scraped gently on some submerged rocks, and picking up the paddle, she began to stroke firmly. The canoe glided out into deeper water, heading around a wooded point of land to the sandy beach in front of the hotel.

Several of the guests were there enjoying the sunshine. They greeted Gina, who accepted gratefully when three of the older children offered to help her beach the canoe and lift out the buckets of berries. They moved with Gina across the lawn to the house, all carrying plastic pails, a ragtag little group in bathing suits and bare feet.

"Just leave them here on the back steps," Gina told the children as she climbed onto the veranda. Two of them already had purple-stained lips and guilty looks. "I'll take them to the kitchen, okay? You guys all have too much sand on your feet."

They stood below her on the grass, looking up at her hopefully.

"Okay," she said with a smile. "You can each take as many berries as you can carry in two hands."

Whooping with delight, they plunged their hands into the brimming pails and raced off toward the beach, trailing blueberries as they ran.

Gina smiled, took up the two heaviest pails and carried them into the hallway, setting them down by the kitchen door, then went back for the rest.

"Mary," she said, popping her head into the kitchen, "I've left some pails of..." Gina's voice failed her and she sagged against the door frame, almost faint with shock.

Alex and Roger sat at the table, sipping coffee. Mary was rolling biscuit dough on the counter then cutting circles of dough with a floured cutter. Perched on a stool nearby was a girl with red hair and a baggy plaid shirt, watching Mary's deft hands as she worked.

"Hello, Gina," Alex said, his face lighting with pleasure. "You're finally back. We were getting worried about you."

Gina licked her lips, trying not to stare at the girl's profile. "There's no need to worry," she said, wondering if she sounded as shaken as she felt. "I've been out in the canoe a hundred times by myself."

"See any bears?" Roger asked.

"No," Gina said. "No, I didn't see any bears."

She hesitated, longing to turn and flee down the hall to her room. But Alex was speaking again.

"Gina, this is my daughter. Steffi, this is Ms. Mitchell, the owner of the place, but I guess we're all on a first-name basis around here, right, Gina?"

"Yes," Gina murmured. "Of course. Hello, Steffi."

"Hi," the girl said.

She turned around on the stool, and the full frontal view of that smooth young face was more than Gina could endure. She felt dizzy. Nausea began to tug urgently at her stomach.

"I have to go," she said in panic. "There's something in my room I have to... to check on."

She turned and stumbled a little, then caught herself and hurried off down the hall to her room while the others in the kitchen exchanged puzzled glances.

CHAPTER EIGHT

ALONE IN HER ROOM, Gina sat on the edge of the bed for a moment, then dropped her head between her knees, fighting the waves of nausea and dizziness. She took a few deep breaths, sat erect to push the hair off her forehead and stared out the window at the shaded yard with its peaceful banks of flowers.

It *couldn't* be. This wasn't happening...

She moaned, still gazing out at the lawn. Finally she heaved herself from the bed and crossed the room to the bureau. Opening a drawer, she took out a photograph of her sister, taken a few years ago at Claudia's high school graduation.

The young face smiled at Gina from behind the glass, softly framed by a vivid mass of red hair. It was the image of Stefanie Colton. The two could have been twins.

Except for the mouth, Gina thought, still examining the photograph in shocked horror. Claudia's mouth was wide and thin-lipped, while Steffi's was the same as Alex's, with that humorous lift at the corners and a full sensuous lower lip.

She shivered, clutching the photograph, her mind reeling with confused images and random thoughts. A knock sounded at the door, jerking her back to reality.

"Gina?" Alex called. "Are you all right?"

She stared wildly at the closed door. "Just ... just a minute," she said, thrusting the photograph hastily back into the drawer and covering it with a pile of sweaters. "I'll be right there."

She struggled to compose herself, leaning against the dresser and staring at her reflection in the mirror. Finally she crossed the room, paused once more to take a couple of deep breaths, then opened the door.

Alex stood in the hallway, his brow creased in concern. "Are you all right?" he asked. "You rushed out of the kitchen so fast we thought something was wrong."

Gina moved aside. He stepped into the room, closing the door behind him, then took her in his arms and held her gently.

"Nothing's wrong. I'm fine," Gina mumbled against his shoulder, trying not to show how distressed she was by his touch. "I just feel a little lightheaded, that's all. Maybe I got too much sun this morning."

"You shouldn't have stayed out so long. I saw all the berries you picked."

"I found another thicket a little farther down the lake and there were so many berries..." Gina was hardly conscious of what she was saying. "I got ... I got started and couldn't stop picking."

"You should have waited till I was back." Alex bent to kiss her cheek. "Steffi and I would have loved to come along and help."

Gina stiffened in his arms, desperately wishing he'd go away and leave her alone.

"Gina, I'm worried about you." He touched her forehead. "You're shivering. Would you like me to call a doctor?"

She drew away and forced herself to smile. "I'm fine," she said again, rubbing her arms nervously. "Really, Alex. I just need...a cool drink or something."

"Should I go and ask if Mary has some lemonade in the fridge?"

"No. No, it's all right. I'll go out there in a minute. Nobody needs to wait on me." Gina hesitated, wondering what to say. "Your daughter is...she's a beautiful girl," she whispered at last, turning away so he couldn't see her face.

"I know," Alex said. "But she doesn't seem any happier after her trip to Disneyland. I don't know what to do, Gina. It feels as if everything I say is wrong these days."

"I suppose..." Gina faltered, then found her voice again. "I suppose it's partly her age."

"Maybe. Fourteen is a difficult age for girls, I've heard."

Although she already knew what the answer would be, Gina asked, "When...when's her birthday?"

She glanced up at him, holding her breath.

"Next month. She'll turn fifteen in August. Just before we leave, in fact."

August twenty-fourth. Gina's heart contracted painfully at the memory. Stefanie Colton's birthday was August twenty-fourth...

"You know, I'm still worried about you," Alex said, taking her in his arms again. "You look so pale."

Gina slipped out of his embrace and crossed the room to look out the window, keeping her back to him. "I'm fine," she repeated, then took a deep breath. "I think," she went on, her voice shaking, "maybe I'm a little upset about... about what happened last night."

"Why?" He came and stood close behind her, but she kept her face resolutely turned to the window.

"It was all so... I think maybe we rushed into things."

"You didn't feel that way last night, Gina," he said quietly. "We had a wonderful time. At least I know I did, and I thought you felt the same."

"I guess I did, but things tend to seem a lot different in the daylight. I just think..." She paused, then forced herself to continue. "I think rushing into a sexual relationship is never a good idea. Maybe we should go back to being friends for a while and see what happens."

"I wasn't aware we'd stopped being friends." His voice was gently teasing, but Gina was in no mood for laughter.

"Please, Alex," she murmured.

"All right," he said. "If you're having second thoughts, of course I won't rush you into anything. But I want you to know..."

He put his arms around her from behind. Gina's whole body ached to lean against him, curl into him, lose herself in his strength and warmth.

But that wasn't possible. Not anymore.

She fought back a sob and, holding her body rigid, made herself keep looking out the window.

"I told you, Gina," Alex went on gravely, "that I've fallen in love with you. I don't fall in love lightly or say anything that isn't true. I care for you very deeply, and I'm hoping you'll decide to give us a chance."

She was silent.

"Do you hear me, Gina?"

Numbly she nodded, moved out of his arms, turned and met his gaze. "Yes, Alex, I hear you," she said. "And I appreciate your patience."

He watched in puzzled silence as she hurried across the room to the door, then waited for him to join her in the hallway.

"So what are you doing this afternoon?" she asked, trying to keep her tone casual. "A lot of the guests are on the beach today. They say the water's perfect."

"I know, but Steffi tells me she forgot to pack a bathing suit. I thought we'd drive into Kelowna and do some shopping, maybe pick her up some snorkeling gear, as well."

"So you'll be gone the rest of the day?"

"Probably. We'll grab dinner in town and maybe go to a movie later. Provided I can find something she'll be interested in. Say," he said, brightening, "why don't you come along?"

"Alex, I don't think—"

"Come on," he urged, taking her arm as they neared the kitchen. "It'll give you a little break, and a chance to get to know Steffi, too. Please, Gina, won't you think about it? We could—"

They were close enough to the kitchen that Roger's voice was clearly audible. He was asking a question, followed by Steffi Colton's muffled reply.

Gina shook her head in sudden panic and pulled away from Alex's hand. "I have to do some work outside," she said abruptly, hurrying down the hall toward the lobby. "Have a nice day in town, Alex. I'll probably see you in the morning."

HALF AN HOUR LATER, Gina stood under the weeping willow in the yard and peered out through the trailing branches, watching while Alex and his daughter got into their car and headed out of the parking lot, down the road toward the highway.

She waited until they were out of sight, pretending to trim the drooping branches with a pair of hedge clippers in case anybody was watching her from the one of the windows.

Finally, her heart pounding, she set the clippers down on the stone ledge and searched in her pockets for the hotel master key. Gripping the key tensely in her hand, Gina hurried across the shaded lawn, feeling furtive and self-conscious as she unlocked the patio room.

The French door opened easily and swung inward. Gina slipped inside, closed the door behind her and leaned against it while she fought another breathless wave of nausea. After a few moments her head cleared and she looked around.

It appeared that Steffi hadn't been able to make a quick decision about what to wear for her trip to the city with her father. An empty duffel bag lay open on the bed, and piles of shirts and jeans were scattered messily nearby, many of them turned inside out. But the girl hadn't yet found time to unpack most of her other things. Two large suitcases sat on the floor, still bulging.

Gina knew it was wrong for her to be here snooping in the girl's room. But she was desperate to learn the truth, and she couldn't think of anything else to do.

She moved farther into the room. Apparently the duffel bag had contained most of the girl's treasures, as well as her favorite clothes. A leather jewelry box was already positioned carefully on the mirrored dressing table, flanked by a couple of photographs in ornate gold frames.

One of the photographs was of a much younger Alex Colton. Gina picked it up and looked with detached sadness at his handsome face, with its square jaw, sober gaze and sensual mouth.

At last, hardly daring to look, she picked up the other photograph.

Janice Colton's face smiled at her from the gold frame. She was delicate, blond and lovely, exactly as she'd looked almost sixteen years ago.

Gina gave a cry of distress and dropped the photograph back on the dresser. She stumbled toward the chintz-covered armchair and huddled in it, drawing her knees up and burying her face against them, whimpering in agony as the memories came flooding back....

GINA HAD BEEN barely twenty-one years old, graduated from college and looking for work, on that lovely summer day when she'd first met Janice Colton in Vancouver.

Of course, the woman wasn't using her real name. She called herself Joanne and said her husband's name was Al. She was a legal assistant, while her husband taught physical education at a local high school.

Joanne and Al.

They sounded like a normal wholesome middle-class couple. The kind of people who could provide a loving home to a child. And they wanted a child so desperately....

Gina rocked in the chair, drowning in memories, so distressed she could hardly breathe.

It was a lawyer who'd first introduced her to
Joanne. Gina had found herself in the lawyer's office
after answering an advertisement in a Vancouver
newspaper.

She could still remember that ad:

Do you need a lot of money? Are you a special
kind of person? Are you bright, competent, re-
sourceful and physically healthy? Do you consider yourself strong and independent? If so, we
have a challenging, interesting project that will
earn you a salary beyond your wildest dreams....

Gina had been sitting in the dingy bedroom in her
aunt's basement apartment when she saw the ad.
She'd studied it, wondering what kind of work it could
possibly be.

Salary beyond your wildest dreams. Well, her
dreams had once been pretty wild, all right. She'd actually dreamed of buying Edgewood Manor and running her own bed-and-breakfast. But now all those
hopes were shattered, swept away by the appalling reality of her sister's medical bills.

Maybe this newspaper ad was some kind of a sign.

So Gina sent off a letter of application with her ré-
sumé to the box number at the bottom of the ad, then
waited and hoped for an interview.

The call finally came about two weeks later from a
woman who sounded mysterious and noncommittal
over the phone. "I can't tell you anything about the
job," the woman said. "You'll have to talk to Mr.
Harwood. He's the one doing the screening."

Mr. Harwood's office was more opulent than anything Gina had ever seen. She sat and looked in awe at

the green plush carpet, the Turkish rugs, the heavy oak furniture and glass-fronted bar.

There had to be something wrong with this deal, Gina thought nervously. She didn't belong here. What could she possibly offer these people when she didn't even—

"Miss Mitchell. Nice to see you. I'm John Harwood." A man entered, looking at Gina with undisguised pleasure and a kind of frank appraisal that made her nervous.

He was small and balding, with a round plump belly that strained at the belt of his expensive suit trousers. But his dark eyes were keen and shrewd.

"We were very impressed with your application," he said.

"I didn't even know what I was applying for," Gina told him bluntly. "But I was completely honest in my application, Mr. Harwood. My degree is in hotel management, not law."

"We know that." Harwood seated himself across the desk and continued to study her. "We're not particularly interested in your academic field, Miss Mitchell. We're more interested in *you.*"

Gina's nervousness increased. "I don't understand. How could you be—"

He raised a hand to cut her off. "Now, you probably wouldn't have answered our advertisement unless you were interested in making a lot of money. Why do you happen to want all that money, Miss Mitchell?"

"My mother needs fifty thousand dollars to pay my little sister's medical bills. I received an inheritance from my grandmother on my twenty-first birthday, but it's not enough."

The lawyer looked sympathetic, so Gina told him the details about Claudia's accident, the costly reconstructive surgery and the fact that her mother had no medical insurance.

"So your need for this money is totally altruistic?" the lawyer said at last, still watching her closely. "There's nothing you want for yourself?"

"Well, there used to be. I wanted to buy an old hotel near Kelowna. With the thirty thousand dollars I inherited from my grandmother, I almost would have had enough."

Gina found herself relaxing a little as she told the lawyer about Edgewood Manor, the tumbledown old mansion on the shores of Okanagan Lake that she'd dreamed of purchasing and renovating.

"But you've changed your mind about wanting the hotel?"

"That was all a fantasy of mine before... before Claudia's accident. Now I need to give the whole inheritance to my mother and somehow find another twenty thousand to go with it."

He studied her thoughtfully. "You're twenty-one, you said?"

Gina nodded. "My birthday was in June."

"Well, suppose I told you, Gina, that you could earn enough to pay your sister's medical bills *and* make the down payment on your hotel, as well as provide a wonderful service to some very deserving people at the same time."

"How could I possibly do all that?"

"If we can work out the details, my clients would be prepared to reimburse you up to seventy thousand dollars for a one-time project. Would that be interesting to you?"

Gina's mouth dropped open. "But . . . I don't understand. What kind of project? What would you want me to do?"

"Something," he said with a brief smile, "that you are supremely well equipped to perform."

Suddenly uneasy, Gina got up and began to move toward the door. "I'm afraid we're probably just wasting each other's time, Mr. Harwood."

"Listen to me for minute, please, Miss Mitchell. Sit down and let me outline the project."

When he told her, Gina's head began to spin and she was forced to grip the arms of her chair to keep herself steady. She stared at the lawyer in disbelief, searching for words.

"You . . . you want me to have this man's *baby?* And then give it to him and his wife?"

"Please don't look so horrified," he said gently. "This is not such a terribly outlandish proposition, you know. As a matter of fact, it's done all the time."

"But I couldn't . . . I don't see how I could possibly . . ." Again Gina got to her feet, holding her handbag close to her chest.

"If it's impossible for you to consider our proposal," the lawyer said pleasantly, leaning back in his chair, "then our interview is over, Miss Mitchell. Did you come here by car?"

"I don't have a car," Gina muttered. "I came on the bus."

"Then I will arrange to have you driven home." The lawyer picked up his telephone and smiled at her. "Thank you for your time."

"Wait . . ." She sank into the chair again, her cheeks flaming with agitation. The lawyer gave her an alert glance and slowly hung up the receiver.

"Yes, Miss Mitchell?"

"How would I ... Would I have to..." She shuddered, then composed herself and went on. "Would I have to sleep with this man? To get pregnant, I mean."

He smiled, but sobered instantly when he met her eyes. "Of course not. Fertilization would be achieved by artificial insemination. You would never, at any time, meet or see the child's father. All arrangements would be done through the mother."

"Wouldn't *I* be the mother?"

"Not in this case," Harwood said quietly. "You would merely be the surrogate. The real mother is my client. She intends to be involved at every stage of the pregnancy, including the childbirth itself, and will take the baby home from the hospital immediately afterward."

"Leaving me with seventy thousand dollars?"

"You would be paid twenty thousand on conception. I believe that's enough, along with your own inheritance, to cover your sister's medical expenses. An additional twenty thousand would be paid at the end of the sixth month and the balance on delivery of the baby. In addition, all your expenses would be looked after during the pregnancy, and your health and welfare would be carefully monitored."

"By this woman?"

"And a doctor of her choice. As well as my office, of course. We would all be very concerned with your comfort and happiness."

Gina shook her head, unable to believe she was hearing this proposition. Even more incredible, to realize she was actually considering it.

All her mother's worries would be laid to rest, Claudia's future welfare would be assured, thanks to continuing physical therapy, and the balance of the money would guarantee her ownership of Edgewood Manor. And all she'd be doing in return was offering a wonderful once-in-a-lifetime chance at happiness for a childless couple.

"Why can't they have a baby of their own?" she asked abruptly. "What's wrong with them?"

"There's a possibility that the wife has a defective gene that might be passed on to their natural child. They're both too responsible to take such a risk, even though it's minimal. They're very nice, highly moral people, Gina."

"What kind of defective gene?"

"It causes the carrier to develop a rare neurological disease, but usually quite late in life. So even if the mother does have it, it's nothing that would interfere with her capacity to be an excellent parent."

"And the man? Her husband? What about him?"

"He's a very bright powerful man," the lawyer said easily. "They're both professional people, with a comfortable financial situation."

"They must be," Gina said, "if they can afford to pay seventy thousand dollars for a baby."

"The wife's family has considerable resources. I believe she intends to look after these . . . financial arrangements on her own. She's desperate to have a child. I can certainly assure you that the child will have a wonderful home and family."

Gina toyed with the leather fringe on her handbag, staring out the window in brooding silence.

"What are their names?" she asked at last.

"I can't tell you their full names. The privacy of all parties will be carefully guarded throughout the entire process. For your purposes, their names are Joanne and Al.''

"And I'd never meet Al, right?" Gina asked cautiously. "I'd just talk to Joanne?"

"Are you considering the idea, Miss Mitchell?"

She looked at him in silence, her eyes wide and troubled. "Yes," she said at last. "Yes, I think maybe I am."

Shortly afterward, Gina was introduced to the woman she knew only as Joanne. The two of them embarked on a course that still seemed incredible whenever Gina stopped to think about it.

But like any bizarre situation, familiarity had gradually made it seem less strange. Eventually the whole thing became more like a creative project, an interesting challenge that absorbed much of her thoughts and attention.

Three tedious anxious months passed before the attempts at artificial insemination were successful. Joanne was present at each trial, comforting Gina when she felt frightened, encouraging her as the test results showed yet another failure.

Though she was older and much more sophisticated, the dainty blonde became almost a friend, someone Gina could talk with easily. Only Joanne's steely dedication, her obsessive determination to have this baby, made her seem a little intimidating at times.

Early in December, Gina finally missed her period. Joanne was almost beside herself with excitement. When the test results came back positive, Joanne hugged her and wept, thanking Gina for the most wonderful Christmas present she'd ever received.

Gina sent fifty thousand dollars to her mother, saying only that the inheritance from Grandmother

Mitchell had turned out to be larger than they'd expected. Her mother's tears of relief and gratitude were almost enough to ease the doubts Gina had about what she was doing.

Gina made arrangements to move into a comfortable studio apartment provided by Joanne and her husband, and settled down to wait. She enrolled in the winter semester at UBC, taking extra courses in hotel management to upgrade her degree.

Finally she received an assurance from the bank that if she could provide the necessary funds by the following summer, she would be able to get a mortgage on Edgewood Manor. The thought of the baby still seemed dreamy and unreal, but the old Victorian mansion obsessed her more and more.

Gina's feelings about her pregnancy didn't become really troublesome until one morning in early spring, when she felt the baby move for the first time.

She'd been lying in bed, looking at the soft green buds on the trees outside the window, resting her hand on her swelling abdomen with a kind of wondering awe. Somehow she'd never allowed herself to realize that an actual human being was developing in there, a living, growing entity. But the ultrasound test Joanne ordered had already revealed that the baby was a girl, and she was healthy and normal.

Gina felt a gentle flutter. She pictured the baby swimming in her watery world, safe and warm, cradled within her mother's body.

She felt another little movement within her, perhaps a kick from a tiny foot. Gina's heart swelled with emotion, and her eyes filled with tears. This child was hers—no, not hers. She was Joanne's. *Joanne* was this baby's mother.

"But I love you," she whispered into the stillness, her voice breaking into a sob. "You'll never know it, my darling, but I love you very much."

She cried for a long time in the soft gray light of dawn. Finally she got up and took out her pictures of Edgewood Manor. She wiped her eyes and opened the album, forcing herself to concentrate on her real dream, the thing she wanted more than anything.

After that moment of wrenching sorrow, Gina forbade herself to think about the baby or talk to her or even imagine what she looked like. The movements inside her grew stronger and more vigorous all the time, but she tried to ignore them.

For her part, Joanne got more and more excited as the pregnancy advanced. She often came to the apartment and lay next to Gina on the bed, her blond head cradled on Gina's abdomen so she could feel and hear the baby's movements.

"I wish you didn't have to go through it," she told Gina passionately when the early summer months grew long and tedious. "If there were any way, I'd take this burden away from you."

"I know you would."

"It won't be like this all summer. You'll feel better as soon as the baby drops into the birth canal."

Joanne knew everything about the pregnancy. Apparently she spent most of her free time studying medical books so she could learn what was happening to Gina's body at every stage.

"When will that happen?" Gina asked.

"It could be any time now," Joanne promised. "With subsequent pregnancies, it doesn't happen until just before labor starts. But when it's a first baby, the fetus can move down into the birth canal as early as a month before the birth. Won't that be exciting?"

"I suppose so." Gina looked gloomily at the massive bulge of her abdomen. "I just want all this to be over."

"It will be, dear." Joanne hugged her and smoothed her hair. "Would you like to go somewhere for a holiday these final few weeks to help pass the time? Maybe we could rent a place at the beach or something."

Gina shook her head, feeling ashamed. "It's okay, Joanne. I don't mean to be such a whiner. I'll quit thinking about it and concentrate on my work. I have tons of things to do."

In fact, Gina was close to becoming the actual owner of Edgewood Manor. She needed only the final payment after the baby's birth to secure the mortgage. Claudia was in physical therapy and doing better all the time. Their mother was safely out of debt and absorbed in her beloved chemistry again. And Joanne was wild with excitement over the coming birth.

Everything was going well. By September Gina would be free, thin and in charge of her own body again.

And I'll be happy, she told herself fiercely. *I'll be happy, just like everybody else.*

She buried herself in plans for the hotel renovations, spending her days reviewing price quotes, looking at floor plans, going though catalogs and instructional books on period restorations.

Joanne leafed idly through the stack of books on Gina's desk. "My goodness, you're brave," she murmured. "I'm really impressed with you, Gina."

"Me?" Gina asked in surprise, shifting her bulk to a more comfortable position on the bed. "What's impressive about me?"

"You're so determined and so capable. I can hardly imagine anyone, especially someone as young as you are, actually being able to buy and renovate that huge old building."

"You think *I'm* determined? Joanne, you're probably the most single-minded person in the whole world."

The slim blonde came over to pat Gina's stomach in a fond proprietary manner. "I admit it," she said. "I wanted this baby, and I was prepared to move heaven and earth to get her."

Gina looked away. "What about your husband?" she asked, concentrating on the carton of ice cream in her hand.

"What about him?" Joanne moved back to the desk and picked up a roll of fabric swatches, giving each a perfunctory examination.

"Is he as excited about the baby as you are?"

"Of course he is," Joanne said. "It's his baby, after all."

An awkward silence fell. This was something they'd never discussed, the fact that the baby Gina carried was the biological child of Joanne's husband. Gina knew instinctively that it pained the other woman to be physically excluded from the miracle of reproduction.

Sometimes she wondered what he was like, that shadowy man known to her only as Al. Was he tall or short, dark or fair, laughing or solemn? Would the baby resemble him or look more like her, Gina?

But, of course, she would never know, for Joanne didn't talk about her husband. And the lawyer had told Gina that the baby's father knew nothing about her, the surrogate mother, except that she was healthy and young. He hadn't even been told her name.

Apparently Joanne was obsessed with the need to keep her husband completely separate from the mother of their child. She seemed to be consumed with a deep fear, the lawyer told Gina, that all their careful attempts at secrecy would somehow fail if he knew, endangering the security of the adoption.

Remembering, Gina set the empty carton on the bedside table. "It's all right, Joanne," she said quietly. "It's really all right."

Joanne turned to look at her. "What do you mean, honey?"

"You never ever have to worry about me," Gina told her. "I signed those legal papers for Mr. Harwood, promising I'd never try to find out who you are or have any contact with you or your family ever again. But even if there were no legal papers, you could still count on me."

Joanne came back and sat on the edge of the bed, her face drawn with worry. "I do think about it sometimes," she confessed. "I lie awake at night and wonder how I could bear it if you decided someday that you wanted the baby, after all. I think about your coming back to find us and trying to get custody."

Gina patted the woman's shoulder under the expensive linen suit jacket. "Don't worry," she repeated. "Please, Joanne. I knew exactly what I was getting into, and you know why I'm doing this. I'll keep my part of the bargain until I die, no matter what happens. After this baby is born, I'll never have anything to do with you or your family again. And I swear to you that I'll never assert any claim over the baby."

Joanne's eyes sparkled with tears. "Do you promise, Gina?" she asked, her face suddenly intense. "Do you really, really promise?"

"I really, really promise," Gina said solemnly.

As August wore on, Joanne began to spend almost all her time with Gina. When she had to be away from the apartment, she'd leave lists of telephone numbers where she could be reached at a moment's notice.

While Gina ballooned, Joanne actually grew thinner with anxiety and anticipation.

"You're fading away to a shadow," Gina told her, heaving herself from the bed one morning and waddling to the bathroom. "If I'm overdue, you'll probably disappear altogether."

"Oh, God, don't say that! If you're overdue, I don't think I can bear it."

Joanne had spent the night on a couch by the bay window, and she still lay under a mound of blankets. She lifted the curtain to stare gloomily at the riot of flowers in the garden.

"I'm half out of my mind already," she added. "This summer feels like it's been two years long. I can only imagine what it's like for you."

Gina paused in the doorway, looking at the other woman. "Doesn't your husband miss you? I mean, you're with me practically all the time. He must be getting lonely for you."

Joanne shook her head and let the curtain fall. "He's with a group of other teachers taking their students on a camping trip in the Rockies. But he checks in by telephone every day, so he can be back at a moment's notice when our baby arrives."

Gina closed the bathroom door behind her and leaned against it wearily, then began to unfasten the buttons on her nightgown.

A few moments later, she opened the door and looked out, wide-eyed and shaking with alarm. "Joanne," she whispered.

"Yes, dear?" Instantly alert, Joanne leapt from the couch and came running across the room. "What is it?"

"I think it's starting."

They looked at each other for a long frightened moment.

Gina couldn't remember much about that last day except that Joanne was with her every second, timing the contractions, helping her to pack a bag for the hospital, giving her encouragement when she began to feel tired and scared.

They checked into the hospital just after six in the evening and were moved at once to the labor room. Joanne hovered over Gina's bed, held her hand and whispered to her, brought her glasses full of ice chips, brushed the damp hair back from her forehead and helped her to breathe properly.

The situation had apparently been explained to the hospital staff. They were quiet and tolerant, allowing Joanne to stay nearby, though Gina wondered at times if she didn't catch a glint of cold disapproval in the eyes of some of the older nurses.

But soon she was aware of nothing at all but a wide sea of pain, and strong hands that kept her from drowning.

"Hang on, sweetie," a voice urged, distant and faint. "Hang on. You're doing great."

"Hurts. So much..."

"I know, darling, I know. But you're so brave..."

There was a final wrenching pain, an agony so intense that Gina knew her body could endure no more. Then it was over, and the room was wrapped in peace and stillness. Moments later the peace was disturbed by a frantic wailing sound.

"That's her," Joanne whispered, her face wet with tears. "It's our baby, Gina. She's crying."

Gina strained briefly to see, then fell back onto the cot and turned her head away.

Joanne crossed the room, still in hospital gown and mask. She took the blanket-wrapped bundle from the nurse's arms, cradling it tenderly.

At that moment, watching Joanne take the baby into her arms, Gina realized with crushing finality that the pain wasn't over at all. The worst pain lay ahead, through all the dark nights and long years of her life. But it was too late.

Too late to change anything.

Joanne came to her, holding the baby. She had carefully adjusted the pink blanket so Gina couldn't see the child's face.

"Thank you, Gina," she whispered. "I love you, and I'll never forget you as long as I live."

Then she was gone, almost running as she carried the baby out of the delivery room.

Gina recovered quickly from the trauma of birth and went back to the apartment to pack her things before the month's end. She collected the final payment, plus a generous bonus she hadn't expected, and left Vancouver for Azure Bay.

All the business details were handled by the lawyer. After that final brief moment in the delivery room, Gina had never seen Joanne again.

At least, she told herself, still huddling in the armchair, not until this moment, when Joanne's face smiled at her from the gold-framed photograph on Steffi Colton's dresser.

CHAPTER NINE

SEVERAL CHILDREN were out in the lake, splashing and shouting as they clung to a raft made of heavy logs lashed together.

"Hey, come on, Steffi," one of the boys jeered, flinging his long wet hair out of his eyes. "Why don't you come in and swim with us, chicken? I'll bet you can't even swim."

From her perch on the shore under a spreading maple tree, Steffi put down her book with calm deliberation and glared at the boy.

They were all so dumb, the kids at this hotel. For one thing, most of them were younger than Steffi, and they acted like such babies. But there was something else about these kids that bothered Steffi even more, and that was the way they all had normal families. A mother and father, maybe a sister or brother, as well. She ignored their shouts and rested her head against the tree trunk.

Once, a long time ago before her mother got sick, Steffi could remember having a normal family, too. When she was little, what she'd loved best in the world was having her parents walking on each side of her, holding her hands. There'd be a puddle or a crack in the sidewalk and they'd lift her up, laughing, and swing her through the air, then set her down again.

How wonderful it used to feel, that magical sensation of balance and utter safety. One strong parent on each side, carrying you though the air like a feather—

"Steffi can't swim," a little girl chanted from the water. "Steffi can't swim."

She looked at the child in distaste.

None of these kids knew anything. They had their fathers and mothers waiting for them in the hotel, and all their little friends to play with. They didn't know what it was like to live for years and years in a house that was more like a hospital, full of gross medical equipment. They'd never watched while the person you loved and depended on died.

Most of all, they didn't know how it felt to carry something horrible in your own body, something that was going to kill you the very same way it had killed your mother.

"Steffi can't swim," the cry echoed.

Didn't they ever get tired of being stupid?

Angrily Steffi got up and pulled her T-shirt over her head, then stepped out of her cutoffs and kicked them aside, revealing the sleek yellow maillot her father had bought for her.

A couple of the boys whistled awkwardly, but the rest of the children watched in nervous silence as Steffi climbed deliberately onto a rocky outcropping to one side of the sandy beach, poised for a moment against the sky, then arched and dived.

She surfaced partway out in the lake, dropped her head and started to swim with an effortless crawl, heading for the opposite shoreline.

The children exchanged disbelieving glances, then watched in growing awe as her mass of red hair grew smaller and smaller across the shining water.

But Steffi wasn't aware of her audience. She moved through the water with slow powerful strokes, lifting her face at intervals to breathe deeply and rhythmically as she'd been taught. The far shore still looked impossibly distant, just a line of green as thin as a pencil slash. She was fairly certain she could reach it.

Actually, she didn't care very much if she failed.

She was often haunted by such dark thoughts, especially late at night. She kept having images of how restful it would be to lose herself in the waters of the lake, or fling herself over a cliff to shatter her body on the rocks, or steal some pills from her father's medicine cabinet and swallow enough of them to go to sleep forever.

Then she wouldn't have to live all the time with the terror of knowing she'd inherited that awful disease from her mother and wondering when it would finally strike.

Steffi kicked and stroked, kicked and stroked, moving through the water like a slim golden fish. She was beginning to feel tired when the lake grew warmer and she realized she was nearing the shallows.

She rolled over and began to do a lazy backstroke, letting the sun fall on her face. At last she put her feet down and walked up onto the shore, shaking her long red hair back over shoulders, looking around with detached interest.

Back across the lake she could see the massive bulk of Edgewood Manor, so distant it looked like a toy castle in a storybook. The taunting children were nothing more than bright dots around the old gray raft.

Steffi turned to look behind her. There was a highway somewhere above the beach on the wooded hillside, and she could hear the faint sound of an occasional car. Otherwise it was peaceful on this side of the lake, pleasantly deserted. She liked the feeling of solitude and isolation.

Gina Mitchell, the lady who owned the hotel, said that the hills over here were mostly untracked wilderness, full of bears and cougars and deep treacherous swamps.

"People get lost in there every year," Roger had told Steffi the day before, while she helped him pick apricots for jam. "It's a pretty rugged place. Except for that lakeshore highway, there aren't any roads. Not even logging trails."

"What happens to the people who get lost?" Steffi had asked.

"Sometimes hunters find a bit of their skeleton or a piece of clothing a few years later. Most often there's never any trace of them again."

Steffi looked up at the woods, the forbidding band of trees and the scary caverns of darkness under their overhanging branches.

Something drew and pulled at her, made her want to plunge into those black caverns and disappear forever. She liked the idea of vanishing so completely that nobody would ever find any trace of her. It seemed infinitely better than waiting to die, being afraid all the time.

At last, almost reluctantly, she turned and looked back at Edgewood Manor. Her father was there, and he needed her. He was a really strong man, but even he couldn't survive the loss of both his wife and daughter within a few months.

He'd be all alone if he didn't have her.

Steffi hesitated a moment longer, then waded into the lake and stood with the water lapping around her thighs. She took a couple of deep breaths, dropped into position and began to swim, heading back across the lake.

"GINA MAKES great fishing flies. She could sell them for a pretty penny if she ever decided to open a fly shop in town."

"No kidding?" Lounging in the passenger seat, Alex looked over at Roger, who was driving the hotel truck off the road and down onto the beach.

Roger nodded and squinted at the side mirror as he backed up near the shore, then activated the hydraulic to hoist the truck box upward.

"Gina's an amazing woman," Alex said thoughtfully. "Really amazing."

"She is indeed." Roger opened the door and grinned back over his shoulder. "Come on, time to do some shoveling."

After three days of hauling sand, Alex was familiar with his part in the routine. He got out and rounded the back of the truck, hoisting himself lightly over the boards and into the heavy load of sand. Roger handed a shovel up to him. Alex gripped it and waded through the heavy mass, struggling up the incline toward the top of the box.

"Ready?" Roger shouted from below.

"Ready," Alex called back, clinging to the boards with one hand as he plied the shovel with the other. "Let her rip."

Roger opened the small tailgate. The sand began to flow downward in sluggish rivers, assisted by Alex, who worked energetically with his shovel. He could hear the sound of the engine starting, then a jolt when Roger began to move the truck slowly along the waterfront, spilling sand as they went.

When the truck box was empty, Alex put one hand on the boards and vaulted down onto the beach. Roger parked the truck, then returned with another shovel. They worked together amiably, spreading the neat trails of sand across the expanse of beach, talking about books, music and politics.

Roger paused, resting on his shovel handle, and smiled at the other man.

"You know, Alex, for an academic kind of guy, you make a pretty good laborer," he said.

Alex continued to work. He liked the feeling of hard physical labor, of peace and silence and the warm sun on his back.

"I can see why you quit your job and stayed here," he told Roger. "Sometimes I'm tempted to do the same thing myself."

Roger gave him a keen glance. "Well, now, I'm not too sure about that idea," he said. "My job's already filled, and I don't think Gina needs two handymen around the place."

"I'm not sure if Gina knows what she needs," Alex said quietly, earning another thoughtful look from his companion.

"Gina's not like other women," Roger began after a brief silence. "She's always been—"

He was interrupted by a commotion near the part of the beach where the children were swimming. Gina had come running down from the hotel and stood near the water's edge, accompanied by a pair of little girls in bathing suits who were talking and gesturing excitedly.

"Alex! Roger!" Gina called. "Come here!"

Alarmed by the panic in her voice, the two men dropped their shovels and ran toward her, awkward in their heavy boots.

"Steffi's out there in the water," one of the little girls told Alex. "She swam all the way across the lake. Now she's swimming back."

He looked down at the wide-eyed child, then at the glistening expanse of water. In the distance he could make out the faint outline of his daughter's head moving closer and the lazy splash of her arms.

"We have to go out in the boat and get her!" Gina rummaged frantically in her pockets. "Roger, do you know where the key is? I can't—"

Alex moved over beside her and put a hand on her shoulder. "Don't panic," he said. "She's okay. Look how strongly she's swimming. Her stroke isn't faltering at all."

"But the kids told me she swam all the way across just a few minutes ago. Alex, she's got to be exhausted! We can't take the risk."

He smiled and shook his head. "If I know Steffi, she'd be furious to have us go out there. She'd probably just keep swimming and make us follow her all the way back to shore."

"At least we'd be close by if she had problems. What if she gets a cramp or something?"

"Then we'll go out in the boat. Gina, she's been swimming since she was three months old. She knows everything there is to know about water-safety techniques."

Gina and Roger stood next to him with the children lined up on the beach in silent awe. They all held their breaths as Steffi drew nearer and nearer, her arms still lifting and bending in clean steady motions.

"I don't know how you can stand it," Gina muttered. "It terrifies me, thinking about her swimming all that way."

"Lots of times she scares me, too," Alex confessed, watching his daughter. "One of the hardest things about parenting is learning when to interfere and when to back off. I'm still not very good at it."

Steffi was almost at the shore. She took a few last strokes, stood up and waded onto the beach, pausing to double over and gasp for breath while the water dripped from her slim body and her tangled hair.

At last she straightened and cast a brief contemptuous glance at the silent group of adults and children on the beach, then headed for the maple tree, picked up her book and clothes and walked to the hotel.

Roger cleared his throat awkwardly. "Well, I'd better get back to town," he said. "We've got one more load to haul. Coming, Alex?"

"Not this time. I'll stay down here and finish spreading all this."

"Okay." Roger strolled off toward the truck. The children dispersed, shouting and pushing as they, too, headed to the hotel for afternoon tea and cookies.

Gina and Alex were left alone on the beach.

She still looked shaken, so pale that the freckles seemed to stand out on her cheekbones in sharp relief.

"Are you all right?" Alex asked, putting his arm around her.

"I'm not sure." She tensed at his touch, but allowed him to walk her away from the beach and into the shade of the maple.

Alex lowered himself to the sand and pulled her down beside him. "Have a rest and talk with me for a while."

She looked at his jeans and sand-covered hiking boots and tried to smile. "Aren't you supposed to be shoveling?"

"Even unpaid laborers get coffee breaks."

Gina squinted at the calm surface of the lake. "That was such a terrifying stunt," she murmured. "Swimming all the way across the lake and back. I can't believe she did that."

"I can't believe a lot of the things she does lately." Alex picked up a fallen leaf and smoothed it between his fingers. "Steffi and I used to be able to talk about everything in the world. Now there's some kind of huge wall between us, and I don't know how to get through it."

Gina was quiet so long that he wondered what she was thinking. Finally she glanced over at him.

"You told me Steffi was adopted, didn't you?"

"Yes," he said.

That wasn't technically a lie. After all, they'd been required to file legal adoption papers for Steffi after her birth.

"I see." Gina still gazed across the lake. "Does she know?"

"You mean, does she know she's adopted?"

"Yes."

Alex shook his head, wondering what Gina would think if he told her the whole truth.

How could they ever have explained it all to Steffi? Of course a child had the right to know she'd been adopted. But how would she deal with the reality of knowing that her biological mother had been hired like a brood animal and artificially inseminated with her father's sperm? At what point in her life did you tell a child that kind of truth?

"Janice never wanted her to know," he said at last. "It was like an obsession with Jan, the need to keep Steffi from finding out the truth. She loved that girl so much you just can't imagine."

"But doesn't Steffi have the right to know the truth about herself?"

"Janice made me promise we wouldn't tell her until she was an adult. After Jan got sick, I couldn't betray that promise. And now, when Steffi's grieving so much, I'm afraid I'd be piling more bereavement on her if I was to tell her that Janice wasn't even her natural mother. It would just be another kind of loss."

Gina nodded slowly. "I can see how you'd feel that. But still . . ."

Alex toyed with the leaf, wishing she'd drop the subject. Gina would never understand unless she knew all the details. But how could he tell her the truth when he hadn't even told Steffi?

"You know, it's funny," she was saying. "About Steffi, I mean."

"What about her?"

"The way she looks. If you hadn't told me she was adopted, I would have sworn she was your natural child. Her mouth is exactly like yours."

He drew his breath in sharply. But Gina was still gazing across the lake, her delicate profile sharply etched against the sun-dappled wash of blue.

"We knew quite a lot about Steffi's background," Alex said carefully, "even before she was born. We were careful to pick a . . . a birth mother who was compatible with us."

"Did you ever meet the birth mother?"

Alex recalled how secretive Janice had been about the young woman who'd borne his child. He'd never even learned the girl's name; he'd known only her age and race.

Sometimes he found himself wondering where she was now, that mysterious young woman, and if she ever thought about her child....

"Janice and our lawyer managed all the contacts with the birth mother," he said. "I trusted their judgment."

"I see."

Gina got to her feet and looked out across the lake, hesitating as if about to say something else. Whatever it was, she seemed to think better of it.

"I have to help Mary with the tea," she said, starting down the beach toward the hotel. "Are you coming?"

Alex shook his head. "Roger's going to be back soon with another load of sand. I'd better finish spreading these piles."

She nodded and hurried away. Alex watched her slender form as she vanished, longing to run after her and pull her into his arms.

He hungered for her all the time, yearned to hold her and kiss her. But she was obviously having second thoughts about their relationship. Ever since that night of wild sweet passion, she'd been slipping farther away from him. Alex could almost feel her retreating into some mysterious place where he didn't seem able to follow.

GINA LAY IN BED, holding her book open on the dark green quilt. She turned her head and looked out the window beside the bed at the silent yard. Though it was almost midnight, the neat banks of shrubs and flowers were still clearly visible in the moonlight. But the beauty of the scene didn't register with her. Her thoughts were all turned inward, replaying the events of the afternoon.

Over and over she saw Steffi's bright head far out on the lake and recalled the heart-stopping terror she'd felt when she realized what the girl was doing.

This must be the way it was for parents all the time, this intense love and panicky concern for another person's safety. But Gina had never expected to feel those emotions.

She picked up her book and tried to read again, then set it down. With a frown, she recalled her conversation with Alex that afternoon.

For the past few days, she'd been struggling to understand the bizarre situation she found herself in. She'd even begun to wonder if Alex knew the truth about her background, and that was why he'd come to Edgewood Manor.

Maybe his wife had told him Gina's identity before she died, and he'd brought Steffi here for some purpose of his own....

But their talk had dispelled those theories. Alex was too blunt and straightforward a man to lie so readily. Gina believed him when he said he'd never learned any details about Steffi's mother.

Janice Colton had carried the secret to her grave. Still, she must have taken an interest in Gina's life after the birth of the child, because she'd kept that brochure about Edgewood Manor.

Maybe it was just a precaution, Gina thought. Perhaps Janice had continued to be afraid of her and reasoned that it was safest to keep track of her because then she wouldn't be taken unawares if Steffi's biological mother suddenly reappeared.

Whatever the reason, Janice Colton's possession of that brochure and Alex's subsequent discovery of it had now created a situation that could be utterly devastating to all of them.

Most troubling, of course, was the simple fact that Gina had fallen in love with the man.

All her years of single-minded effort, all the sacrifice and loneliness, had been swept away in the passion she felt for Alex Colton. No other man had ever made her feel so alive, so breathless and happy and rich with fulfillment.

Added to those feelings was the astounding knowledge that, all those years ago, Alex and Gina had been joined together to create Steffi. Learning about the girl had added a depth and sweetness to Gina's passion, making her fall so deeply in love with Alex that she sometimes feared she would drown in emotion.

But she knew there was no hope for this love. In fact, Alex Colton was the one man in all the world denied to her. Gina brushed at the hot tears that stung in her eyes.

Back in Mr. Harwood's office, long before the baby's birth, she'd signed mountains of legal papers promising she would never in future have anything to do with her child or the adoptive family. Perhaps she was no longer legally bound by those documents now that Janice was dead, but regardless, there was no way she could bring herself to tell Alex the truth.

She switched off her lamp, got out of bed and moved across the room to the other window, standing in the silvered darkness as she looked wistfully over at the patio door.

A soft light glimmered through the panes of frosted glass. Steffi must still be awake, despite the hour.

Gina watched a dim shape move behind the glowing rectangles of the French door. She had to battle a sudden fierce longing to run over there, take the girl in her arms and tell her the truth.

But Gina knew she could never be that self-indulgent.

Steffi was still grieving. At this stage it would be cruel to tell her that Janice Colton hadn't been her mother at all, that her birth mother had been a stranger who'd made a business deal.

While Gina stood there brooding, the patio door opened and Steffi appeared suddenly in the square of light. Gina caught her breath and leaned forward.

The girl wore jogging pants and a baggy plaid nightshirt, and her hair was pulled back into a ponytail. She hesitated on the doorstep, looking around at the darkened mansion. At last she took something from her pocket and moved cautiously into the yard.

All at once a white shape erupted from the shadows near the back porch and hurtled toward the girl. Gina smiled when she recognized Annabel, the overweight poodle. Steffi looked around furtively and knelt to pat the dog, then extended her hand and waited patiently while Annabel gobbled whatever it was she was holding.

Finally Steffi went back into her room, carrying Annabel, and closed the door behind her. Gina leaned against the window frame, smiling though her tears.

All she could do was try somehow to get through this terrible summer, then pick up the shreds of her life after Alex and Steffi went away. In the meantime she certainly couldn't have anything more to do with Alex. She would never hold him, kiss him, feel his arms around her and his body close to hers—

A knock sounded at the door. Gina whirled around, her heart pounding.

"Yes?" she called. "Who is it?"

"It's Mary. Are you in bed?"

Gina felt a sharp mixture of disappointment and relief. She crossed the room to switch on the light, then opened the door.

Mary stood in the hallway, carrying a tray with two cocoa mugs and a plate of butter tarts. She looked in alarm at Gina, who was pulling on her old terry-cloth robe.

"I didn't wake you, did I?"

Gina shook her head. "I was in bed, but not asleep yet."

"I couldn't sleep tonight, either," Mary murmured.

Gina took the tray and set it on the small drum table next to her bed. "This looks good," she said. "I'm glad you came, Mary. I was lying here wide-awake and thinking a whole lot of mournful thoughts."

The older woman gave her a curious glance. "Are you all right, honey? You've been so quiet lately."

"I'm just tired. Every summer seems busier than the last, doesn't it?"

"Maybe we need a little more help. How about a full-time desk clerk and housemaid to take some of the burden off your shoulders?"

Gina shook her head. "You know I can't afford another salary. Maybe in a few more years, when I've managed to pay down the mortgage a little more and reduce the payments.''

Mary watched while Gina sipped her cocoa and picked at one of the rich tarts. ''You're not eating, either,'' she said. ''I'm getting worried about you, Gina. Something's the matter.''

Gina was almost tempted to tell the whole story, just for the relief of sharing her unhappiness. But the luxury of confiding in somebody, even a good friend like Mary, was another thing that was denied her. She'd vowed to protect the details of Steffi's birth, and she couldn't break that promise.

Instead, she took a healthy bite of the pastry, then another.

''See?'' she told Mary. ''I'm eating. And every one of these things is at least two thousand calories, you know.''

''Hardly,'' Mary said. But she seemed pacified and leaned back in the armchair to sip her cocoa.

''Where's Annabel?'' Gina glanced innocently toward the window. ''I thought I heard her outside a few minutes ago.''

''She's sleeping under the porch.''

''How's her diet coming along?''

''A lot better,'' Mary said with satisfaction. ''She doesn't seem nearly as hungry anymore. She's stopped whimpering all the time.''

''That's good.'' Gina looked down at her mug, trying not to smile. ''Is she losing any weight?''

Mary frowned. ''A little. Steffi takes her out for long walks every day. I'm hoping the exercise will do her some good.''

It wouldn't do much good if Steffi kept sneaking bits of sausage to the poodle under cover of darkness, Gina thought wryly.

"Steffi's...she's quite nice," she said, struggling to sound casual. "Don't you think?"

"Once you get to know her. She's a prickly little one, though, that girl. She seems awfully unhappy."

Gina thought once again about that slim body moving though the glistening lake waters.

"You know, she reminds me of somebody," Mary said with a frown. "It's driving me crazy. I can't seem to put my finger on it."

"She looks a lot like her father," Gina said, concentrating on her pastry.

Mary looked over at her in surprise. "Do you think so? I wouldn't say that."

"They have different coloring, but a lot of their features are the same."

Mary shook her head, still frowning. "No, it's not Alex. She looks like somebody else. I have the feeling it's somebody I saw a long time ago, but I can't seem to remember."

Claudia, Gina thought. *Steffi's aunt. She was here eight years ago, just after she graduated from high school.*

She felt a chill of fear and glanced nervously at the other woman. But Mary was putting the empty mugs on the tray and briskly sweeping pastry crumbs from the table.

"We'd better get to sleep," the housekeeper said, standing. "Tomorrow's a busy day."

"What's happening tomorrow?"

"Laundry, bread baking and washing all the lower windows."

Gina sighed. "I thought Roger was doing the windows this year."

"Just on the outside. Stacy and Kim are going to help us do the inside ones. *And*—" Mary paused in the doorway "—we're having company for tea."

"You mean besides the regular guests? Company for us in the kitchen?"

"Oh, yes," Mary said darkly. "Don't you remember? Ms. Lacey Franks is coming to see us. It's time for us to meet Roger's girlfriend."

CHAPTER TEN

"MY GOODNESS, this is just *so* delicious. Isn't it, Roger?"

Lacey Franks nibbled at an oatmeal scone, liberally smeared with fresh butter, and beamed at the group assembled around the kitchen table. She wore dainty leather sandals, madras walking shorts and a white tank top that displayed an impressive tan. Her gold hair was as carefully groomed as ever, and her face seemed to glow.

She really was quite attractive, Gina thought, noting the woman's trim figure as she sat perched in childlike fashion on one of the high wooden stools near the table.

Roger sprawled on a chair next to their guest, his arm dangling over the chair back, and looked out the window. Mary moved back and forth between the table and the cupboards, saying nothing, her face carefully expressionless.

Alex was with them, eating scones and trying manfully to help Lacey carry the conversation, while Steffi lounged at the small worktable in the corner. The girl toyed with Gina's vise in a bored fashion, rummaging through the tackle box full of neatly arranged feathers and other supplies used to make fishing flies.

"I *adore* these scones," Lacey continued. "Don't you, Alex?"

He nodded. "Mary's scones are the best."

"I simply don't know how you do it, Mary." Lacey gave the housekeeper a look of guileless admiration. "Taking care of all these people and keeping the place clean and cooking such wonderful things. You must be Superwoman."

Mary turned her back to the room, standing rigidly by the stove as she adjusted the heat under the kettle.

Gina sipped her tea and looked around cautiously at the others. It was easy to see that Mary was unnerved by their glamorous visitor.

Roger, too, seemed unlike his normal easygoing self. Every now and then Lacey reached over to stroke his arm or pat his shoulder possessively. He didn't seem to mind, yet his gaze frequently swung to Mary as she worked at the counter or refilled their teacups, and the expression in his eyes was impossible to read.

Gina exchanged an involuntary glance with Alex, who raised an eyebrow, showing her he was having similar thoughts. Even that brief moment of communion and understanding was enough to set Gina's pulse racing and make her throat go tight with yearning.

Oh, God, she thought in despair. *I love him so much it's all I can do to keep my hands off him. How will I ever be able to get through the summer?*

"By the way, Gina," Lacey was saying, "did you know that you're one of the reasons I coaxed Roger into bringing me here today?"

"I am?"

"I just *adore* this place," Lacey said. "Azure Bay, I mean. But—" she rolled her eyes "—I'm not all that thrilled with Fred's motel, if you know what I mean."

"I think I do," Gina said cautiously. "Fred's service standards are . . . fairly basic."

Lacey gave a dramatic shudder. "Now *that's* the understatement of the year! So—" she looked up at Gina with a dazzling smile "—I was wondering if you might have some teensy tiny little room I could move into for . . . oh, say a month or so. Even a little cubbyhole under the attic?"

Mary's head jerked erect. She gave Gina a look with such naked appeal it was almost comical. Roger, too, looked at his employer in alarm.

"Why, Lacey," he protested, turning to her, "you never said anything about this to me."

She leaned over to pat his cheek, smiling fondly. "I wanted to surprise you, sweetie. Won't it be a hoot, having me living right here where we can see each other all the time?"

Alex and Gina exchanged another glance. His eyes sparkled so brightly with teasing it was all she could do to stifle her laughter.

"I'm sorry, Lacey," Gina said when she could trust her voice. "But, really, I'm booked solid for the whole summer. In fact, we even have a waiting list this year."

Lacey's pout became somewhat less attractive, almost sullen. But she recovered quickly and smiled at Roger.

"Well, that's too bad," she said. "I suppose I'll just have to find a good friend who can stand to have me around the house for a few weeks."

Roger got hastily to his feet and, with old-fashioned courtesy, extended his hand to Lacey to assist her off the stool. "I'm afraid it's time to get back to town," he announced. "The chamber group has a practice at the church hall in twenty minutes." He urged Lacey forward. "See you later, folks."

Mary ducked her head in a wordless goodbye. Alex walked down the hall with Roger and Lacey, while Gina crossed the room to sit at the side table with Steffi.

"Hi," she said nervously, clenching her hands and hiding them in her lap so Steffi wouldn't see how they were shaking. This was the first time Gina had made any kind of direct overture to Steffi Colton since she'd realized the girl's identity.

Steffi glanced up casually, then peered at the vise again. "How does this thing work?"

"It holds the base of the fly." Gina hitched her chair closer. "Let's make a simple nymph just to show you the procedure. See, I start with a bit of wire to give some shape to the body, and then I wind it into a long, thin..."

She worked carefully, conscious of the girl's nearness. At one point she felt almost overcome with emotion and had to fight back tears. Yes, the love she felt for Alex was rich and exciting, springing from the depths of her womanhood, but the feeling she had for this child was even more profound in its way, a steady flow that had no beginning or end. After all, she'd carried her for nine long months, felt the first tiny kicks of her little feet. She'd given her away, but had yearned for her ever since....

"What are those?"

"Antennae. My own invention. They wobble and attract the fish."

"I tried fly-fishing once," Steffi said in a neutral tone. "Dad took us on a fishing holiday in Montana one summer before my mom got really sick."

Gina cleared her throat, surprised by this small overture. "Did you like it?"

Steffi shrugged, the noncommittal mask settling over her face again. "It was okay, I guess. But I wasn't very good."

Don't do this, Gina warned herself in mounting desperation. *Stay away from her. If you let yourself get involved, there's going to be heartache for everyone.*

But she couldn't stop herself. The words seemed to come of their own volition. "Roger and I are planning a fly-fishing trip up to Bear Creek this weekend if we can get away. Would you like to come with us?"

Steffi's eyes widened in surprise. "Me?"

She looked so sad and lonely it was all Gina could do not to gather the girl in her arms and cuddle her tenderly.

"Yes, you," she said, forcing a smile. "Roger loves teaching people to fly-fish. Probably because it gives him a chance to show off."

Steffi actually smiled back, a fleeting rearrangement of her features that was gone almost as soon as it appeared.

"Roger's kind of neat," the girl said.

"He is, isn't he."

"But I didn't like that other lady who came today. She was really dumb."

Mary was passing by at just that moment with a tray of warm macaroons. She paused, then placed two of the fluffy cookies next to Steffi on the table.

"Thanks, Mary." The girl looked in surprise at the cook's back as she returned to the stove.

"I guess Mary agrees with you," Gina said with a smile. "So, how about it, Steffi? Would you like to come fishing with us?"

The girl shrugged. "I guess there's nothing else to do."

But the glow on her face belied her words. She leaned forward with interest, munching a cookie and watching as Gina's skillful fingers shaped the body and wings of the nymph.

ALEX WALKED along the path from town, carrying a box containing half a pizza. In the west, the setting sun crept below the hills and painted the clouds pink and orange, spilling colored light across the lake.

The evening was mild and calm, and the valley at sunset was like a bowl filled with gold. The place seemed enchanted, a scene lifted from another age. He wouldn't have been surprised to see a band of warriors riding down to the lake on their painted ponies, or a brontosaurus wading out of the water to browse among the trees.

Alex smiled at his fancies, then noticed a slim figure sitting quietly on a big flat rock down by the shore. His pulse quickened when he recognized Gina, and he hurried toward her.

"Hi there," he said, sitting next to her on the rock, careful not to touch her. "A penny for your thoughts, my love."

She turned with a start, then smiled at him automatically. "Alex. Did you have a nice dinner?"

"Pizza and a salad. It was great." He held up the box to show her. "I brought half the pizza back for Steffi."

"Why didn't she go with you?"

"She was reading. She said she didn't feel like walking all the way into town."

Gina nodded and continued hugging her knees, resting her chin on them as she stared out at the darkening water.

Alex watched her, longing to take her in his arms. He'd never known this kind of fierce attraction to another person. He yearned constantly to hold her, caress her, drown her in kisses. But he also wanted to know everything she was thinking, how she felt about the people around her, how she felt about the world. He wanted to talk with her for hours, learn about her past, share his own thoughts and dreams.

But since their night of lovemaking and Steffi's arrival the next day, Gina had deliberately shut him out. Obviously she was nervous about getting too close to him, and Alex was afraid of losing her altogether if he tried to force a reaction from her.

You've got the whole summer, he told himself. *Be patient.* A woman like this was worth waiting for. And she was too strong to respond to any kind of heavy-handed approach.

"Okay," he said. "I'll make it a dollar."

"For what?"

"Your thoughts."

Gina shifted on the rock. "Actually I was thinking about Roger."

"What about him?"

"This new girlfriend of his. I'm worried about the whole situation."

"Why?"

"What if he gets married and moves away? I'd hate to try to run the hotel without him. Besides—" Gina frowned "—I don't think Lacey Franks is right for Roger."

"I see. Still, you have to admit she's attractive, don't you?"

Gina turned to look at him fully, her eyes searching. "Did you like her?"

"Not much. Personally I prefer the kind of woman who paddles her own canoe and carries a lot of junk around in her pockets."

Gina's cheeks turned faintly pink, an encouraging sign to Alex. But she looked so adorable he was forced to struggle even more against the urge to touch her.

"Do you think Roger's in love with her?" Gina asked, studying the lake with a brooding expression.

"No, I don't. I think she's latched on to him with some firmness, and he's too much of a gentleman to know how to get himself free. It's possible he's even a bit flattered by all the attention. But I don't believe he's in love."

"How can you be so sure?"

"I've been speculating about the whole situation. What if Roger were actually in love with Mary?"

Gina turned to stare at him. "Of course! Why didn't I think of that?"

"Maybe because you're too close to them. You can't be objective. But it makes sense, doesn't it? Mary's a nice-looking woman, and she and Roger have a lot in common. I've watched them when they're together, Gina. And I believe there definitely could be something there."

"Roger and Mary." Gina nodded slowly. "Yes, I think you could be right."

Alex added more weight to his theory. "They read the same things. They share a lot of the same interests, including this old hotel of yours. They like to argue about politics and everything else under the sun. It's only natural they'd fall in love."

"But why would it have taken them fifteen years to realize how they felt?"

"Maybe it just sneaked up on them," Alex said. "Maybe they haven't fully realized it yet. Working together for so long can do that to people, know what I mean?"

Gina nodded again. "Yes, and Mary's been really upset about this woman coming along. I was thinking it was just a…sisterly kind of response, but now, well, I see it could be much more than that. And did you notice the way Roger kept glancing at Mary the whole time Lacey was there?"

Alex nodded. "We could be wrong, of course. But I've sensed something between those two ever since I first saw them together. Having Lacey Franks here today just helped to confirm my suspicions."

Gina's brow wrinkled in thought. "What can I do about this?"

"Should you do something?"

"I *have* to," she said. "I can't let Lacey get her hooks into Roger even deeper. Not if there's any possibility that it's Mary he really wants. I have to find a way to… to force Roger to make some kind of move. But he's so shy, and Mary's even worse."

"The innkeeper becomes a matchmaker," Alex mused. "I get to see yet another aspect of the world's most fascinating woman."

She looked down at her denim shorts, her bare tanned legs and ragged sneakers. "Fascinating?" she muttered. "What a laugh."

Alex put an arm around her and drew her toward him. "Gina..."

But she pulled away and changed the subject. "Guess what happened today? Steffi's agreed to go fly-fishing this weekend with Roger and me."

"No kidding," Alex said in surprise. "How come I can't get her to do anything, but you can?"

"I think maybe she's angry with you," Gina murmured, avoiding his eyes.

"Why?" Alex was truly puzzled.

"Have you considered that maybe she blames you somehow for her mother's death? Subconsciously, I mean. I'm not a psychologist, but I suppose it's possible she thinks her father should have been able to protect her from all that pain."

Alex nodded thoughtfully. "She's had some counseling in the past few months. The therapist suggested much the same thing, but he also told me he felt something else was at the root of Steffi's withdrawal. Something she won't talk about with anybody."

"Maybe she just needs to work through her feelings. It must have been awful to realize that your parent had a disease like Huntington's."

"But she doesn't know anything about that. About the Huntington's, I mean. Janice felt Steffi was too young to understand, so we were careful to keep the details from her."

"Really?" Gina asked, obviously startled. "Then what does she think her mother died of?"

"Just a serious disease of some kind. I heard her telling one of her friends last year that it was 'sort of like cancer.' I assume that's still what she thinks."

"Alex...don't you think she has a right to know the truth? It seems there are a lot of things she hasn't been told."

"You sound critical."

"I believe children have a right to know the truth, that's all."

"Not if it's going to cause them terrible pain," Alex said firmly. "When she's older and less troubled, I intend to tell Steffi all about her birth and the details of her mother's death. In the meantime I don't want her burdened with even more things she'll find hard to bear."

"I guess it's your decision," Gina said after a brief strained silence. "Anyway, she seems to be interested in going fishing with us, and that's a good sign, right?"

"Where will you be going?"

"Up to Bear Creek." Gina waved her hand to indicate the brooding hills across the lake. "It's a beautiful little trout stream, really isolated. We have to go over in the canoe and then hike up to the stream."

"I wish I could come along," Alex said wistfully. "I love fly-fishing."

"I think it's best if you don't. She might open up more if it's just Roger and me."

"You're probably right about that," Alex said. "I'll take advantage of the day by myself to get a whole lot of work done."

"Okay. And we'll bring back a mess of trout and invite you down to eat dinner with us in the kitchen. Mary's baked trout with basil is a dream come true."

She smiled, and once again Alex couldn't resist pulling her into his arms. This time she didn't push away, and when he lowered his mouth to hers, she yielded completely to the kiss, her mouth opening under his, her body warm and pliant. Alex felt a surge of desire so intense he was breathless.

"Gina," he whispered against her neck, his hand sliding beneath the cotton fabric of her shirt and cupping her breast. "I want you so much I can't bear it...."

She tensed suddenly, a reaction that was becoming wearily familiar to him. Then she pulled away and sat upright on the rock, rubbing her arms.

"Gina, tell me what's wrong. What are you afraid of?"

"What makes you so certain I'm afraid?" she asked, turning away.

"Because I can feel your response. I know you want me as much as I want you. But when we're together, something always happens to make you draw back. I want to know what it is."

She was silent, gazing out across the water into the gathering darkness.

"Why can't you trust me? Whatever it is," he said passionately, "I know we could work it out, if only you'd let me help."

Gina climbed down from the rock and started to head back up the slope toward the hotel. He hurried after her.

"Gina—"

"Some things can never be worked out, Alex," she said without turning around. "There are...situations in people's lives that make it impossible for them to be together, and this is one of them. Please don't keep..."

Her voice broke and she began to run. After a moment she rounded a bend in the path and vanished, leaving him alone in the shadows.

THE NEXT MORNING after breakfast, Gina walked into the kitchen to see Mary chopping vegetables at the table and dropping them into a blue enamel mixing bowl.

Mary looked up. "So tomorrow's the fishing trip?"

"Bright and early." Gina crossed to the table. "What's in the bowl?"

"Tomatoes, red and green peppers, onions and a few other things. I'm making Edgewood salsa."

"One of my favorites." Gina sniffed at the rich scents of spice and fresh vegetables.

"How much food will you need for the day? I guess I should pack the big picnic basket."

"No, you shouldn't," Gina said firmly. "You should make us look after ourselves. Roger and I are perfectly capable of packing our own food, and so is Steffi."

Mary smiled. "If I leave it up to the three of you, you'll spend the whole day eating packaged doughnuts and apples."

"Maybe," Gina admitted, settling at the table to help cut up the piles of tomatoes and peppers. "But think how much fun we'll have."

"I'm surprised Steffi agreed to go along." Mary carried the bowl over to the big Dutch oven on the stove and added its contents to the simmering pot. "She spends all her time alone, poor little thing. I didn't think she'd ever want to do anything as sociable as going fishing with you two."

"Yes, she does seem unhappy." Gina stared at the paring knife in her hand.

"It can't be easy, losing your mother at fourteen. I still remember how terrible I felt when my mother died, and I was over forty."

Gina was silent, picking up another tomato from the basket.

"There's always a special bond between a mother and daughter, don't you think?" Mary measured vinegar into the bowl of sliced tomatoes and peppers. "Something that goes so deep it's hard to understand."

Gina nodded a little desperately, searching for a way to change the subject. "You know, I've never had the chance to ask you," she said at last, "what you thought of Lacey Franks."

Mary turned away, but not before Gina caught the look of pain on the older woman's face.

"I take it," Gina said with a brief smile, "that you don't approve of her."

Mary displayed a rare flash of anger. "Of course I don't approve! That woman isn't good enough to shine Roger's shoes. She's not worth one of his little fingers."

Gina kept her head carefully lowered and concentrated on the green pepper she was slicing. "I always thought you and Roger argued so much you wouldn't mind if he left. He seems to get on your nerves all the time."

Mary was at the stove, stirring the bubbling pot. All Gina could see was her rigid back.

"I never meant a lot of those things I said." Mary's voice was low and muffled, almost as if she was fighting back tears. "About being so upset with him, I mean. I've really enjoyed Roger's company over the years. I...I don't think I could bear to see him go away with...with that woman."

Gina got up and crossed to the stove. "Mary..." she said gently, putting her arm around the other woman's shoulder.

Mary rummaged in the pockets of her apron, looking in vain for a tissue. Finally she used the corner of the apron to wipe her eyes.

"Mary... why don't you tell Roger how you feel?" Gina asked.

Mary looked at her in horror. "Oh, I wouldn't make a fool of myself like that. Not while..." She couldn't, it seemed, bear to finish. *Not while Roger is seeing another woman.*

"He doesn't care about Lacey Franks," Gina said. "He's just flattered by her, that's all, and lonely enough to be vulnerable. But Roger's a smart man, Mary. He must know he and Lacey have almost nothing in common."

Mary dabbed at her eyes again and went over to the table, aimlessly picking up her paring knife.

"Besides," Gina said with deliberate casualness, "you know what Alex thinks?"

Mary turned away and shook her head.

"Alex thinks Roger's in love with you."

"With *me?*" Mary's face drained of color. She stared at Gina, her eyes blazing with emotion. "Alex said that? He thinks Roger's..."

Suddenly Mary fled. She left the kitchen and ran down the hall to her own room, leaving Gina alone with the bubbling salsa and the piles of vegetables.

"Well, well," Gina said thoughtfully, picking up a wooden spoon to stir the simmering mass. "So that's how it is."

She smiled, thinking how right Alex had been. Then her smile faded and she frowned thoughtfully, trying to think of a way to get Roger and Mary together after all these years. She was still pondering that when she heard the sound of a truck outside.

"Mail time!" a voice shouted cheerily. Gina glanced out the open window to see the mailman heading down the flagstone path toward the front of the mansion.

"Thanks, Elliott!" Gina called.

She turned down the heat under the salsa, wiped her hands on her shorts and headed for the lobby, where she encountered a scene of unusual activity.

Six of the couples currently in residence at the hotel were gathered in the sun room and the library.

"My goodness," Gina said, smiling at them. "You all look so festive. What's going on?"

"We're waiting for the bus we chartered. We're going on a tour of the valley wineries," one of the men told her. "We're visiting six of them between here and Penticton."

"And you'll be having free samples at every winery, I suppose?"

"Of course," he agreed happily.

Gina grinned, then looked around at the rest of the group. "Does Alex know about your trip? He'd love to test all those wines."

"We asked him, but he said he wants to work."

"The poor man works all the time," one of the women said, looking annoyed. She was single and fortyish, quite attractive. Gina had noticed her efforts in the past few days to draw Alex into conversation.

But Alex had made it very clear there was only one woman he was interested in . . .

Gina's cheeks warmed at the thought, and she moved hastily through the group to pick up the mail scattered on the hardwood floor.

"Well," she said, straightening, "I'm sure you'll have a good time." She watched while the little tour bus pulled up into the drive and her guests climbed aboard. Then she carried the mail into her office and sat at the desk, slitting envelopes.

One of them, she noted with pleasure, was a personal note from her sister, Claudia. She set the letter aside to read after she'd dealt with the rest of the correspondence.

The bills went into a wire basket, receipts and invoices into their respective folders, reservation forms and inquiries into a ledger that handled the hotel traffic.

Finally, after all the business was taken care of, Gina opened her sister's letter and began to read it eagerly. Though slapdash and inconsistent, Claudia was still a better correspondent than their mother, so Gina relied on her sister for most of the news from home. Claudia's letter informed her that their mother was well, and busily involved in a project with her students: a summer course of environmental studies designed to become a prototype for the New Brunswick school system.

It sounded so typical of their mother, giving up her summer to work with the same kids she taught during the school year. Alice Mitchell was a person who truly loved her work. Furthermore, she hadn't had a man in her life for more than twenty years and certainly didn't appear to be suffering from the lack of one, Gina reminded herself.

She read on. Her sister had finally made the decision to go back to college and get a second degree in speech therapy so she could do clinical work. Gina nodded approvingly and flipped to the next page.

"But I want a little fun before I put my nose to that particular grindstone," Claudia wrote. "So guess what? I've met this wonderful guy named Jerry, and he and I are traveling across Canada on his motorcycle! We should be dropping in on you sometime in the last week of July, maybe a bit earlier if we don't have a hard time getting through the mountains. I'm putting you on notice that we want the blue room, sis, so keep it open, okay?"

Gina felt her face drain of color when she read the last paragraph. Then she stared at the postmark on the envelope. Her sister's letter had been mailed from a small town in Manitoba.

Claudia was on her way to Edgewood Manor! It was possible she might arrive in less than two weeks. There was no way to get hold of her and warn her not to come.

And despite the fact that Claudia was now a grown woman in her mid-twenties, there wouldn't be a shadow of doubt in anybody's mind. When people looked at Claudia Mitchell and Steffi Colton side by side, they were going to know at once that the uncanny physical similarity was far more than a coincidence.

CHAPTER ELEVEN

HIDDEN AMONG DARK STANDS of evergreen trees, the trout stream danced and sparkled over rocks and submerged logs. It was midsummer and the woods were rich with flowers of all kinds, from mountain lupine to dainty orchids that clung to the trunks of the trees.

Roger stood in the water in a pair of hip waders, making a few experimental casts with his long fly rod while Steffi watched him from the bank. A little farther upstream, Gina rummaged in her tackle box for the flies she wanted to use.

Suddenly Roger lifted his hand and pointed. Gina and Steffi followed the direction of his finger. A young mule deer emerged from the trees across the stream and sniffed the air cautiously, then approached the water, apparently unaware of their presence on the opposite bank.

Gina glanced at Steffi, who was watching the deer raptly. The girl wore jeans and her usual baggy plaid shirt. She had a baseball cap pulled low over her eyes, with a long ponytail drawn through the opening at the back. Except for that rich fall of red hair, she could have been a boy.

Oh, God, Gina thought. Claudia had looked exactly the same when she was a young teenager. What was she going to do about her sister's impending visit?

How had this nightmare ever happened to her?

Back on that pleasant June afternoon she'd been working happily in the gold room, putting up new wallpaper. Then Alex Colton had arrived on the scene, and her life had been turned upside down.

But looking at Steffi now, Gina had to admit she wouldn't have changed a thing. It was worth all the anguish to see the girl and hear her voice. Gina knew that she was going to suffer for the rest of her life after Alex and Steffi were gone, but she wouldn't have traded this experience for anything.

I love you, Gina told the girl silently. *You'll never know how much....*

The deer threw up his head, sniffed the air for a moment, then turned and bounded gracefully back into the woods. The spell was broken.

Roger reeled in his line and waded out onto the shore, approaching Gina.

"Did you remember the insect repellent?"

She handed him a plastic tube from her tackle box. "Use lots of it," she warned. "Those mosquitoes are going to be wicked today. Better give some to Steffi, too."

Roger glanced over at the girl, who was busy attaching a fly to her own line.

"She's a bright little thing," he said fondly, rubbing the repellent cream on his hands and neck. "She picked all that up in a few minutes, when I took the time to show her last night."

Now was her chance, Gina thought, to learn how he felt about Mary. She looked down at the tackle box to hide her face. "Roger—"

"Do you have any of those new nymphs?" he interrupted, peering into her tackle box. "Might as well give them a try."

Silently she gave him a handful of the fluffy nymphs. He took off his cotton hat and stuck the flies into the hatband, his bald head gleaming in the sunlight.

"Roger, are you in love?" Gina asked abruptly.

He looked at her in comical surprise. "Gina Mitchell!" he said after a moment's shocked silence. "What kind of question is that to ask a man?"

"I want to know," she said. "We've always been honest with each other, haven't we?"

"Sure we have. But we don't sit around discussing our love lives."

"That's because neither of us has ever really had one," Gina said dryly. "But now you're going out on dates and bringing girlfriends to the house...I want to know what's going on."

Roger settled on the bank next to her and plucked at a blade of grass. "I don't consider Lacey Franks a girlfriend," he said at last.

"Then what is she?"

"I don't know." He gave Gina a troubled glance. "I don't really understand the etiquette of these situations," he confessed. "When I was young, a girl waited for the man to make some kind of move. Now they just call up and ask you out."

"And if you're a gentleman, it's hard to say no for fear of hurting their feelings," Gina offered.

Roger nodded gloomily.

"And then," Gina said, "you find yourself getting deeper and deeper involved in something that wasn't your idea in the first place, and you don't know how to stop it. Right?"

"Pretty much," he agreed.

Gina selected another fly and held it up, squinting at it thoughtfully. "And meantime," she went on, "the person you really care about is left behind. That's not a very good situation, is it?"

Roger looked at her sharply. "What are you talking about, Gina?"

She stood up and made a couple of experimental casts with her rod. "I'm talking about Mary," she said.

"What about her?"

"Alex and I think it's Mary you really care about, but you're too shy to tell her."

Roger snorted, but Gina noticed he didn't deny her suggestion. She took the fly off her line and replaced it with a different one, then said, "I was talking to Mary yesterday. We discussed Lacey Franks and what was going on between the two of you."

"I doubt Mary approved of Lacey."

"She certainly didn't. She said Lacey Franks wasn't even worth one of your little fingers."

"Really?" Roger looked pleased. "Mary actually said that?"

Gina nodded. "And then I told her what Alex and I believed, how we both thought it was Mary you really cared about."

"Quite the pair of meddlers, aren't you?" Roger said, his pleased expression changing to a look of uneasiness. "I'll bet she had a good laugh over that."

"She cried," Gina said quietly.

Roger stared at her. "Mary *cried?* Over me?"

"She burst into tears and ran out of the kitchen. I had to finish making the salsa for her."

"What did she say afterward?"

"I haven't had a chance to talk to her since then. She's been very careful to avoid me."

"My God," Roger breathed, staring at the rippling water. "I can't imagine Mary in tears over a man, let alone me."

"Well," Gina said briskly, "maybe it's time you smartened up and started using your imagination a little more, Roger Appleby."

"You could be right." He got to his feet, still looking stunned, then gathered himself together and grinned at Gina. "Maybe I could give you the same advice," he said, his face creasing with humor.

She gripped her fishing rod tensely. "What do you mean?"

"Just what I said. I've got eyes in my head, you know."

Gina's thoughts began to whirl. Was Roger talking about her and Alex?

Or had he remembered what her sister, Claudia, looked like, and noticed the similarity to Steffi?

"Roger," she whispered, "I don't...know what you mean."

"Sure you do," he said calmly.

He started to move away, then came back and handed her the plastic tube.

"Here," he said. "Give some of this to Steffi. I'm taking my gear downstream a bit to see if I can find any deeper pools."

While Gina watched, he picked up his rod and basket and headed out of sight around the bend of the stream, leaving her alone with the girl.

Nervously clutching the tube of insect repellent, Gina set down her rod and made her way across the grassy bank to Steffi.

"Hi," she said. "How are you doing?"

Steffi stood up and flexed the rod in her hand. "I got the fly tied on. Now I'm trying some casting to see if I can do it right."

"Roger showed you how, didn't he?"

Steffi nodded. "I practiced for quite a while last night, but that was just out on the lawn by my room. I don't know how it's going to work when I'm really in the water."

"I'll help you," Gina said, almost wishing Roger would come back. She was afraid of getting too involved with this girl. The more time they spent together, the harder it would be for Gina to remain detached.

"What's that?" Steffi asked, looking at the tube in Gina's hand.

"Insect repellent. Want some?"

Steffi nodded. "Those mosquitoes are awful. I've got about a thousand bites already."

Gina opened the tube and squeezed some cream onto her hand. "Here," she said, trying to sound casual. "Let me put some on your neck."

Steffi came nearer and stood obediently while Gina rubbed the cream on the girl's throat and the back of her neck.

Gina's hands trembled at the feel of the soft warm skin. It was all she could do not to gather her daughter in her arms and stroke her beautiful hair.

"They bite right through my shirt," Steffi complained.

"I know." Gina put more cream on her palms and rubbed them lightly over the girl's arms and the back of her plaid shirt. "There," she said brusquely, turning away. "That should help."

"Did you ever get married?" Steffi suddenly asked.

Startled, Gina shook her head.

"Why not? I mean—" The girl's face colored with embarrassment. "Didn't you want a husband and kids and all that?"

"I guess I did. But it just never happened somehow. I was always too busy with my hotel to...to meet anybody I cared about."

"You could still have kids," Steffi said, concentrating on a kink in her line. "You're not so old, and you're really pretty."

Gina looked at the girl in surprise. "Why, thank you, Steffi," she said awkwardly. "If I were to have a daughter," she added, her heart pounding, "I'd want her to be just like you."

The girl's face darkened. She turned away, bending to pick up her fishing rod. "Nobody would ever want a daughter like me."

Gina was shocked by the pain in her voice. "Why not? Steffi, why would you say such a thing?"

Steffi shrugged and walked down to the water's edge, carrying her fishing rod.

Gina followed. "Steffi?" she said again.

"What?" The girl made a clumsy cast with her rod, dropping the fly near the edge of the stream. She reeled her line in and prepared to try again.

"Why do you think nobody would want you as a daughter? I happen to know," Gina added, "that your father is crazy about you. Before you came to Edgewood Manor, he could hardly wait for you to get here. He talked about you all the time."

"That doesn't mean anything," Steffi muttered. "He *has* to care about me. He's my father."

"But I still don't understand what you meant. Why do you think—"

"Does anybody else ever come up here?" Steffi interrupted.

"To Bear Creek?"

The girl nodded.

"Not much," Gina said. "Roger and I found the trout pools one summer when we were hiking. But it's fairly isolated. The only way to get here is the way we did this morning."

"You mean, bring the canoe across the lake and then climb that big hill?"

"That's right. We usually manage to get up here once or twice a season, but I've never seen anybody else while we're here."

"What's over there?" Steffi waved her hand across the stream at the woods where the mule deer had vanished a few minutes earlier.

"Wilderness," Gina told her. "Trees and mountains and lots of black bears. You'd cross a mountain range and run across some high ranching country if you were to keep going west, and then more mountains."

Steffi nodded, looking thoughtfully at the dense banks of evergreens.

Gina moved closer to her. "Look, honey," she said awkwardly, "I don't want to keep bothering you, but I'd really like to know why you said that—about nobody wanting you."

"I didn't actually mean it that way." Steffi stared down at her feet. "I know how much my dad cares about me. It's just that . . . nobody else would if they knew."

"Knew what?"

She looked up, her eyes dark with pain under the brim of the cap. "I've got something wrong with me. I'm probably going to die."

Gina stared at her, appalled. "Steffi," she whispered. "What are you talking about?"

Steffi dropped to the grass, set her rod aside and sat hugging her knees. "Do you know what Huntington's disease is?"

Gina, her heart pounding, sat down next to her daughter. "Yes," she said. "I know what it is."

"Woody Guthrie died of it. Quite a few people have Huntington's," Steffi said. "It's an awful sickness. If you have it, you die."

"I know," Gina said.

"Do you know how people get it?"

"It's inherited," Gina said. "Huntington's is a dominant gene."

"That means if one of your parents has it, you're going to get it, too."

"That's not exactly true," Gina said carefully. "If one of your parents carries the gene, you only have a fifty percent chance of inheriting the disease. It's..."

The girl cast her a bleak glance. Gina fell silent, knowing how little comfort those odds would be to anyone in Steffi's situation.

"My mother had Huntington's," Steffi said after a long silence. "That's what she died of."

Gina moved closer and put her arm around the girl's shoulder, wondering desperately what to do.

Damn you, Alex, she thought. *Why haven't you talked to this poor girl, told her the truth? Why are you allowing her to suffer like this?*

But Alex had no idea that Steffi knew the truth about Janice Colton's illness. Like so many parents, he'd underestimated his child's level of maturity and awareness. In his mind Steffi believed that her mother had died of "some kind of cancer."

"I don't think..." Gina began cautiously, then paused and cleared her throat. "I talked with your father once about how your mother died. He said you didn't know anything about Huntington's."

Steffi waved her hand in dismissal. "They never told me, but I found out, anyhow. I've known for a long time. I heard Dad talking with the doctor one day, and then I looked it up at the school library."

"Why didn't you talk to your father about it?"

"I couldn't. He was really unhappy a lot of the time when my mother was sick, and it would've been worse if I told him. Then he would've been unhappy about me, too."

"So you've just been worrying about it and not telling anybody?"

Steffi nodded. "I can't stand it anymore," she whispered, staring at the water. "I can't die the way my mother did. It was so awful." She turned to look directly at Gina, her face white with suffering. "She got all twisted and jerky, and toward the end she couldn't eat or talk or anything. She didn't even know us."

Gina forgot all her resolutions in a flood of sympathy and love. She put her arms around Steffi and held her, patting the girl's back tenderly.

"Oh, Steffi," she whispered. "I'm so sorry."

She held her daughter and gazed over her head at the trees, wondering what to do. She wanted to tell Steffi the truth, but she couldn't. Even if she wasn't bound by her promises, it was Alex's responsibility to tell his daughter the circumstances of her birth.

He'd already told Gina that the girl was adopted, so she had at least a basis to approach him on the topic.

Gina needed to talk with him right away, let him know what Steffi was thinking and feeling. Then it would be Alex's decision, how much of the truth he was going to tell his daughter.

And after that, Gina thought grimly, *I have to figure out how to get both of them away from here before my sister comes to visit.*

THAT EVENING, after their day of trout fishing, Roger dressed in his corduroy slacks and a neatly pressed sports shirt. He packed his cello in his truck and drove into town to the church hall, where his chamber group had gathered to practice a set of Mozart selections they were working on for a midsummer recital.

As he'd expected, Lacey Franks appeared soon after their practice began. She made her way down the aisle to a seat in a front pew and smiled up at him.

She was dressed even more stylishly than usual, wearing a mauve-and-yellow flowered sundress with a mauve blazer and a pair of mauve high-heeled shoes. She crossed her legs in a provocative fashion and listened with rapt attention while the group ran through its new repertoire.

At the end of the practice, Roger packed his cello and met her near the door.

"Hello, stranger." Lacey took his arm and gave him a dazzling intimate smile. "It seems like ages since I saw you last. Where shall we go?"

Roger paused outside the church to put the cello case away in his truck.

"I feel like doing something romantic," Lacey said, not waiting for his answer. "And you're all dressed up tonight. Let's drive down to the yacht club and go dancing.''

Roger's heart sank. She looked so bright and eager, all ready to enjoy the evening. It seemed cruel to disappoint her.

He squared his shoulders, reminding himself that such cowardly weakness was the whole reason for his current dilemma. He'd spent far too much time drifting along without protest, allowing Lacey to call all the shots.

It was time to speak his mind.

"I don't think so," he said quietly, locking the door of his truck. "I don't feel like dancing tonight. Let's just go for a walk, all right?"

She gave him another melting smile. "As long as I'm with you, honey, it doesn't matter what we do."

Roger forced himself to smile back, then turned and strolled along the walkway leading down to the beach, with Lacey still clinging to his arm.

"How was your day?" she asked.

"Pretty good. We went fishing."

"We? Who else was there?"

"Gina and Steffi Colton. Remember that red-headed girl? She's the daughter of the writer who's staying at the hotel."

Lacey pouted, clearly not all that pleased to hear about Roger's fishing companions. "You always have so much time to spend with other women. Why don't you ever invite me to go fishing?"

Roger pictured Lacey hiking up the mountain trail to the trout stream in her mauve high heels. Tickled by the image, he laughed.

Lacey looked injured. "What's so funny?"

"Nothing," he said, sobering hastily. "Just a thought."

"Did you catch lots of fish?"

"We had a pretty nice mess of trout when we left. Mary was planning to cook them for dinner tonight, along with vegetables from the garden."

"I see." Lacey sounded a little sharp at his mention of the hotel cook. "So, did the ladies have a good time on this fishing trip?"

"I'm not sure," Roger said. "They were both kind of quiet all day. I think Gina's worried about something," he added. "And Steffi never says much, anyway."

Lacey nodded, seeming somewhat mollified. "Oh, well," she said with a bright smile, "at least you didn't enjoy yourself *too* much, then."

Roger was silent as they crossed the grassy expanse and seated themselves on a wrought-iron bench that faced the darkening waters.

"It's so peaceful." She sighed, resting her head on his shoulder. "I could almost get used to this country living."

"No, you couldn't. You'll always be a city girl, Lacey."

She laughed and snuggled closer. "I guess you're right," she admitted. "You can take the girl from the city, but it's pretty hard to take the city from the girl. Still, I can always keep my apartment in West Vancouver and go out there for a shopping trip every few weeks. I think that should be enough to keep me contented, don't you?"

Roger braced himself. "What are you talking about?" he said. "Are you planning to move to Azure Bay?"

She gave him a hesitant glance. "Oh, *you,*" she said at last with a tinkling little laugh. "You're such a tease."

"I'm not teasing," Roger said quietly. "I'm asking you what you're talking about."

She pulled away and sat up, rubbing her arms nervously under the thin fabric of her jacket. "You know perfectly well what I'm talking about, Roger Appleby. After all this time together, how can you pretend **you** don't know?"

"We haven't spent a lot of time together," he said. "And when we do get together, it's been mostly your doing. I've never pretended to be making any plans for the future."

Lacey stared at him, aghast. "How can you *say* that?" Her eyes filled with tears. "You mean you've just been leading me on? And all this time I thought . . ."

She began to sob.

Roger was surprised and distressed by her tears. He felt a jolt of sympathy and a brief weakening of resolve, but forced himself to continue. "I haven't been leading you on," he said. "This whole relationship between the two of us has mostly been a figment of your imagination, that's all."

"A figment of my *imagination?* Why, that's just the meanest, coldest—"

"Please," Roger said wearily, "I don't want any more drama, Lacey. I'm not the kind of guy who enjoys drama. The truth is, you don't know anything about the kind of man I am. You just picked me out of the crowd and decided you wanted me for some reason, but we don't know each other at all. We aren't having some wild passionate love affair. Let's not pretend that we are."

Lacey dabbed her eyes with a tissue, her look of shock changing to an angry scowl.

"Well!" she said, getting to her feet. "If *that's* the kind of man you are, I'm just as glad I found out early."

She began to walk away. Roger didn't move, just sat and watched her.

After a few steps she stopped and turned to give him a searching look. "Is that all you've got to say?"

He nodded. "Pretty much."

She clutched her handbag, obviously taken aback by his matter-of-fact attitude. "You know what I think?" she said at last.

"What?"

"I think you're just having a bad day. You're tired from all that fishing and then having to come here for your practice right afterward." Lacey brightened and smiled. "Let's just forget all about this, and I'll give you a call tomorrow."

Roger took a deep breath. "No, Lacey," he said gently. "Don't call me tomorrow. Forget all about me. You're a good-looking woman, and you'd be a fine companion for the right man. Go back to the city and find somebody who can appreciate you."

She stared at him, her eyes dark. Roger forced himself to keep his face impassive. At last she muttered something bitter and walked as quickly as her high heels would allow across the grass, heading for her car.

After a long time Roger twisted cautiously around and looked toward the church-hall parking lot to make sure Lacey was actually gone. The place where her car had been was empty, and his truck sat alone nearby.

Roger smiled, feeling his spirits begin to lift. For the first time he allowed himself to think about the other amazing thing Gina had said.

When she'd told Mary that Roger cared for her, Mary hadn't laughed or said something scornful.

Mary had cried.

Roger stretched out comfortably on the bench, gazing at the dark line of trees across the lake. He smiled, then began to hum one of the Mozart pieces. At last, when the world was dark and the moon started to climb, he got to his feet and strolled to his truck, still humming softly.

GINA SAT at the kitchen table leafing through Mary's recipe books and menus.

"All right," she said, making a couple of notes. "Here's our list of breakfasts for the next two weeks. Are we agreed?"

Mary glanced over from the sink, where she was polishing a copper skillet. "As long as you don't think it's too much, serving eggs three times in the second week."

Gina frowned and tapped her pen on the table. "I don't think so. None of the guests will be staying long enough to be served all three of those breakfasts."

"Except for Alex and Steffi." Mary hung the skillet on a rack along with her other saucepans.

Gina didn't answer.

Privately she hoped that Alex and his daughter would be gone in a few days. She couldn't bear any more of this stress, and she couldn't see any other way out of their situation. She intended to tell Alex about Steffi's private anguish and then find some excuse to ask him to leave.

The best approach, she decided, was to tell him that their personal relationship was interfering with her ability to conduct her business properly.

Alex would be hurt and angry, but that was just as well. If Gina could goad him into a really bitter argument, he'd be less likely to come back.

And it was vitally important that after he and Steffi left, they never, ever came back. Gina couldn't bear to lose them both again. It was going to be hard enough this time.

"The trout was good, wasn't it?" Mary asked, breaking into her gloomy thoughts.

Gina nodded absently. "It was delicious."

"I wonder why Roger didn't come over for dinner. He loves baked trout."

Gina looked down at the table, thinking about her conversation with Roger that morning. No wonder he was avoiding the kitchen. At this point his natural reserve would probably keep him away forever unless Mary gave him some encouragement.

She glanced over cautiously, but the cook's face was unrevealing as she worked over the sink.

"Did Steffi have a good time today?" Mary asked.

Gina remembered the girl's pale miserable face and her silence for the rest of the day while they were fishing. "Steffi's not a very happy girl," she said at last. "She's suffered a lot in the past few years."

"Poor little thing." Mary wrung out her dishcloth and gazed through the window at the rising moon.

"Mary..." Gina began.

"Yes?" Mary gathered up the cookbooks and put them away on a shelf above the counter.

"Yesterday when we talked about Roger, you seemed quite emotional. I just wondered—"

"Please, Gina," Mary said without turning around. "Don't talk about that anymore. Roger's got a girl-friend. He's obviously made his choice."

"But I don't believe that's true. I think he really cares about you."

"I don't want to talk about it," Mary repeated, then paused by the window again. "Where is that dog of mine?" she added. "I've been looking all over for her. Half the time I don't know where she is anymore."

Gina thought about Steffi in the moonlit backyard, picking up the fat poodle and heading into her room. "Oh," she said casually, "you know Annabel. She's probably sound asleep under the kitchen steps."

"I suppose so."

Gina studied the housekeeper's rigid back, feeling troubled and uncertain. But she didn't know what else to say, and she had enough complications in her own life without worrying about Roger and Mary.

Finally she pushed her chair back and got to her feet. "Well, good night," she said. "I guess I'll see you in the morning."

"Are you watching television for a while? There's a Pavarotti concert on public television."

Gina shook her head and moved reluctantly toward the door. "Maybe later. Right now I have to go up and see Alex for a minute. There's . . . something I need to talk to him about."

CHAPTER TWELVE

ALEX'S DOOR STOOD partly open when Gina approached and knocked.

"Come in," he called.

She pushed the door open and stepped inside. Alex sat near the window at his computer, wearing a pair of horn-rimmed glasses, jeans and a navy blue sweatshirt.

"Gina!" he said in delight. "I was just thinking about you."

She smiled uncertainly and closed the door behind her, then moved across the gold-bordered oriental carpet to sit in an armchair near the desk.

Alex smiled back at her, his eyes warm with affection. "I wanted to tell you at dinner how beautiful you looked after your day of fishing—all suntanned and wholesome—but there were others around." He leaned back with his hands braced against the keyboard.

"You're not so bad yourself."

What an understatement, Gina thought in despair. Everything about this man looked wonderful, from his wavy graying hair and vigorous body to the keenly intelligent blue eyes behind those glasses. Since his arrival at the hotel, Alex had also acquired a healthy tan, and he smiled much more readily.

God, he had a gorgeous smile.

Alex took off his glasses and set them aside, then stood and pulled Gina out of the chair to give her a hug. "You smell good," he whispered, nuzzling hungrily at her neck. "Like pine trees and flowers."

Gina felt all her resolve melting in a flood of desire. She wanted him so much it was all she could do to keep herself from reaching out to fumble at his clothes. She'd never known such overwhelming sexual desire, such passion.

Why not tell him? a voice whispered inside her head. *Tell the man you're Steffi's mother. You have a right to let him know the truth. Janice is gone now. If you want, you can have both of them. You can hold on to this man you love so much and have your daughter, too.*

She was horrified by the treacherous thoughts. Sternly she reminded herself she didn't have any rights at all in this situation. She'd signed those rights away fifteen years ago—for a payment of seventy thousand dollars.

And that, of course, was the reason she couldn't tell Alex the truth. He was such an honorable, upright, fair-minded kind of person, with a strong sense of loyalty and responsibility. She loved him for all those sterling qualities.

He thought she was the same kind of person.

How would he feel about her if he knew the truth? Gina had a pretty good idea. Alex Colton would be utterly appalled to learn that this woman he loved and admired wasn't a paragon of virtue at all. Instead, she was the kind of person who would sell her own flesh and blood for a bundle of cash.

Shame gripped her, deep and sickening. All her passion turned to grayness and sorrow.

Reluctantly she pulled herself out of his embrace and turned away to look out the window. "We have to talk about something, Alex," she said.

"We have to talk about a lot of things." He came up behind her and put his arms around her, resting his chin against her hair. "But at least you're willing to talk. That's an encouraging sign."

"It's not about us," she said. "I want to tell you something about Steffi."

Alex's hold tightened. "What about her?"

"Let's sit down for a minute." Gina took a deep breath. "This is . . . kind of hard."

He released her, then took her elbow and led her across the room to the upholstered love seat. "Let's sit here," he said, lowering himself next to her and resting one arm lightly along the back of the couch behind her shoulders. "Tell me what's on your mind."

Gina looked down at her folded hands. "I had a talk with Steffi this morning while we were up at the trout stream. I . . . learned something pretty upsetting from her."

"What?"

Gina took another deep breath. "Steffi knows the truth about your wife's illness, Alex. She says she's known for a long time."

Alex drew away and stared at Gina, his face turning white beneath the tan. "What do you mean?"

"She knows that her mother died of Huntington's. And she knows exactly what Huntington's is."

"How could she know? I was so careful to protect her!"

Gina shrugged. "How do kids learn things? She listened at the door, saw some mail or read the medical literature. The fact is, she knows exactly how her mother died. She believes Janice was her natural mother, and she's aware of what Huntington's is. She's known for at least a year. So, what do you think would be uppermost on her mind right now?"

"My God," Alex breathed. "Of course! Steffi thinks *she's* carrying the gene, too. She believes she's going to die the same way her mother did."

"I'm afraid so," Gina said quietly.

Abruptly he got to his feet. "The poor kid. I've got to find her right away. Talk to her."

He hurried from the room. Gina followed him down the stairs and watched as he strode through the hall, heading for the backyard.

ALEX RAPPED on his daughter's door, then pushed it open and looked inside. The room was in its usual wild disorder, but there was no sign of Steffi.

She was a night owl, he knew. She liked to roam around in the moonlight and take Annabel out for walks. There were times when Alex suspected that Steffi even slipped out and went swimming in the lake after dark, though she'd been expressly forbidden to do anything so risky.

Alex wandered down to the beach, but there was no sign of Steffi or the white poodle. Maybe his daughter was visiting Mary in her suite, or maybe she was curled up with a book in some corner of the old mansion.

He sank onto the flat rock at the water's edge and looked across the lake.

Perhaps it was just as well he hadn't been able to find her. After all, he needed a little time to think about what he was going to tell her.

His first impulse of course had merely been to ease Steffi's pain by reassuring her that she couldn't possibly carry the gene for Huntington's. But how much was he going to tell her? When she learned that she'd been adopted, she would certainly want to know some details about her birth parents.

Alex shook his head, frowning. He had usually tried hard not to lie to his daughter. Still, could his child stand to know the whole reality of her birth?

Alex wasn't entirely convinced that complete honesty was the best policy in this case. Steffi was exceptionally mature and intelligent, true, but to learn that she'd been the result of a surrogate pregnancy, a cold-blooded financial transaction, might be too much. He *could* just tell her she was adopted. . . .

But she and her father had an undeniable physical resemblance. People had often commented on it, especially when she was younger. How did he intend to explain that likeness?

At last, feeling confused and miserable, Alex got to his feet and trudged back toward the house.

Maybe, since it was already so late and Steffi was nowhere to be found, it would be a better idea to wait until morning before he talked with her. Then he'd have a chance to figure out exactly what he wanted to say.

Steffi was a late riser, so it would have to be sometime after breakfast.

Right after breakfast.

In the lobby he paused and looked around, hoping to catch a glimpse of Gina, but she seemed to have vanished, too. Finally he climbed the stairs to his room, still deep in thought.

GINA WAS IN THE LIBRARY sorting through piles of old magazines when she heard Alex going up the stairs. After a moment she stacked the magazines on a shelf and went up to his room.

"What happened?" she asked tensely when he answered her knock. "You're back so soon. What did she say?"

"I couldn't find her—she's no doubt out walking Annabel. Anyway, I wanted to think a little more about what I'm going to tell her. I've decided to talk to her first thing in the morning."

Gina moved past him into the room. "What's to think about? Can't you just tell her she's adopted?"

"It's not that simple."

No, it sure isn't, Gina thought, understanding his dilemma. Should he tell Steffi *all* the details of the adoption? About the surrogacy? He clearly had problems with admitting the surrogacy—certainly he hadn't told *her.*

Alex watched her as she went over to the window. "Thank God you found out about this, Gina. How were you able to get her to confide in you?"

Gina frowned, trying to remember their conversation. "She asked if I'd ever been married or had children. I told her I hadn't, but that if I ever had a daughter, I'd want one just like her. Steffi got really unhappy and said nobody would want a daughter like her if they knew the truth about her."

"Oh, no. My poor little girl," he whispered in agony.

Since her conversation with Steffi, Gina had felt some impatience toward Alex about what he had chosen to tell his daughter. In her private thoughts she'd accused him of carelessness, at the least. But now, seeing how deeply he was suffering at the knowledge of Steffi's pain, all her resentment vanished.

"Alex," she whispered, getting to her feet and putting her arms around him. "You mustn't feel so terrible about this. You didn't know how Steffi was feeling. You were only trying to do the best thing for her. And soon she'll know the truth."

"But I knew she was troubled. I should have talked with her and forced her to tell me. You know, Gina," he added, "I think I was really a little afraid of her grief. I've always wanted her to be happy. And for the first ten years of her life, she was the happiest child you could ever meet."

He held Gina close and kept talking wistfully.

"You should have seen her when she was a little girl. Steffi was the most beautiful baby you ever saw. Plump and healthy, with that rose-petal skin and a mop of curly red hair that took your breath away. She was bright, too, talking in full sentences before she was two. And then when she got a little older . . ."

Gina listened hungrily, knowing that these few whispered memories were all she would ever learn about her daughter's childhood. She brushed at her tears and pressed closer to Alex, hiding her face against his shirtfront, grateful for the strength of his arms around her.

"It'll be hard for both of us, the things I have to tell her," he said. "But at least there'll be a heavy load off her mind."

"Poor Steffi. I wonder how it would feel to learn after all those years that the person you'd loved as your mother wasn't actually your real mother."

"I think she's mature enough to understand," Alex said. "She knows how much she was loved and cherished. I think she can recognize the difference between biology and nurturing.''

Biology.

That's what I provided, Gina thought bitterly. *Just the biology. I could have been a machine in a laboratory. Janice was the one who did all the nurturing and teaching, all the loving and hugging and caring....*

Gina wanted to shout the injustice of it all, to rail at the world and burst into noisy sobs to ease her breaking heart. This constant need to suppress her emotions was getting to be more than she could endure.

Suddenly Alex bent his head and began to kiss her passionately. Gina found herself responding with a savagery that surprised both of them. Almost frantic, needing an outlet for her pain and the love she would never be allowed to express, she kissed him back and rumpled his hair with her fingers, then tore at his shirtfront and fumbled with the waistband on his pants.

''Gina,'' he whispered, astounded. ''Gina, darling...''

''Please, Alex,'' she gasped, her face streaming with tears. ''Please, I need you so much.''

He responded at once, helping her to undress. Then he stripped off his own clothes, carried her across the room and lowered her into the soft shadowed depths of the big four-poster.

This time, their lovemaking wasn't at all like the gentle interlude they'd enjoyed the first time, when they were caught up with the wonder of discovery. Then, both had felt a little shy and awkward, knowing how long it had been since their last sexual encounter.

Tonight there was a kind of hungry lustful desperation to their coupling, as if each of them wanted to drown a sea of emotional pain in the other's body.

They rolled around in a hot tangle of arms and legs, panting noisily while they kissed and embraced. Gina clawed at his back, and Alex seized her earlobe in his teeth. He gripped one of her breasts tightly, and she tugged at the mat of hair on his chest.

Both of them were so excited that when he entered her they moaned aloud, and exploded together in orgasm just seconds later.

Soon, incredibly, he was aroused once more, and it all started again.

After what seemed like hours, an immeasurable time, the tumult stilled and the room was finally quiet and peaceful. They lay together, exhausted and limp in each other's arms.

He stroked her face with his fingers and whispered, "Do you think they heard us downstairs? We were pretty wild, I'm afraid."

Gina smiled ruefully. "I think they probably heard us across the lake. What on earth got into us?"

He drew away to grin at her. "Well, sweetheart, I'm not sure. But I know what got into *you*. In fact, it's still there."

She blushed, making him laugh.

"After what just happened in this bed, the woman still has the grace to blush. I can't believe it."

"That wasn't me," Gina murmured. "I mean, the woman who was in this bed a few minutes ago. I don't know who she was, but I must have some kind of multiple-personality disorder. That other Gina comes out every now and then, and she does shocking things just to embarrass me."

Alex stroked her cheek again, his eyes bright with teasing. "Just for future reference," he whispered, "can you tell me how to make her appear? I kind of like that other Gina."

She laughed, snuggling in his arms, drowsy and rich with fulfillment. But gradually reality came creeping back and cast dark shadows of misery over her.

She hadn't come up to his room to make love. She'd only wanted to know how Steffi had taken his news, but of course nothing had changed yet; Alex hadn't told his daughter. And despite the ecstasy of their sexual union, Gina was still shut out of their relationship, denied access to the two people she loved most in the world.

And to make matters worse, Gina's sister was on her way to Edgewood Manor, with that hair and skin and eyes that would point like a beacon to Steffi Colton, shouting the girl's heritage to the world.

Gina frowned and shifted in Alex's embrace. He was so protective of Steffi. Even now he might not intend to tell his daughter the whole truth, that he and Janice had hired a surrogate mother. That meant, Gina realized, that he was prepared to sacrifice the truth of his own fatherhood in Steffi's eyes just to protect her from a reality she might find unsettling.

And why would it be unsettling?

Relentlessly Gina forced herself to continue with her line of reasoning.

Because the girl would learn that her birth mother had, in effect, sold her child to the highest bidder.

No wonder Alex might want to keep the information from Steffi.

But if Claudia arrived before the Coltons left, there would be no way to hide the truth from anybody.

Steffi would be terribly wounded, Alex would feel angry and betrayed, and Gina would be shamed beyond endurance.

That disaster must never be allowed to happen. Somehow, after Alex told his daughter that she was adopted, they would both have to be persuaded to cut short their holiday and go home to Vancouver.

Gina nestled in her lover's embrace, making plans to drive him from her life.

And after that was accomplished, she knew she would never again lie in a man's arms like this, feeling such bliss, such a deep rich flood of love....

ROGER PARKED his truck outside Edgewood Manor and sat behind the wheel looking up at the vine-covered bulk of the old mansion. A full moon drifted high above the mountains now, etching trees and windows with a sharp clear radiance.

He could see the silhouettes of a couple of guests behind the sheer curtains in the library, and some guest rooms with lights on upstairs. But except for the sound of bullfrogs by the lake and the occasional cry of a nighthawk, the whole place was silent, wrapped in the stillness of the summer evening.

Finally Roger got out and closed his truck door quietly, not wanting to disturb the peace. He went around to the side of the mansion, letting himself in through the entrance there. Then he walked softly toward the kitchen, where a faint aroma of the trout dinner Mary had cooked still lingered in the air.

Wistfully Roger imagined how the trout would have looked, all browned and crispy around the edges, sprinkled with basil and parsley. At last he let the kitchen door close gently behind him and tiptoed down the hall to where Gina's and Mary's doors faced each other.

Gina's room appeared to be dark, but there was still a line of light under Mary's door. Roger moved closer to the oak panels, straining to listen.

Maybe both women were in there, watching television as they often did in the evening. But he couldn't hear any voices, just a rich swell of music.

He recognized Pavarotti and forgot all his troubles for a moment in his pleasure at the soaring tenor voice. Gina didn't like opera, so Mary was probably listening to Pavarotti on her own.

Roger smiled, imagining how she looked.

No doubt she was wearing one of the sensible flannel nightgowns, high-necked and lace-trimmed, he'd seen once or twice when he surprised her early in the morning while she was brewing coffee. Mary had an old red housecoat, too, once cherry-colored but now faded to a kind of dark pink, that she wore belted over her nightgown. In the soft robe and furry white slippers she looked cuddly and feminine.

She'd be sitting in one of her comfortable little armchairs drinking hot chocolate and listening to the television program, with Annabel in a drowsy lump at her feet.

The whole image was so cozy and appealing that Roger felt an urgent longing to be part of it. Holding his breath, his heart pounding noisily, he lifted a hand to knock.

"Hi," a voice whispered behind him.

Roger whirled around, startled. Steffi Colton stood in the hallway, wearing a baggy much-patched sweat suit of navy blue. Her spectacular hair was jammed out of sight beneath a baseball cap, and her feet were bare. She stood on one foot like a stork, with her toes curling away from the chilly hardwood and the sole of the other foot pressed against her leg for warmth.

"Hi, Steffi," he whispered back. "What's the matter? Are you hungry?"

She shook her head. "I'm looking for Annabel. Have you seen her?"

Roger took the girl's arm and moved down the hall with her, away from Mary's door, till the sounds of that rich tenor voice faded.

"I think Annabel's probably in there with Mary," he said, gesturing back down the hallway.

Steffi's face creased with disappointment. "I was hoping I could take her to my room for a few minutes. I took her for a walk a little while ago and promised her I'd give her some of that fish we had at suppertime. I saved some for her."

"Steffi Colton!" Roger said in mock outrage. "Mary would have your hide if she knew you were smuggling food to that overweight dog."

Steffi looked unrepentant. "Poor Annabel. She cries all the time like she's starving to death. And I never give her unhealthy stuff like pie or cookies even when she begs for them. I just give her low-calorie nourishing things."

Roger patted her shoulder. "You're a good girl, Steffi. But, I'm afraid you're out of luck tonight. Mary's watching a concert on TV and she'll probably keep Annabel with her until the program ends in a couple of hours. You'd better go to bed and sneak her that piece of fish in the morning."

Steffi considered, then nodded. "Okay. Thanks, Roger."

She gave him a strained smile, then moved toward the stairs.

"Where are you going, honey?" Roger asked.

"I just wanted to run upstairs and talk to my dad for a minute. I'll be right down."

Roger nodded and watched her till she disappeared up the stairs. Then he stood alone in the darkened lobby, looking wistfully down the hallway toward Mary's room.

But the mood was broken, and he couldn't get it back tonight. Tomorrow would be soon enough to approach her, he decided. He'd spend one more day getting his courage up.

And then tomorrow night, without fail, he'd knock on that door, go into Mary's room and tell her exactly how he felt.

STEFFI TIPTOED down the hall toward her father's room, conscious of the other closed doors along the corridor. Some had slits of light at the bottom that showed the occupants were still awake, reading or watching television. Others were already dark, though it didn't seem all that late to Steffi, who'd always been a night owl and liked to wander around after everybody else was asleep.

She was constantly astonished by how early people went to bed here at Edgewood Manor. Maybe they got really tired from long days spent out in the sun, hiking and fishing and swimming in the lake.

Her father's room was one of the darkened ones. Steffi paused uncertainly, reluctant to bother him if he was already in bed.

But when she bent over to peer at the doorsill, she could see a faint glow. Maybe it was his reading lamp, or perhaps just bright moonlight, since he never bothered to close the curtains.

She decided not to risk waking him by knocking. Instead, she turned the knob carefully and pushed the door open a crack, then leaned forward to peer into the room.

Steffi caught her breath in shock. The room was softly illuminated by the moonlight. She could see her father in his bed—and he wasn't alone.

Gina Mitchell lay in his arms, snuggled closely against him, her curly head buried in the hollow of his neck. Their tangled bodies were partly covered with a sheet, and both of them were clearly naked.

Steffi gaped at them as they lay there together, serenely unaware of her presence. Finally she eased the door shut and stood in the quiet hallway, taking great gulps of air to calm herself.

When she felt able to move again, she crept back along the hallway, hoping Roger wasn't still waiting down in the lobby. How could she ever face anybody or manage to carry on a conversation? Roger was so smart he'd know right away that she'd seen something shocking.

But to her immense relief, the lobby was empty. In the distance she could hear the sound of a truck retreating along the road. Roger, no doubt, heading for his little farm.

Steffi hurried through the silent corridors to the back of the house. She passed by Gina's closed door and listened for a moment to the throb of music from Mary's room. The man who was singing sounded mournful and troubled, as if he'd just suffered some kind of tragedy.

Outside in the moonlight, Steffi looked around with growing desperation, wishing that Annabel would appear. If she had that warm little body to hold, maybe she wouldn't feel so lonely and chilled.

"Annabel?" she whispered in the stillness. "Annabel, where are you? Come here."

But there was no sign of the little dog. She must be with Mary, as Roger said. At last Steffi wandered across the yard and let herself into her own room. She climbed onto the middle of the bed and buried her face against her knees, still trying to recover from the shock of stumbling onto that scene in her father's room.

There was no mistaking what was going on. Steffi was a voracious reader, and she knew considerably more than any of the adults in her life suspected. For instance, she understood what was involved in an adult sexual relationship, and she also had a fair idea of how difficult it must have been for her father to endure those years while her mother was sick.

He'd been faithful and patient, never complaining, always there to help his family without any thought for himself. But he must have been awfully lonely.

It's no excuse, Steffi thought, lifting her face and wiping furiously at the tears that sprang to her eyes. *My mother just died a few months ago. What they're doing is wrong.* She would have liked to despise both of them, but hurt as she was, she still found it difficult to feel hatred for her father. Or for Gina, who was an outdoor person and knew all kinds of neat things about fishing and gardening and looking after a big place like this.

Gradually Steffi's sense of pain and betrayal gave way to a cold bitter determination. She began to realize that what she'd seen in her father's bedroom was a liberating thing. Now that he had somebody else, he didn't need her anymore.

It was time for her to take action. She'd always known this day would come, ever since she'd learned the truth about the disease that killed her mother. She just hadn't expected it to come so soon.

Steffi thought about the time they'd spent by the trout stream, and how Gina had said that if she ever had a daughter, she'd want one like Steffi. It felt so good to hear somebody say that, even though Gina hadn't known the truth about her at the time.

She'd been surprised and distressed to find herself confiding in Gina about the disease she'd inherited. It was the first time she'd ever told anybody, and she still couldn't understand why she'd done it.

Up until now, she'd kept that dreadful secret locked away. She'd had the feeling, somehow, that keeping it hidden would make it less real. But telling the truth to a sympathetic listener had actually been a relief.

And now she'd learned that her sympathetic listener was her father's lover. No doubt they talked about all kinds of things. By now Gina had probably told him that Steffi knew about her mother's illness.

She moaned aloud and covered her face with her hands, thinking about what was going to happen next.

Tomorrow her father would come and talk to her about it. Maybe Gina would want to talk to her again, too. Everybody would be discussing this horrible thing, dragging it out into the open after all the time Steffi had spent trying so hard to bury the reality.

She knew, absolutely, that she couldn't bear the thought. It was bad enough to know that she lived every day with a death sentence, and a terrible painful one at that. She would never live to be old or marry and have children. She'd never enjoy a happy normal life like other girls. But to have people talking about her sickness, trying to comfort her, looking at her and talking about the defect she carried...it was more than she could stand.

Months ago, before her mother's death, Steffi had begun planning what she was going to do. She'd been putting it off because she was scared, but now it was time for that plan to be carried out. She just had to be brave and strong for a little while longer.

Galvanized into action, she climbed down from the bed, stripped off her sweat suit and dressed warmly in jeans, a flannel shirt and hiking boots. She pulled on a heavy down-filled jacket and jammed a few things into her backpack.

Extra socks, some of the luncheon meat she kept in her room for Annabel's visits, as well as the fish, a few pieces of fruit, her favorite book.

After a moment's hesitation, Steffi jammed her old stuffed bunny into the depths of the pack, along with the gold-framed pictures of her father and mother.

She went to the door, opened it and peered out at the yard, silent and bright in the moonlight. She started to step out, then reluctantly closed the door and crossed to her desk. She took a pen and a sheet of paper from the drawer.

Nibbling the pen, she frowned and thought about what she wanted to say. At last she took a deep breath and began to write.

Dear Dad,
I'm really sorry to cause trouble for everybody, but it's better to do this now than wait for years and years when I know I'm going to die anyway.

I've known about Mom's sickness for a long time, and I have it, too. Sometimes my hands shake and I feel really dizzy. I don't want you to go through it all over again when it was so hard for you while Mom was sick. I know you have Gina now, and that's okay, because she's really nice. But you don't need me anymore now, so I can go away. Please don't look for me or feel sorry. Honestly, it's a lot better this way. I'm going to die anyway, so it's better to do it fast, instead of waiting and getting all sick and ugly.

Steffi hesitated, biting her lip, then returned to the notepaper.

I really love you, Dad. You were always so good to me. Thank you for everything, and please, please don't feel sad.

Love, Steffi

P.S. Please give Annabel a hug for me. She's such a nice dog. And say goodbye to Mary and to Roger and Gina. Tell them I really liked fishing with them.

She read the letter a couple of times, trying not to think about her father's reaction. This really was the best thing to do, Steffi told herself firmly. It was better for everybody. Besides, she simply couldn't bear the pain any longer. And when you couldn't bear something, it was time to leave.

She capped the pen, set it prominently on top of the letter and removed everything else from her desk so the note was clearly visible. Finally she switched the light off and left her room.

She crept among the trees and along the lilac hedge that bordered the orchard, keeping to the shadows where she wouldn't be seen. She made her way through the darkness toward the black water of the lake, then walked along the water's edge, wishing she'd thought to bring a flashlight.

Steffi shivered and hesitated, wondering if she should run back to her room and find the little camping flashlight her father had given her. Despite her fear of the darkness, she was reluctant to go back now that she'd found the courage to get away.

At last she squared her shoulders and kept working her way up the lakeshore. A few minutes later she found the canoe pulled up where Roger and Gina had left it earlier that day, with the bowline tied to a tree near the water.

Steffi untied the line, pushed the canoe completely into the shallow water, then tossed her backpack into the bottom of the canoe and climbed in behind it. She picked up one of the paddles from beneath the thwarts, turned the canoe around, then headed out across the lake, feeling vulnerable and conspicuous in the moonlight, expecting at any moment to hear shouts of alarm and the sounds of pursuit. But the mansion remained silent behind her, its windows glittering coldly with silver as she pulled away from the shore.

Her paddle dipped and stroked, dipped and stroked, carrying her smoothly across the lake toward the remote forbidding expanse of evergreen forest on the opposite shore.

CHAPTER THIRTEEN

GINA PAUSED by Alex's chair with the coffeepot and refilled his cup. He reached out to put an arm around her, cuddling her briefly while the other guests dispersed. She yielded to his embrace, reluctant to move away even though her heart ached at his touch.

They had so little time left . . .

"Steffi didn't come to breakfast," she murmured, pulling away and sitting for a moment in the opposite chair. "Is she all right?"

Alex nodded, sipping his coffee. "If you recall, she hasn't made it for breakfast all week, except yesterday. My girl's not an early riser. She usually stays awake until after midnight, reading and wandering around. Then she sleeps until I go and wake her up."

"When are you going to talk with her?"

"Right away." Alex put down the cup and got to his feet. His smile faded as he looked down at Gina. "I should have done this years ago, shouldn't I?"

"I think so." Gina fingered the edge of one of the place mats, keeping her head lowered.

He reached out to touch her, lifting her face so he could look into her eyes. She met his gaze steadily, hoping her emotions didn't show.

"I love you, darling," Alex told her softly. "I know it's too soon to press you about anything, but I want to start making some plans for the future."

She blinked, fighting back tears. At last she managed to find her voice. "Please, don't think about anything like that right now," she whispered. "Just go and talk to Steffi."

Gina watched his square erect figure as he left the dining room. She thought about what he'd said, her heart aching with love and sorrow.

When you get back, she told him silently, *we'll talk about the future. I'll tell you it's impossible. I'll say I don't love you and I want you both to go away.*

And then you'll leave.

She swallowed a sob and got to her feet, moved the coffeepot to the sideboard and began to clear the tables.

After a few minutes, much sooner than she'd expected, Alex was back. He carried a sheet of notepaper, and his face was white.

"What's the matter?" Gina asked. "Isn't she awake yet?"

Wordlessly he held out the paper. Gina took it and read Steffi's neat upright handwriting. Her mouth went dry with fear. She felt a wave of dizziness and clutched at the back of a chair.

"Alex," she whispered, staring at him. "What can we do? When do you think she left?"

"I don't know," he said tensely. "We have to get everybody together and find out if anybody saw her last night. Oh, God—" his voice broke "—you were right. If only..."

Gina forgot her resolve and put her arms around him, holding him fiercely. "Don't start blaming yourself, Alex. You've been through enough. There's no time for if onlys. We just have to find her, that's all."

Alex held her gratefully for a moment, then released her and examined the note again.

Roger strolled into the room, carrying a toolbox and set of hinges.

"What's up?" he asked in alarm, seeing their faces.

"Steffi's run away," Gina told him.

Alex handed him the note and Roger scanned it quickly, his callused hands trembling. "What does she mean, all this stuff about dying?" he asked Gina.

She glanced at Alex. "Steffi's mother had a serious disease. Steffi thinks she's inherited it and that she's going to die exactly the same way. Apparently brooding over the prospect has made her suicidal."

"The poor little kid." Roger turned to Alex. "Does Steffi actually have this disease she's so worried about?"

"It's impossible for her to have it." Alex looked at the note in despair. "Steffi wasn't even my wife's natural child. She was...adopted at birth, but we never told her."

Roger nodded. "Then we'd better hurry up and find her. That sounds like something the girl needs to know."

"When did you last see her, Roger?" Alex asked.

"Let me think. It would have been pretty late last night, close to eleven. She came into the house from the backyard looking for Annabel."

"Eleven? I didn't know you were here that late," Gina said.

Roger looked uncomfortable. "I stopped by hoping to...have a little chat with Mary, but I didn't get the chance. Mary was already tucked away in her room, listening to Pavarotti."

"What about Steffi?" Gina asked tensely. "Where did she go after you saw her?"

"She went upstairs to talk to you, Alex. She said she had something to tell you and she'd be down right away. I left before she got back."

Alex and Gina exchanged a horrified glance.

"She went upstairs to my room?" Alex asked. "What time?"

"About eleven," Roger repeated patiently.

"Oh, no!" Gina clutched Alex's sleeve. "We were still... Oh, Alex!"

Alex put his arm around Gina and held her for a moment, his jaw tight with worry. "Don't worry about it, darling," he whispered. "This has been coming on for a long time."

"But I hate to think..."

All at once Alex was galvanized into action. "Roger," he said, "you check the grounds and out-buildings. I'll go up the beach toward the dock and check the woods and shoreline. Gina, you do the inside of the house, since you know all the closets and cubbyholes. She could just be hiding somewhere to give us a scare, though chances are more likely that she set off hitchhiking somewhere. Her boots and backpack are both missing. By the way, Gina," he added, "can you ask Mary to call the police? Tell them to get somebody out here right away. Describe the whole situation. Maybe we'll need a search dog."

"The police!" Gina said in alarm. "But, Alex, don't you think that might just frighten her even more? If she's hiding somewhere—"

Alex made a curt gesture. "We have to take drastic measures. If she's really as suicidal as she sounds in that note, we might not have a lot of time."

"Oh, God," Gina whispered. "Please, God..."

While the two men dispersed to begin their search, Gina raced through the house, pausing in the kitchen to tell Mary what was happening. She watched while Mary dialed the police, then began a frantic search of the old building from cellars to attic.

LESS THAN AN HOUR LATER, the four of them met again in the lobby. Gina was hot and frantic, trailing cobwebs and smeared with dust. Roger, too, looked dirty and harried. Mary's face was tight with fear.

Only Alex seemed calm, but Gina knew that his controlled manner was hiding an unendurable level of anguish.

"No luck?" he asked, looking around at their worried faces.

The others shook their heads.

"Damn," he muttered. "I was hoping... The canoe's missing," he said, his voice tight with pain. "I was thinking that maybe some of the other children took it as a prank or something, and that Steffi was still hiding somewhere around the mansion. But if you haven't found her..."

"The *canoe?*" Gina gasped. "Roger, we left it tied up near the cove, didn't we?"

"It's missing," Alex repeated. "I can see tracks in the sand where somebody untied it and shoved it into the water. But if it really was Steffi, where would she go?"

"Maybe up the lake to where you picked those blueberries," Roger suggested. "She knows about the berry groves, doesn't she? Maybe she just paddled a little ways up the shore and dragged the canoe into the brush. She could be hiding somewhere and watching us from the trees right now.''

"She's been crying out for help and attention, the poor little thing.''

This was Mary, speaking for the first time. The housekeeper was haggard with worry.

"I should have spent more time with Steffi,'' she said miserably. "The child liked to be in the kitchen, watching and asking questions while I worked, but I was always so busy. Sometimes,'' she confessed, her voice quivering on the verge of tears, "I was even cross with her because I suspected she was giving food to Annabel. And now she's...''

Roger moved over and put his arm around Mary, patting her back tenderly. Mary glanced at him in surprise, then leaned against him and allowed his awkward caress.

"The police are radioing for backup,'' Alex said. "They've got a dog handler on the way, too. When he gets here, we can make some determination what direction she headed and get search crews started.''

"I think she went across the lake,'' Gina said quietly, startling the others. "She went over to the other side and hiked up to Bear Creek.''

Roger looked genuinely alarmed. "Gina, surely you don't think she'd do something that dangerous?''

"I'm sure of it. I remember the way she looked around while we were up there, all the questions she asked.'' Gina was struck by a sudden thought. "Maybe she was planning this already. And then after she saw us together, Alex, it was more than she could bear. She had to do something.''

"That's not what the note says.'' Alex's jaw was rigid, his eyes dark with fear. "It sounds more like she was actually relieved to find us together, because then she could go away without having to worry about leaving me all alone.''

"Poor, poor Steffi." Gina was still gazing at the dark line of trees. "Think how unhappy she must have been all those months."

The uniformed police officer appeared in the door to the lobby with a handful of curious guests pressing behind him on the veranda.

"Mr. Colton?" he said. "Our dog man's arrived."

The group moved outside to watch as another RCMP officer unloaded his big German shepherd from the back of a police van.

Alex took them down to the lake and showed them the empty mooring for the canoe. The dog sniffed frantically, then began to dance and whine at the water's edge. He made little forays out into the shallows and turned back reluctantly at his master's command.

"Can he track across water?" Gina asked the young policeman.

"For a little ways if the trail's fairly recent. Far enough to give us an idea of the direction she went, at least. Does that motorboat up by the dock belong to you people?"

Roger ran along the shore, fumbling in his pocket for the boat keys as he went, and climbed into their small outboard.

"Bring it down as close as you can," the officer called, while the big dog strained eagerly at his harness. "Try not to swirl around and stir the water up any more than you have to."

Roger brought the boat slowly toward the shore. Gina and Alex climbed on board, along with the dog and his handler.

The animal immediately clambered over the seats and across the deck, whining eagerly, his paws on the bow as he stared out into the water.

"What's over there?" the officer asked, waving a hand at the opposite shore.

"Not much," Gina said gloomily. "Beyond that ridge there's a deep chasm and two hundred miles of wilderness. Lots of bears, swamps and bottomless lakes. Swarms of blackflies and mosquitoes."

"Organize a couple of search parties," the officer called to his partner, who still waited on shore. "As many men as the detachment can spare. Roger here will call up all the locals he can think of. We should try to get a few other boats down here, too, from summer places along the lake. If we locate the canoe on the other side, we'll radio back and mobilize the teams of searchers while we still have plenty of daylight."

Roger handed the motor's tiller to Alex, climbed out of the boat and waded onto the beach, moving close to Mary again.

"What can I do?" Mary asked the policeman.

"Make coffee," the officer told her. "Gallons of it. And sandwiches, too. Get some of the neighbors and hotel guests to help you. This could be a long hard day for everybody."

Roger and Mary disappeared inside the house, their arms entwined, while the boat began to throb across the water toward the opposite shore. The dog sniffed at the water, whining anxiously with his paws on the railing, then strained toward the front again. Alex followed where he pointed.

"That's amazing," Gina murmured to the police officer. "I had no idea a dog could follow a scent across water."

"Only if the conditions are just right. The water has to be undisturbed and the air completely still. You know, we even have some dogs that can find a body under hundreds of feet of water. They hang their head over the edge of the boat and tell the handler when they scent something different."

She shuddered and the officer fell silent, obviously regretting his words.

Alex cut the power and the boat drifted toward the shore in a direction that was apparently satisfying to the dog. As soon as the hull grated on gravel, the animal scrambled from the boat with his handler close behind and began running along the shore, his tail rotating wildly.

Alex and Gina followed, keeping close to the police team. All of them stopped and watched while the dog scratched at a messy pile of cedar branches. In just a few moments the bright yellow stern of the canoe was revealed.

"She's a smart little worker, this girl of yours," the officer commented, moving forward to lift away more of the concealing branches. "Without Rex, here, we'd probably never have found this canoe unless somebody fell right over it."

"Yes, she's a really smart girl," Gina whispered in agony. She looked at the forbidding expanse of dark pine on the hills above them, then shivered and rubbed her arms. "But she's only fourteen, and she's up there all alone."

STEFFI CLIMBED DOGGEDLY, working her way up the steep hillside through the pines. The trees were so thick that most of the time she couldn't use the sun for a guide. Her only navigational aid was the incline itself and the knowledge that as long as she kept climbing, she'd probably be heading west.

So she clambered over boulders and through dense stands of brush that scratched her face and arms, deviating from the upward course only when she came to streams that trickled and danced over rocks, like the trout stream they'd fished the day before.

Each time she encountered running water, Steffi waded in and followed the creek up- or downstream, sometimes as far as a mile, knowing that the swift-moving current would help to throw pursuers off her trail if they were using tracking dogs.

Sometimes she paused to glance back over her shoulder, wondering if anybody had even found her note yet, or if they'd discovered the missing canoe and suspected where she'd gone. But all she could see was a thick wall of pine and brush.

After she'd beached the canoe, the moon had stayed bright for a long time, allowing her to hike for several hours. When it got dark she'd made a nest of pine boughs near a rock outcropping, curled up and covered her face with her jacket, trying not to hear the sounds out there in that terrifying black void.

She retained her childhood fear of the dark.

But it was midsummer, and the night had only lasted for a few hours. She'd been awake at the first faint rays of dawn, and after eating the fish, started climbing again, heading for the rocky summit that still looked impossibly far away.

When her watch told her it was noon, she paused in a patch of light among the trees, took out a chocolate bar and some trail mix, then allowed herself a couple of sips of water from the rapidly dwindling supply in her canteen.

If she ran out of water, she'd have to refill the canteen at one of the mountain streams. They looked so clean and sparkling, but Gina had warned her not to drink the water. Microbes from decaying plant and animal matter infected the streams and made people sick.

Not that it mattered, Steffi told herself grimly. Nothing in this water could make her any sicker than she already was.

She finished her meal, stored the wrappers neatly in her backpack and removed all traces of her presence from the clearing. Finally she pulled her cap low over her eyes and resumed her climb.

Her goal was the rugged expanse of cliffs at the summit of the mountain range, faintly visible through swirls of noonday mist. On the other side, according to Roger, was a sheer rock face that plunged more than a thousand feet into a desolate chasm that nobody had ever penetrated.

Steffi expected to arrive at the rocky summit before sunset. She planned to spend some time looking around at the world, thinking about her life and the people she loved, having a little ceremony to say goodbye. Then she was going to walk forward, spread her arms and dive into nothingness.

She was actually looking forward to those final moments of her life. When she took off and soared down into the chasm, it would be just like flying. And after falling all those hundreds of feet, she wouldn't even feel the impact. Her life would be over before she hit bottom.

And then, finally, there'd be no more pain, no more worry and fear, no more hours spent lying awake at night and wondering what was happening inside her body...

Steffi's pace quickened. Feeling hot even though the air was cool at this elevation, she took off her jacket and shoved it into her pack, then lifted her cap to wipe her damp forehead.

Suddenly a noise startled her, a snuffling grunting noise in the thicket nearby. Before she could decide what to do, the bushes parted and she found herself confronted by a huge black bear.

Steffi gaped at the animal, frozen with terror. He stood on his hind legs at the edge of the thicket, no more than twenty or thirty feet away from her.

She couldn't believe how big he was. In his upright position, he seemed at least a couple of feet taller than a man. His teeth were bared and dripping blood.

A sickening smell drifted out of the thicket behind him, warm and metallic, like the scent of a butcher shop. Steffi realized that the bear had probably been feeding on fresh kill and she'd interrupted him at his meal.

His dark piglike eyes were fixed on her with a look of outrage. He growled low in his throat, dropped onto all fours and advanced a couple of paces, then reared up on his hind legs again.

Steffi's mind whirled with random disconnected thoughts. Frantically she tried to remember everything she'd been taught about dealing with bears in wilderness settings.

Have to get out of his sight. Run away from him. No, don't run. If I run, he'll chase me. Climb a tree. It's impossible to climb a tree. He'll catch me before I even get started. Have to drop and play dead. Lie facedown and stay very still. . . .

But the bear charged before she could even do this. With unbelievable speed, he came bursting across the clearing and lunged toward her, knocking her to the ground.

Instinctively she lay still, only reaching her hands behind her neck, locking them and guarding her face with her elbows. The bear swiped at her body with his paw, and she could hear the sound of ripping.

She wondered what part of her body was being torn open and felt briefly amazed that she experienced no pain. After a moment she realized the animal was tearing at her backpack. She heard the big jaws snapping, and a lot of grunting and snuffling.

The worst thing, surprisingly, was the smell.

The bear had a rank musty scent, coupled with the smell of the fresh kill. Its breath was hot against her arms and body, and unbelievably foul. Steffi was so sickened she had to fight back waves of nausea, knowing it would probably be fatal if she threw up.

She lay for what seemed like hours while the bear ripped and scattered her pack and took a few more glancing swipes at her legs and back. Any second she expected to have the huge jaws close over her skull, to feel the crunching of bone and the blood spurting as her life ebbed away.

She didn't want to die this way, even though her goal for the present journey was to end her life. She still wanted to make the departure on her own terms. She dreamed of flying gracefully and painlessly out into that sun-sparkled void, vanishing forever in the chasm below.

She didn't want to be mangled and left in pieces in the woods, where a search party would find her body in a couple of days and her father would have to feel terrible forever about the way she'd died.

The bear swiped at her again, sending a harsh jolt of pain through her body. Then he moved away to nose among the scattered belongings from her pack. Still lying on her face in the sharp pine needles, Steffi lifted an elbow and peeked underneath it. She knew the bear was nearby because the rank heavy scent still filled her nostrils.

In fact he was almost close enough to touch, just a few feet to her left, gobbling the last of her trail mix. His shaggy bulk filled her whole line of vision.

She moaned silently and tightened her arms around her face again, wondering how long this nightmare could last. She felt as if she'd been here for hours, even days. She couldn't remember anything but lying among the pine needles and moss-covered rocks, waiting for the bear to kill her.

Desperately she forced herself to think of other things. She pictured Annabel's tail wagging and her father's beloved face and the way Gina had smiled yesterday when Steffi made a perfect cast and a trout rose to her fly. She thought about her father and Gina lying in each other's arms and hoped they'd stay together and find happiness.

Maybe her father would sell the house in Vancouver and move out here to live with Gina.

That would be a good thing. She and her father had been so unhappy in the other house, and her mother was never coming back....

The bear stumbled and fell against her for a moment, his immense bulk almost crushing her legs. Steffi bit her lip so hard she tasted blood.

Mercifully the animal rolled off her legs. She could hear him as he snuffled and rooted at something nearby. But her courage was beginning to falter. In a minute she'd go crazy, scramble away and begin screaming, and that would mean certain death. So she forced herself, by a mighty effort of will, to keep thinking about her father.

It would be nice for him to live with Gina. He loved Edgewood Manor, and he could write his column no matter where he lived. Wistfully Steffi wondered if perhaps that had been her mother's plan. The hotel brochure her father found in the desk had been only a few years old. Maybe Mom had somehow learned about the manor and decided it would be a nice place for her husband and daughter to live after she was gone. Maybe she'd realized that Alex and Gina would fall in love, and she'd left the brochure as a sign that she didn't mind.

Not likely, Steffi decided, although it was a pleasant thought. But there was no way Gina could ever have met Janice and Alex Colton. Steffi's parents had never even been to Edgewood Manor.

Steffi shifted cautiously on the ground, trying not to attract the bear's attention, and struggled to keep her mind on the familiar soothing train of thought while she waited.

If her father lived at the old hotel, he could help Gina a lot, especially with financial matters. Gina seemed to spend a lot of time worrying about money.

Her father had all kinds of money—

Suddenly she felt a ripping pain in her left thigh. The bear had returned and slashed at her leg. Pain rushed though her, hot and sickening. She clamped her jaws, trying not to scream.

Steffi braced herself, waiting for the next blow, her heart pounding wildly.

After a long, long time, she eased her arms away and peeked out to one side, then the other. There was no sign of the bear.

She struggled to her feet, looking in dismay at the scattered remnants of her pack and her slashed denim jeans soaked in blood. The clearing was silent and deserted, so peaceful she could hear the warbling of birds in the trees overhead and the distant chatter of a magpie.

Whimpering and sick with terror, Steffi gathered up the shredded remains of her jacket and ran unsteadily into the trees, away from the clearing, heading toward the sound of running water.

In minutes she reached another stream and waded in, then sat down to let the icy water flow over the burning throb of her leg. The tanned skin of her thigh was marred by a row of deep gashes, welling blood.

When the wound felt numb and somewhat eased by the cold water, she tore the remains of her jacket into strips and applied a clumsy bandage, tying it tightly enough to stanch the flow of blood.

At last, her face twisted and white with pain, she left the stream and continued her dogged upward climb. The sun was dropping below the cliffs, and the shadows had begun to lengthen all around her....

LOWER ON THE MOUNTAIN, the police dog ran frantically along the water's edge, making little forays in both directions. At regular intervals Rex followed animal trails into the woods, then came back out again, looking disconsolate, his ears drooping.

Grim-faced and intent, the trainer followed.

"Your daughter's really throwing us off the track," he told Alex, who stood with Gina at the edge of the stream. "Every time there's a creek, she's used the running water to cover her tracks. We're probably hours behind her by now."

In the distance, all over the woods, they could hear the sound of brush crashing, of distant shouts and the occasional sharp crack of a gunshot, a signal to other searchers, as volunteers fanned out, combing the dense undergrowth of the hillside.

"We have to keep trying," Alex said tightly. "We've picked up her scent before. It's just a matter of ranging up- and downstream with the dog until we find where she came out."

"But every time we do that, it wastes time and she gets farther ahead," Gina said.

Alex looked at her in concern. She was drooping with weariness, and so pale that her freckles were dark against her cheeks. But she refused to go back to the mansion to rest. She'd been with Alex and the dog handler ever since morning, and now it was almost sunset.

"Where do you think she's going?" he asked, afraid to hear the answer.

Gina hesitated, her eyes enormous and tragic. "Up there," she said at last, waving her hand at the rocky summit above the trees, stark and forbidding against the twilight swirl of color.

"You think she's . . ."

"I'd bet on it," Gina said wearily. "I think she's chosen that place because she can jump off the cliff's edge and nobody will ever find her body. She doesn't want to hurt you any more than she has to."

Tears ran down her face unchecked. She was in such anguish that Alex wanted to gather her in his arms and hold her, whisper words of comfort to her. But ever since Steffi's disappearance, Gina seemed to have withdrawn into some private hell of her own, where she was alone with her pain and fear. He couldn't reach her, and he couldn't understand the passionate intensity of her terror.

"Okay!" the policeman called. "We've got it back again." He plunged after the dog, who was bounding eagerly up the hillside through a dense stand of birch trees.

Alex and Gina ran to catch up.

"She stopped here for a while," the dog handler said, indicating a compressed area in the grass where the dog was scratching and whining in a frenzy of excitement. "Probably had a bite of lunch, maybe a little rest."

"How long ago?" Alex asked tensely.

"Quite a few hours. I'd say around noon."

Alex knelt with the policeman to touch the flattened grass, thinking about his daughter's precious body. She'd been in this very place just hours ago, and yet it seemed impossible to find her.

So near and yet so far.

"At least it's something," he muttered, getting to his feet again and shouldering his pack. "Let's hurry, so we don't waste any more daylight."

Gina fell into step behind him, climbing lightly and easily despite her fatigue.

What a woman she was, Alex thought. She was the kind of woman who would follow a man through the worst life had to offer, stand shoulder to shoulder through any kind of danger or turmoil.

He felt another flood of love for her, so intense it was almost dizzying. But now was neither the time nor the place. When they found Steffi, after she was well and safely back at home and all her fears had been cleared up, then it would be time for him and Gina.

Steffi had to come first.

"I love you, honey," he whispered to his absent daughter. "I love you so much. Please, please hang on till we can get there. Don't do anything until I've had the chance to talk to you."

Behind him, Gina reached forward to grip his hand. Alex responded gratefully, squeezing her hand for a moment, then letting it fall as they both shifted their packs and began to climb over an outcropping of rock.

Ahead of them, the dog was barking hysterically. He stood near a thicket, his hackles raised, growling deep in his throat.

The police officer turned to Alex, his face ashen. "Mr. Colton," he said reluctantly, "I don't know if you want to see this, but..."

"What?" Alex shouldered his way forward. "What is it? Have you found her?"

Gina moved up beside him and stood gazing at the scattered objects in the clearing. Alex could feel her sharp intake of breath and the violent trembling of her body.

"I don't know if she's nearby." The policeman cleared his throat awkwardly. "But it looks like she's tangled with a bear. A big male, judging by the tracks."

"Oh, no!" Gina gasped, her voice breaking as she moved forward into the clearing. "Oh, my God, Alex . . ."

"The scenario looks pretty clear," the officer said. "There's a half-eaten deer carcass in the thicket. She must have come on the bear while it was feeding—and been attacked."

Mutely, her eyes streaming with tears, Gina held up the remains of a stuffed pink rabbit in a velvet waistcoat. Steffi's beloved old toy was shredded and limp, its stuffing trailing on the ground.

Alex's head began to swim sickeningly. "How do you know she was attacked?"

The policeman indicated the other scattered remains of the backpack and the ripped food packages.

Alex shook his head. "Maybe she tossed her pack away to distract the bear."

Wordlessly the officer held up a long shred of denim, heavily stained with blood. Alex's terror hardened slowly into a bitter rage. If the monster that had hurt his daughter confronted him at this moment, he felt able to rip it apart with his bare hands. He'd never known such fury.

"What happened?" he asked grimly. "Did the bear drag her away?"

"I don't think so. There'd be more of a trail if he had. I think he roughed her up a bit, then ran off. You know," he added with a bleak smile, "I'm getting more impressed all the time by this kid of yours. It looks like she was smart enough to lie here and play dead until the bear got bored."

"Then where is she?" Gina wailed.

"Rex found a trail of blood leading up toward that stream above us. She was obviously injured, but able to get away under her own steam."

"That means she's bleeding from her wounds but still climbing," Gina said.

"Right. For some reason she seems real anxious to get to those cliffs before dark."

Gina and Alex exchanged a despairing glance.

"Steffi's afraid of the dark," he murmured. "If she's planning what you think she is, Gina, she'd want to do it before nightfall."

Gina turned to the officer. "Can you get us there before dark?"

He looked at them uncertainly, then up at the rocky summit. "We have to keep following her trail," he said. "There's no telling where she came out of the water this time. And it's damned rugged up there. Unless we have a warm trail to follow, we could wander around for days without finding her."

"We'll keep looking," Alex said. "If need be, we'll spend the night up here and hunt by moonlight. It's imperative we find her soon."

"Okay." The policeman whipped out his radio and barked some instructions. He gave their approximate location and requested backup, along with some food and hot drinks.

Then he splashed across the stream and went back to the routine of roaming up and down the opposite bank with the police dog, trying to pick up the scent again.

Gina and Alex sank onto a big flat rock at the water's edge, huddling against each other as they waited.

Alex put an arm around her shoulders and bent to kiss her cheek, but she pulled away.

"Alex," she said, "when we find her, if she's still...if she's all right, then I want to be the one to talk to her."

He looked at Gina in surprise.

"I have something to tell her," Gina went on, her voice low and unsteady. "It's a story she should have heard a long time ago."

She paused to take a deep breath while he waited, puzzled and frightened by her intensity.

"But first, Alex," she said, "I need to tell you the same story."

CHAPTER FOURTEEN

"WHAT IS IT, Gina?" he asked. "What do you want to tell me?"

"It's about Steffi. I should have told you before, but I was..."

Her voice broke. She rummaged in the pocket of her jeans and took out her billfold.

Across the stream, Rex and his handler emerged from the brush.

"Any luck?" Alex called.

"Not in that direction. We're going to work our way upstream for a while. I'll give you a shout if we raise the scent again."

Gina opened her billfold and took a photograph from one of the side pockets, handing it wordlessly to Alex.

He studied the smiling girl in the picture, his eyes widening. "It's Steffi," he said, then hesitated. "Isn't it?"

Gina waited while he looked at the photograph again, frowning in concentration.

"But she looks older somehow," he muttered. "Gina, where did you get this?"

"It's my sister, Claudia, when she was seventeen."

"I don't understand. This picture... Your sister looks so much like Steffi. I can hardly tell the difference."

"They're not exactly the same," Gina said quietly. "Their mouths are different." She pointed to the girl's face. "Steffi's mouth is fuller. More like yours," she added.

"But I still don't... How can they look so much alike?"

"Because they're related. Claudia is Steffi's aunt."

"Her *aunt?*" He was staring at Gina, thunderstruck. "What are you saying?"

"I was your surrogate, Alex. Steffi is my biological child."

Alex was apparently too stunned to respond. Gina looked down at her hands, twisted painfully in her lap.

"I want you to know that I had no idea who you were," she said in a low voice. "When you first came and rented those rooms, I didn't connect you at all with...with anything from my past. It wasn't until I came home that day and saw Steffi in the kitchen. Even then, I wasn't sure until I..."

"What?" he asked tensely when she stopped talking. "What did you do?"

"I went into Steffi's room when the two of you were in Kelowna, and looked at her photograph of your wife. Then I knew."

"I don't believe this," he said flatly. "If what you say is true, the coincidence is too weird. How could I have chanced onto this particular hotel, of all the places in the world?"

"But you didn't chance onto it," Gina reminded him. "You came here because you found a brochure about the hotel in your wife's desk. Obviously she kept track of my career after we concluded our... business deal," she said bitterly.

"But this is so... My God," he breathed. "*You* were the surrogate? Jan never told me anything about you, except that you were..."

"A plain mousey little thing?" Gina gave him a bleak smile. "Skinny and covered with freckles? All wrapped up in some kind of impossible dream with no social life to speak of and no prospects of getting married or raising a family?"

"I suppose that was my picture of you," he admitted. "She never did tell me very much about your situation. And after Steffi was born and we took her home, Jan refused to talk about you at all."

"That's understandable. But she was really good to me," Gina said quietly. "I think she almost loved me, because of the baby."

Alex shook his head in wonder. "The two of you spent a lot of time together, didn't you? Especially toward the end. I seem to recall that Janice was practically living with the... with you, for those last five or six weeks."

"She used to lie on the bed next to me," Gina said with a faraway look. "She liked to rest her head on my stomach so she could feel the baby moving. It never seemed like *my* baby," she added. "It was always hers. I was just the package."

"It was my baby, too," Alex said.

Gina nodded. They sat together in silence for a moment, staring at the rippling water, both of them struggling to come to terms with the reality of their situation.

"Why did you do it?" he asked at last.

"I was desperate for money. Claudia had been seriously injured in a car accident, my mother owed fifty thousand dollars in medical bills, and Edgewood

Manor was going to be sold to the highest bidder. The lawyer promised me enough money to take care of everything."

"But…we didn't pay you enough to do all that, did we?"

"I already had an inheritance from my grandmother. That extra seventy thousand was enough to look after Claudia's bills and secure the mortgage on the hotel."

"How did the whole thing get started?" he asked. "I can't remember exactly how Janice found you, except that there was a lawyer involved."

"Weren't you involved in the planning?"

He shook his head. "I found the whole concept sort of…distasteful. I would have preferred to adopt, but Janice wanted so desperately to have *my* baby. I think in retrospect that she was always a little insecure. Maybe she felt that having my biological child would be a way of holding on to me."

"I didn't know anything about your marriage," Gina said. "She never talked about you. It was like she wanted to keep the two of us as far apart as possible, even in her own mind."

"How did the lawyer find you? Was your name on some kind of list?"

"Of course not!" Gina was stung by the question. "The idea of being a surrogate had never crossed my mind. I answered a newspaper ad that gave no details about the job. When I went for the interview and your lawyer told me what was involved, I was shocked."

"But you didn't walk out?"

"I started to. Then I thought it over. I realized this was a way of getting the money my family needed and making a childless couple happy at the same time. I was only twenty-one, Alex. I honestly thought I could have the baby, hand it over to your wife and walk away without any pain."

"Did you?" he asked.

"Did I what?"

"Walk away without pain?"

Gina's throat tightened. "It was awful," she whispered. "I had no idea how it was going to feel. For months I cried myself to sleep every night. My arms felt so empty. I kept wanting to hold my baby, but she was gone. There were lots of times when I had the urge to find you and your wife, march into your house and tell you I'd changed my mind and wanted my baby. But I'd signed those papers, and I had to honor them."

"And you'd already bought your hotel," he said.

"Yes." Gina looked down at her hands again. "I'd bought my hotel. The only way to ease the pain was to bury myself in work, so that's what I did. But every year when her birthday came around, I'd get really depressed and wonder where she was and if she was happy. Lately it's been getting worse, instead of better. And when I saw her..." She glanced up at Alex, searching for some indication of how he felt, but his profile remained cold and unrevealing.

"I knew who she was," Gina went on, looking away from him. "And I knew, of course, all the facts about her birth. So yesterday, when I found out what she was worried about, that she was afraid she'd inherited Huntington's from her mother, I could hardly stand it."

"Why didn't you tell her the truth right then?" he asked.

"It wasn't my place to tell her anything. I'm well aware that I have no rights in this situation, Alex. I signed them all away. In fact, I'm not even supposed to be having any kind of communication with either of you."

"But you made sure I'd tell her."

"I had to. I couldn't bear to think of the way she was suffering."

"I should have told her years ago," Alex said moodily, staring at the water. "But as I said, the whole business was always a little distasteful to me. I thought it would be too painful for a child to learn that—" He stopped abruptly.

Gina looked at him. "To learn what, Alex?" she asked bitterly. "That her mother sold her for seventy thousand dollars?"

He was silent, his gaze fixed on the rushing stream.

"Of course it's a painful thing to learn," Gina said. "If *you* despise me for what I did, think how *she's* going to feel."

"I don't..."

"Never mind," Gina said wearily. "There's no need to say something polite. It's clear how you feel about me and I don't blame you, but I still want Steffi to know the truth. And I want to be the one to tell her, if we can find her in time."

"Why would you put yourself through such a painful experience?"

"Because I won't be able to live with myself unless I *am* able to tell her the truth. After that, you can take her away, and I promise that neither of you will ever have to see me again."

Suddenly Gina could endure no more. Everything crashed in on her at once—days of agonizing worry over Steffi's unhappiness, the girl's disappearance, their long hours of searching, and now the pain of telling Alex the truth and seeing his contempt for her and what she'd done.

She climbed down from the rock and waded quickly across the stream, heading toward the trees where the dog's barking could be heard faintly in the distance.

"We've got it!" the policeman called. "We've raised the scent again. She's still heading up toward the summit."

Gina quickened her pace, running in the direction of the barking.

She could hear Alex as he splashed across the stream and fell into step on the trail behind her. But he said nothing and Gina ignored him, climbing steadfastly toward the high ramparts of stone silhouetted against the darkening sky.

ROGER PLODDED across the hotel yard and climbed the front steps, his shoulders slumped with fatigue. He paused on the veranda to look across the lake at the distant hills, now almost fully shrouded in twilight mists.

Powerboats roared back and forth on the water, carrying fresh search teams into the hills and bringing back others for food and rest. Dozens of volunteers had been arriving throughout the day, neighbors from nearby farms and people from the city, as well, all offering to do what they could.

But as the sun slipped behind the hills and the sky began to darken, the mood of the searchers grew somber. They knew that the police dog had raised a scent high up in the hills near the summit. They'd been warned, as well, that the girl was seriously troubled.

Many of them believed that even if they found her, it was going to be too late.

Roger thought about Steffi's note and the stark words of farewell. He set his jaw and pushed his way through the front doors, heading for the kitchen.

Half a dozen women labored at the counter and sink, making sandwiches and fresh coffee. Teams of searchers sat at the table, tired and dirty, taking a brief time to eat and refresh themselves before they set off across the lake and into the woods again.

Mary carried a coffeepot to the table and set it down, then straightened and pressed her hand into the small of her back. Her face was turned away from the group in the kitchen, but Roger could see the lines of weariness in it as she began to clear a stack of plates and cutlery from the table.

"Here," he said, crossing the room. "Give those to me."

He took the plates and carried them to the sink, then came back and touched her arm.

"Come outside with me," he said. "There're enough people in here to look after things for a while. I want you to sit down and give yourself a little rest."

She didn't argue, which worried him even more. Together they walked out through the hotel and onto the veranda. Roger drew her across the wooden floor to the porch swing, pushed her down gently and arranged the cushions so she could lean back. He settled next to her and started the swing rocking gently.

Mary sat with her hands folded in her lap, staring at the line of misty hills.

"It's going to be cold up there tonight," she said. "Poor little thing."

Roger thought about the girl's note and wondered if Steffi Colton was going to be feeling the cold tonight, or ever again. But he didn't want to say anything to Mary about that.

Instead, he cleared his throat and glanced at her. "Mary..."

She rested her head against the cushions, closing her eyes. "Uh-huh?"

"Do you remember Gina's sister?"

"Claudia?"

"That's right. I've been thinking about her all day. Remember when she came out to the hotel?"

"It was a long time ago. Years and years."

"I know," Roger said. "But do you remember what she looked like?"

Mary frowned in concentration, then opened her eyes and stared at him. "Yes," she whispered. "Now that you mention it, I do remember."

"So, what do you think?"

Mary stared at the shimmering waters of the lake. "I don't know," she said at last. "Do you think Gina is related to the Coltons somehow?"

"Well, I believe she's related to Steffi, at least. There's something going on here we don't know about. I'm hoping Gina's going to tell us when all this is over."

"I've been here for so long," Mary said thoughtfully. "Gina's like a daughter to me. I keep forgetting she had a life before we met her. She's never told us much about it."

"Gina's a good person," Roger said. "Whatever happened in the past, I know she didn't do anything wrong. But I'm beginning to wonder about the way she's been acting the past week or so."

"So moody and unhappy, you mean?"

He nodded.

"You don't think..."

"I'm not sure what I think. But I'm really worried, Mary."

Tears glittered in her eyes. "It's all been so terrible," she said. "I knew Gina was upset, and that little girl's been unhappy, too, ever since she got here. I pray to God she won't hurt herself."

"I don't think we need to worry," Roger said with considerably more optimism than he felt. "This is probably just a kid's stunt, that's all. A way to get some attention. They'll find her and have a long talk about things, and she'll be fine."

"But what if she isn't?" Mary turned her anguished gaze on him. "Roger, what if they're too late?"

He put his arms around her, and once again, to his amazement, she didn't pull away. In fact, she nestled closer to him, burying her face against his shirtfront.

As Roger held her, he felt such a flood of love he could hardly contain himself. She began to cry, her body shuddering deeply with sobs.

"It's all right, Mary," he murmured, still holding her. "It's going to be all right. Don't cry."

After a while she collected herself, sat up and dabbed at her eyes with the hem of her apron. Roger patted her shoulder comfortingly.

Mary looked away from him, cleared her throat and began to toy nervously with one of her apron strings. "I talked to Fred this morning. He brought a couple of boys over from the motel to help with the search."

"I know." Roger lifted his cap and rubbed a hand wearily across his forehead. "Folks have been so good, haven't they?"

"Fred told me..." Mary glanced at him, then quickly looked away again. "He said that Lacey Franks went back to Vancouver today."

Roger nodded, caught off guard by the change of subject. He hadn't given Lacey a thought all day.

"I guess," Mary said with a distant expression, "she's going out there to pack up the rest of her things."

"Pack up her things?" Roger said, puzzled. "Why would she do that?"

Mary's cheeks turned pink with embarrassment. "I thought the two of you were planning to live together."

Roger shook his head. "Well, you thought wrong, Mary. I never had any feelings like that for Lacey Franks."

She forgot her nervousness and stared at him in disbelief. "But you spent all that time with her and went out on dates and everything. You even brought her to the hotel to meet us."

"I didn't invite her," Roger said dryly. "She insisted on coming. There's a big difference."

"But we thought the two of you were..." Mary paused uncertainly.

"I guess Lacey thought so, too," Roger said. "But the whole thing was happening mostly in her imagination. I'll admit," he added, "that it was partly my fault. I should have told her right away I wasn't interested. I just didn't know how to go about it without being rude or looking foolish."

"I really thought you were in love with her," Mary said in wonder.

Roger shook his head. "Well, now, that's just silly. How could I ever fall in love with a woman like her?"

"Why not? She's pretty and sophisticated, and she dresses so well..."

"That's not the sort of thing that attracts me." Roger drew a deep breath and stared across the lake at the distant line of hills. "Besides, I'm already in love. I've been in love for years. And I guess I'm a one-woman man."

He was conscious of Mary turning to gaze at him, her face white and strained in the darkness. Roger put an arm around her and drew her close.

"I love you, Mary," he said against her hair. "I should have told you long ago, but I could never find the words somehow."

"Me?" she said in disbelief. "You're in love with *me?*"

"What man wouldn't love you? You're a wonderful woman, Mary Schick." Roger tightened his embrace and smiled fondly.

But he couldn't get her to smile back. She pulled away and twisted her apron in her hands, not looking at him.

Roger felt a painful stab of fear. "Mary," he said, "please tell me it's not too late. Tell me you could find it in your heart to care about me, too, even if I've been a foolish old man. I don't want to live without you any longer."

"Why are you telling me this now?" she asked, her voice strained. "If you've felt this way for so long, why did you wait?"

"I was afraid you'd turn me down and then I'd have to leave. But lately I've been thinking about things, realizing that it's not right to be a coward about life. And then today, worrying about that poor girl... Mary, I can't stand it anymore. I don't want to spend my life wishing for something and not having the courage to go after it."

She was silent for so long that his fear turned to misery, then resignation.

"I'm sorry," he said at last. "Please, forget I ever said anything, Mary. I don't want to cause you any pain or embarrassment. Just forget about this, and we'll carry on like nothing ever happened."

Mary turned to him with a flash of spirit. "You know, I think you were right, after all," she said, giving him a level measuring glance.

"About what?"

"You're a foolish old man, Roger Appleby," she said.

And then she was in his arms, laughing and crying. Roger could hardly believe the wonder of it as he kissed her and rocked her gently in the swing.

STEFFI MOANED SOFTLY with pain as she clambered toward the sky. This last bit was more like rock climbing than hiking. The summit was a rampart of stone with almost vertical sides that soared above the last of the trees.

From far below it had looked so small, like an uneven fence of rock that you could simply jump over into the void below. But it wasn't that way at all. To reach the top, she had to concentrate on every step, every handhold, clinging to the face of the rock like a fly on a wall.

And her leg was so sore.

She bit her lip and reached up for a handhold, testing it carefully, then dragged her feet into position one after the other, searching for safe places to rest her weight. A few bits of rock loosened somewhere above and trickled down past her face. She was terrified. What if the whole rock face gave way and she plunged back down into the trees?

Maybe that monstrous bear was still roaming around below, following the scent of the blood she'd been shedding along the way.

Steffi had dealt bravely with the bear attack, but that had been in the warm light of day. She didn't know how she could ever survive such a nightmare in the dark. Just the thought of it was enough to make her whimper, then clench her teeth and pull herself up again.

One more handhold, then another...

Cold sweat broke out on her forehead. Her arms ached, her hands felt like open wounds, and her injured leg burned and throbbed.

"I can't do it," Steffi groaned. "I can't. I have to let go."

But her spirit wouldn't let her give up. Somewhere in the darkening sky, drifting on the breeze, she heard her father's voice.

Never give up, Steff. You're not beaten until you allow yourself to be. You can do anything in the world if you don't give up.

"I won't give up, Dad," she promised.

Her heart ached as she thought about him. He'd always been so big and strong, so gentle and full of laughter and wisdom. During the years when her mother began to falter, Steffi's father had gradually become everything to her. He was the one who taught her things, who shared her happy times and her tears. He'd always been there when Steffi needed him.

She simply couldn't stand the thought that she was going to suffer the same illness her mother had, and her father would have to endure that anguish all over again.

"I won't do it," she whispered, gritting her teeth and hauling herself upward. "I won't, I won't, I won't, I *won't*..." With each repetition, she made it farther up the stone face. Finally, with a last surge of effort, she hauled herself over the edge and lay, panting, on the summit.

After a moment she got to her hands and knees and crept forward, looking around timidly.

She seemed to be at the top of the world, where other peaks soared all around her. Some of the nearby mountains had to be even higher than this one, Steffi realized, because their summits were wreathed in clouds. A few of them had a light dusting of snow.

The dizzying sense of height came from the gorge below, falling away at the other side of the mountain-top. The summit itself was like a shallow bowl, about the size of a couple of football fields. Soil had blown in over the ages to fill the bowl, allowing stunted shrubs to grow in places, along with clumps of thick tufty grass.

A high mountain wind howled around her ears, so loud she couldn't hear anything else. The sense of isolation was complete—and strangely soothing.

Steffi limped to the far edge, holding herself well back, and looked down into the darkness. The chasm below was so deep that it brimmed with shadows. She couldn't even see the bottom although she could hear the roar of a swift-flowing river far below.

Carefully she lay full length on the rock and peered into the gorge. If only she could make out where the bottom was, see the trees and water, she would be able to jump. But she couldn't bear the thought of leaping into darkness. All she could see was a rocky ledge about fifteen feet down the sheer rock face. The ledge was quite wide, littered with boulders and large enough that a few pine trees actually grew there, their twisted roots clinging to the stone.

Steffi knew she'd have to find another place. If she jumped here, she might not fly out far enough to miss the ledge. And if she landed on the rock shelf, there was a chance she might bump her head or break a leg or something, and not be able to crawl over to the edge for a second jump. They'd find her for sure if she got stranded on that ledge.

Steffi had a horror of not finishing this job properly now that she'd come so far. She needed to fling herself all the way into that bottomless chasm to be crushed against the rocks below and carried off by the wild cleansing river, so that no part of her would ever be seen again.

That was how she wanted to die.

Reluctantly she decided she'd have to spend the night on the summit. In the morning, when it was bright and clear, when the sun had climbed high enough to fill the valley with light, then she'd find a place along the rocky cliff where the edge was clear and smooth. She'd stand for a moment to say a prayer and think about her father and mother and all the people she cared about. Then she'd spread her arms, leap forward into the wind and let the sunlight carry her off.

Shivering, she drew back from the rim and began to explore the windswept summit, trying to find some shelter from the cold night air.

The shrubs that grew near the rocky ledges looked something like sagebrush, with heavy gnarled stems and dusty leaves. Steffi took a jackknife from her pocket and cut a pile of the stems, planning to make a bed and cover herself with the branches.

She hated the thought of sleeping out here in the wind and the moonlight, fully exposed to whatever predators roamed the mountains at night. But, she reasoned, no predators were going to climb that rugged cliff in pursuit of her.

She was safe up here, all by herself on her lofty peak.

STEFFI PAUSED in her work and rubbed her arms, looking around at the darkening circle of sky. Stars glimmered here and there in the blackness and seemed close enough to reach out and touch.

"I wish the moon would come up," she muttered. "It won't be so scary once it's light enough to see what I'm doing."

The sound of her own voice wasn't comforting at all. The wind whipped the words from her mouth and blew them away as soon as she spoke. She continued to work, mostly by touch, hacking away at the gnarled branches and throwing a pile of them to one side.

She'd find a place near the rocky crags where there'd be a little shelter from the wind and make her bed. Maybe over there on the other side, near the—

Steffi lifted her head and listened. She thought she heard a sound over the howling of the wind, but she wasn't sure. She started to run toward the side of the summit she'd climbed earlier, then stumbled and fell. Her wounded leg felt worse than ever, and the swelling seemed to be straining at the clumsy strips of fabric she'd wrapped tightly around it earlier.

She thought about the bear's sharp claws, dripping blood from whatever animal it had killed back in the thicket. There was no way of knowing how many germs that bear had on its paws, and what kind of infection was now working inside her leg.

But it didn't matter, she told herself. She just had to get through the night, and tomorrow she'd be lost in the sunshine, carried away on the swift flow of the river.

Just one more night and—

The sound came again. Steffi got to her feet and limped closer to the rocky edge of the summit.

Suddenly she shivered and looked around wildly. The sound was a dog barking, and it seemed very close. Farther below, away from the dog, Steffi was almost certain she could hear human voices.

She froze for a moment, her eyes wide with terror. Then she turned and scrambled as best she could back across the summit, heading for the far side.

She reached the place where she'd seen the ledge fifteen feet down the rock face and lay on her stomach to peer over. A plan formed in her mind, but first she had to destroy all trace of her activities up here. Maybe there'd still be time to fool them.

Working feverishly, she grabbed the piles of branches she'd cut, seized armfuls of leaves and branches and tossed them onto the ledge below.

By the time she was finished, the shadows had climbed the valley wall until the ledge, too, was almost completely in darkness. She could hardly make out the detail of the narrow strip of rock, the scattered boulders and stunted trees.

She threw down the last of the brush, then crept right to the very edge. She rolled herself into a ball, hugging her legs, hesitated for a moment, then let herself drop over the edge.

She landed with a thud that knocked the breath from her lungs and wrenched one of her shoulders painfully. Still, the branches seemed to have broken her fall a little. After she got her breath back, Steffi lay and examined herself with care, flexing her arms, moving around gingerly on the prickly stems and leaves.

Everything seemed all right. Except for the throbbing pain in her leg and the wrenched shoulder, she was intact.

She felt a grim surge of hope. They'd never find her down on this ledge in the dark. Even if they did, they couldn't get to her. She just had to crawl under her pile of brush and survive the night.

And then tomorrow, as soon as the sun came up, she'd make her triumphant flight into oblivion.

CHAPTER FIFTEEN

GINA CLUNG to the rock face, climbing behind the young policeman. Alex was a few steps below her, while the dog stayed anxiously at the base of the cliff, barking up at them.

"Are you okay?" the officer called over his shoulder. "We're almost there."

"I'm fine," Gina said. "Just hurry."

He disappeared into the sky. In a few seconds she tumbled over the rim behind him, then waited for Alex to appear.

The officer was ranging around the summit, playing his flashlight over the terrain. He returned to them, looking tense and quiet.

"There's no sign of her."

Gina felt a wave of sorrow so intense that she stumbled blindly and would have fallen if Alex hadn't reached out a hand to steady her.

"Are you sure?" Alex said tightly. "Look, there's some brush over there. Maybe she's hiding."

The policeman shook his head. "There's nothing growing here that's dense enough to hide somebody. I'm afraid we're too late. Mr. Colton."

The moon spilled a wash of silver across the summit. Gina roamed desperately over the tufted grass, searching for any sign of the girl.

"Look!" she called suddenly.

The two men came running over to examine the freshly cut stems of brush.

"Why would she do that?" Alex said. "Unless she wanted to make a shelter somewhere..."

Gina was already following the trail of scattered leaves and stems that led to the other edge of the mountaintop. She shivered, looking down into the yawning chasm where even the brilliant moonlight couldn't penetrate.

Alex and the policeman stood next to her, also gazing down. "There's some kind of ledge," Alex muttered, peering into the darkness. "Do you suppose she could be down there?"

The officer played the beam of his light about the surface of the ledge. They could see a dense pile of brush—and a flash of light blue beneath the matted leaves.

Alex lay full length, looking downward, straining to make out the details of the ledge. "I think it's her," he whispered, his voice tense with excitement. "And I don't think she fell down onto that ledge. She must have tossed the brush down there to break her fall, then jumped down onto it to hide from us."

He straightened and looked at the other two, who watched him silently.

"I'm going down there," he said.

"How?" Gina asked.

"The same way she did. I'll just drop onto the ledge."

The policeman shook his head. "I can't allow you to do that, sir. It's too dangerous."

"Then what do you propose?" Gina asked.

"I'll radio for a helicopter. They can land up here and bring some gear to drop a harness for her."

"If she hears a helicopter," Gina said, "she's going to jump. That's why she's up here on the mountain in the first place. She's hardly going to be willing to ride back up in a harness."

Alex's face was taut with strain, his eyes darkly shadowed in the moonlight. "What do you think, Gina? What should we do?"

"Give me twenty minutes alone with her," Gina said. "Then bring in the helicopter and send down your harness."

"Alone with her?" Alex said. "What do you mean?"

Before either man could react, Gina stepped to the edge, crouched swiftly and jumped over.

FOR A TERRIFYING SECOND she fell through darkness, feeling the cold air rushing past her face. Then she landed with a thump and heard a squeal of pain and surprise from beneath her.

She'd fallen partly on Steffi, who'd been stretched out under the pile of brush but now gathered herself and wriggled away in panic.

"Steffi, it's just me," Gina said. "I guess it would have been more polite to call before I dropped in, right?"

She pushed aside the branches and sat up. Steffi crouched near the edge of the precipice, staring at her.

"Gina? Why...what are you doing here?"

"I was in the neighborhood," Gina said, hoping her lighthearted words might keep Steffi from making any rash moves.

Steffi continued to huddle in the darkness, far too close to the edge for comfort.

"Ow," Gina muttered, reaching behind her. "I hurt my shoulder. Steffi, can you come over here and see if I'm bleeding?"

The girl hesitated, then crawled reluctantly toward her. Gina turned away, waiting tensely while Steffi explored her back.

"It looks okay," she said at last. "Maybe you just got poked by a branch or something."

"What happened to your leg?" Gina settled back against the rock face, hoping Steffi would follow suit. She tried to keep her voice casual as if they were having a conversation on the veranda back at the hotel.

"It was a bear, down there in the trees. He slashed at my leg. It's been bleeding a lot."

"Oh, Steffi…" Gina reached for the girl, but Steffi drew away again.

"Why are you here? Where's my father?"

Gina took a deep breath. "Your father's waiting up there at the top. I came down ahead of him because I wanted to tell you a story." She paused. "It's very, very important for you to listen to me, Steffi. It won't take long."

"What story?"

"It's about me, when I was a few years older than you are."

Steffi leaned back against the wall of rock and said nothing. But sensing the girl was going to listen, Gina went on. "I moved out to Vancouver to live with my aunt when I was seventeen and took a course in hotel management. Just after I finished my course, I came here one day to Azure Bay, saw the hotel and fell in love with it. I wanted to buy Edgewood Manor and spend the rest of my life making it into a profitable business. I was twenty-one."

It seemed Gina had Steffi's interest now, for the girl asked, "How could you buy a big hotel?"

"I had an inheritance from my grandmother that was almost enough to get a mortgage, and I was young and full of energy. I thought that if I could just get a job, work really hard and save every penny, maybe I could raise the rest of the money somehow. But then something terrible happened."

"What?"

"My little sister was in a car accident. She needed all kinds of expensive medical treatments that weren't covered by insurance, and my mother had nobody to help with the bills. It was going to take all the money from my inheritance, and thousands more besides, just to pay the hospital. So I was desperate."

"What did you do?"

"I answered an ad in the newspaper for a job that promised a lot of money."

Gina hesitated, fighting a dizzying sense of unreality. It seemed incredible that they should be together here on this narrow ledge in the dark of night, thousands of feet above a deadly chasm, while Gina told her daughter the story of her birth.

"Gina?" Steffi asked. "What was the job?"

"It was for a couple who badly wanted to have a baby." She paused. "Do you know what artificial insemination is, Steffi?"

"Of course I do," the girl said. "So this couple wanted you to be a surrogate mother, right?"

Gina nodded. She shouldn't have been surprised at Steffi's knowledge. She went on to describe the situation—her relationship with the woman, how she never met the husband, the birth itself.

"What was it like?" Steffi was clearly fascinated. All her wariness seemed to have vanished.

"Well, the pregnancy was surprisingly pleasant," Gina said, "most of the time. And Joanne—that's what the woman said her name was—loved that baby from the moment it was conceived. Both of us did. She spent a lot of time with me while I got bigger and bigger, and we concentrated on having the best, sweetest, healthiest baby we possibly could."

"But after it was born, you had to give it away?"

"Yes," Gina said. "It was the hardest thing I ever did. I gave my baby away and promised I'd never have any contact with the parents as long as I lived."

"Was it a boy or a girl?"

"It was a little girl."

"Wow," Steffi murmured thoughtfully. "And that's the end of the story? You never saw your baby again?"

Gina's heart began to pound. "Not until just a little while ago."

"What happened then?" Steffi's voice had changed. It was softer, incredulous. "Did you actually meet her?"

"Yes," Gina said quietly. "She came to stay at my hotel with her father."

Those words were met by a silence so profound it was almost a tangible thing. Gina's heart seemed to stop beating altogether as she waited.

At last she heard Steffi take a deep breath. "It was me," the girl said. "I was the baby you gave away."

Gina yearned to reach for her, hold her, but instinct warned her to be still. "Yes," she said. "I never knew your family name, so I had no idea who your father was when he first came here and booked the rooms. I suspected the truth, though, as soon as I saw you—because you look exactly like my sister, Claudia. But I wasn't sure until I went into your room and saw the photograph of your mother."

"Why didn't they *tell* me?" Steffi said, her voice choked with pain. "If this is true, why didn't my father ever say anything?"

"Because your mother didn't want you to know. Your father told me she was obsessed with the need to keep the truth from you. Maybe it was because she felt so much like your real mother. She was even with me in the delivery room when you were born. In fact, she was the first person who ever held you."

"So after it was over, they just forgot all about you?"

"I think they tried to." Gina took another deep breath and forced herself to continue. "Probably they wanted to protect you from the fact that your biological mother was the sort of person who'd actually...exchange a baby for money."

"But my father doesn't feel that way about you. He's in love with you."

"I don't think he is anymore," Gina said, her heart aching. "Not since I told him the whole story this afternoon."

"Why would it make any difference?"

Gina felt a warm surge of love for this wonderful child she'd borne all those years ago.

"Because now he knows I'm the kind of person who'd have a baby and exchange it for cash. I don't think he can live with that."

"Nobody should blame you for making a deal and sticking to it." Steffi paused, then said, "Did you love me?"

"Oh, my darling..." Gina's eyes filled with tears. "You'll never know how much I loved you. All these years, hardly a day has passed when I haven't thought about you and wondered how you were and wished I could see you. And every year on your birthday..."

Steffi moved closer and put her arm around Gina's shoulders. "Don't cry," she whispered. "Don't cry, Gina. I was happy. I had a really good life, until—"

Suddenly she tightened her grip. "I'm not sick!" she said in wonder. "If you're my real mother, there's no way I could've inherited Huntington's!"

"That's why your mother arranged for a surrogate," Gina said. "She knew there was a strong possibility she carried the gene and she would never have risked passing it on."

"But why didn't they *tell* me?" Steffi wailed. "All that time, I thought I was going to die the same way she did."

"Your father had no idea you knew about the disease. He was convinced you believed your mother had cancer. If he'd known how you felt, he would never have let you suffer that way."

After a few moments of silence, Steffi said, "Dad came here to your hotel because he found a brochure in my mother's desk, didn't he?"

Gina found a tissue in her pocket and wiped the tears from her eyes. "Yes."

"I think she kept that brochure because she wanted us to find you and be with you after she died."

Gina considered this. "It's possible, but I guess we'll never know. Anyway, your father is never going to..."

Steffi burrowed against her. All at once the strain of the past few days seemed to take its toll. Gina felt her daughter's slender body begin to shake with sobs.

"It's all right," she murmured. "It's all right, sweetheart. I love you, and so does your father. And your mother loved you, too. Nothing can ever change that."

After a long time the storm of weeping subsided. Steffi wiped her eyes on her sleeve. The two of them nestled together for a while, looking at the starlight.

At last Gina asked, "Now that you know the truth, Steffi, does it make you feel differently about yourself? About your parents?"

"I'm just so happy I'm not sick. But I don't feel bad about my parents. Or about you," she added shyly. "I'm glad you told me. It must have been really hard for you."

"Not as hard as keeping quiet all this past week."

They heard the distant throb of a helicopter drifting above the peak behind them.

"They're going to lower a harness to lift us up," Gina said. "Okay?"

"Okay." Steffi sat up. "I feel like such an idiot, causing all this trouble for everyone."

Gina hugged her fiercely. "None of this is your fault. If we'd all been honest with you, told you the truth right from the beginning, it would never have happened."

Steffi nestled gratefully in her arms again. Both of them waited while the sound of activity intensified on the summit above their heads.

A canvas harness began to descend, clattering on the rock face behind them.

"You go first," Gina said, helping the girl into the harness. She frowned anxiously at the makeshift bandage on Steffi's leg, now heavily stained with blood. "I'll see you at the top in a few minutes."

"Gina?" Steffi whispered.

"Yes, darling?"

"I love you," the girl said.

Then she was gone, rising slowly up the mountainside in the moonlight while Gina stood below and watched.

THE FOLLOWING AFTERNOON, Gina parked at the hospital in Kelowna and went inside, carrying a basket of Mary's fresh-baked cookies and a bouquet of wildflowers picked from the hotel garden. As she made her way through the corridors, her heart thudded anxiously.

Outside Steffi's room, Gina hesitated for a moment, then pushed the door open and stepped in.

Alex sat at the bedside reading a magazine, looking tired but peaceful. Steffi lay with her eyes closed, pale and still under the covers, with an intravenous drip attached to her arm. The red cloud of her hair flamed brilliantly against the white hospital pillows.

Gina looked at the two of them for a moment, tears stinging in her eyes. Finally she took a deep breath and crossed the room.

Alex glanced up, startled, then set down the magazine and got to his feet.

"Hello, Gina," he whispered. "She's been asleep for an hour or so."

"How is she?" Gina whispered back.

"A lot better. They gave her two blood transfusions last night, and she's getting stronger."

"Is there any infection?"

Alex shook his head. "She was smart enough to clean the wound in cold running water. The doctor says it looks really good."

"The poor darling. What a nightmare she's been through." Gina put the cookies and flowers on the bedside table, then reached out gently to touch the glorious red hair, lifting a strand and letting it fall again. "She's so beautiful, isn't she?"

"Yes," Alex said. "She's beautiful."

"All those years—" Gina studied the girl's delicate features "—I kept trying to imagine what she looked like, and what kind of person she'd grown up to be. It was so hard, not knowing. I used to lie in my bed and cry because I knew I'd never ever get to see her."

Alex stood next to Gina, watching her face as she went on, talking to herself as much as to him.

"I had this fantasy about going to the city and finding your house somehow. I pictured myself hiding outside in the bushes just so I could get a look at her. And now..."

She took a deep breath, still studying Steffi's pale face. "Is she really all right, Alex?"

"It's like a miracle," he said with a tired relieved smile. "When I talk with her now, it's as if she's come back from some distant place. She's herself again. I can hardly believe it."

Gina shivered and hugged her arms. "I lay awake all last night, brooding about how close we came to losing her, Alex. Now that the nightmare's over, I can't bear to think about what happened, but I can't seem to get it out of my mind, either."

He put an arm around her shoulders, but she drew away and moved to the window to look out at the hospital grounds. On the lawns below, sprinklers cast a bright drift of rainbows into the warm summer air.

Alex came over to stand beside her. "You did an incredible thing last night," he said. "Jumping down to that ledge to talk to her."

"I had no choice." Gina pressed her forehead against the coolness of the glass. "After what I did to her all those years ago..." Her voice broke.

Alex stayed next to Gina, but didn't touch her. "Steffi and I talked for quite a while this morning," he said. "We talked about everything."

"How does she feel?"

"She's been thinking it all through, and she's very accepting. Steffi has a lot of understanding for a girl her age."

"I know. She's wonderful."

"She told me her theory—that maybe Janice left the brochure where I'd find it so we could be reunited with you."

Gina cast him a quick glance, then turned her gaze away. "What do you think?"

"I don't know. But it's certainly a possibility. I think Steffi wants to believe it."

"Does she?" Gina swallowed hard. "Do you mean that Steffi... Does she still want to have some kind of relationship with me?"

"Of course she does. In fact, she can hardly wait for next winter."

"Why?" Gina asked, bewildered. "What's happening next winter?"

Alex smiled. "Don't you remember? The three of us are going to Costa Rica. We're going to hike through the rain forest and spend two weeks in a tent. Steffi thinks that's going to be great."

Gina stared up at him, trying to read his expression. But the sunlight glanced in through the window and dazzled her. She couldn't see his face clearly.

"Alex?"

He put his arms around her and drew her close. "I love you, Gina."

She felt a shock of disbelief, then a sudden dawning of joy.

"You still *love* me?" she whispered. "After everything I've told you?"

"Why wouldn't I?"

"But I . . . I sold my baby."

"What about me? I bought a baby," he said quietly. "Are you going to hold that against me, Gina? I knew it wasn't right, but I still let my wife bully me into paying hard cash for another woman's child. Wasn't that an unforgivable thing to do?"

She stood in his arms, considering. "If none of us had done what we did," she said at last, "then Steffi wouldn't exist today."

"I know. So let's quit blaming ourselves for everything that happened so many years ago and concentrate on making Steffi happy from now on. What do you say?"

She snuggled into his chest, too overcome to speak.

"Gina? I asked you something a while ago, but you never gave me an answer, so I'm asking again."

"What?"

"Will you marry me? I don't want to rush you into anything, but I think Steffi's going to demand that we get this whole thing settled pretty quickly."

Gina could hardly comprehend the blissful prospect being offered to her. A lifetime not only with the man she loved, but with the daughter she'd thought was lost to her forever.

"Where would we live?"

He laughed softly. "Well, I don't think I'll ever pry you away from your hotel for more than a short vacation, and Steffi doesn't want to go back to the city. So I guess you'll probably have to find room for us somewhere. It's a good thing you've got a big house."

"Oh, Alex, I love you so much. I can't..."

"Gina?" he asked in alarm. "Darling, what's the matter? Are you crying?"

"It's all so wonderful," she said, struggling to control her voice. "I don't deserve something this wonderful."

"Oh, Gina, you deserve the very best," he whispered. "And I'm going to see that you get it."

Gina took his hand and drew him with her toward the bed. Wrapped in the warm afternoon sunlight, she smiled mistily at their daughter's sleeping face, then at Alex, the two people she loved more than life itself.

Merry Christmas, Baby! ★

A romantic collection filled with the magic
of Christmas and the joy of children.

SUSAN WIGGS, Karen Young and
Bobby Hutchinson bring you Christmas wishes,
weddings and romance, in a charming
trio of stories that will warm up your
holiday season.

MERRY CHRISTMAS, BABY! also contains
Harlequin's special gift to you—a set of
FREE GIFT TAGS included in every book.

Brighten up your holiday season with
MERRY CHRISTMAS, BABY!

Available in November at
your favorite retail store.

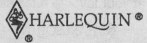

HARLEQUIN ®

The collection of the year!
NEW YORK TIMES BESTSELLING AUTHORS

Linda Lael Miller
Wild About Harry

Janet Dailey
Sweet Promise

Elizabeth Lowell
Reckless Love

Penny Jordan
Love's Choices

and featuring
Nora Roberts
The Calhoun Women

This special trade-size edition features four of the wildly popular titles in the Calhoun miniseries together in one volume—a true collector's item!

Pick up these great authors and a chance to win a weekend for two in New York City at the Marriott Marquis Hotel on Broadway! We'll pay for your flight, your hotel—even a Broadway show!

Available in December at your favorite retail outlet.

HARLEQUIN ®

Scandals

A passionate story of romance, where bold, daring characters
set out to defy their world of propriety and strict social codes.

"Scandals—a story that will make your heart race and your
pulse pound. Spectacular!"   —Suzanne Forster

"Devon is daring, dangerous and altogether delicious."
                                              —Amanda Quick

Don't miss this wonderful full-length novel from Regency
favorite Georgina Devon.

Available in December, wherever Harlequin books are sold.

Look us up on-line at: http://www.romance.net

1997
Reader's Engagement Book
A calendar of important dates
and anniversaries for readers to use!

Informative and entertaining—with notable
dates and trivia highlighted throughout the year.

Handy, convenient, pocketbook size to help you
keep track of your own personal important dates.

Added bonus—contains $5.00 worth of coupons
for upcoming Harlequin and Silhouette books.
This calendar more than pays for itself!

 Available beginning in November at
your favorite retail outlet.